SPACE
ADVENTURE

FIRST BOOK OF THE SPACE TRILOGY

TALES FROM GRANDAD

SPACE ADVENTURE

Don Keirle

authorHOUSE®

AuthorHouse™ UK
1663 Liberty Drive
Bloomington, IN 47403 USA
www.authorhouse.co.uk
Phone: 0800.197.4150

© 2015 Don Keirle. All rights reserved.

No part of this book may be reproduced, stored in a retrieval system, or transmitted by any means without the written permission of the author.

Published by AuthorHouse 10/06/2015

ISBN: 978-1-5049-8747-9 (sc)
ISBN: 978-1-5049-8748-6 (hc)
ISBN: 978-1-5049-8749-3 (e)

Print information available on the last page.

Any people depicted in stock imagery provided by Thinkstock are models, and such images are being used for illustrative purposes only. Certain stock imagery © Thinkstock.

This book is printed on acid-free paper.

Because of the dynamic nature of the Internet, any web addresses or links contained in this book may have changed since publication and may no longer be valid. The views expressed in this work are solely those of the author and do not necessarily reflect the views of the publisher, and the publisher hereby disclaims any responsibility for them.

To Kevin

this book is part of a trilogy.

from

[signature]

14/APRIL/2019

CHAPTER 1

SPACE TRAVEL

I am a fairly old man now, and I do not know if I will have time to finish this account, but as I found myself privy to a unique store of information I decided to try to elicit the story behind the myriad of reports stored in my personal copy of the Space Library. The library has paper and computor copies but I will use the computer to source the information unless it breaks down. I was an electrical engineer during my working life and I became accustomed to writing detailed reports. If this account seems like a report, well too bad, I am doing my best! Almost at retiring age I successfully applied to the space authorities for the job of Space Librarian and thus found work archiving the various space reports. Many would find this boring, but I can tell you it was a severe mental challenge. I had the responsibility of creating an archive structure that would make the documents easily retrievable, with both computor and hard copies required. It was and is a well paid job and I still haven't retired. Like most lads of my age group I knew about stars, planets, moons, comets and asteroids, but during the record compiling I discovered other things like centaurs, (half planet half comet), and Greeks and Trojans, (asteroids in Jupiter's orbit), and a fair few other things like the Oort cloud, which allegedly produces comets. As I got into the story I decided that I ought to know more about subatomic activity. I read up on quarks and bosons and in particular the Higgs boson but after only a few days I realized that such stuff was best left to the few who can claim to have a glimmer of understanding about such things. The most senior of the people who I think do have the requisite education to grasp the fundamentals would be a gentleman generally known as the Whistler. He will appear in due course.

I had the extreme good fortune to see the reports as they were written, slowly at first but then at an ever increasing rate as space exploration began to gather pace and so I already have a good notion of the story of events, just from memories of significant events as they occurred. For anyone else, they would have to read the myriad of small reports as well as the plethora of large ones that came to me over a thirty year period, before they would have any chance of eliciting the storyline. The initial phases of space travel are probably of low interest and, well, boring, but the storyline does hot up! As the personalities emerge, the unending changes in technology take perhaps a back seat, but initially the technology holds centre stage, for without it we have no story to tell.

With regard to the archived reports, bear in mind that many senior wallahs will use ten words when one will do, though Shakespearian is not how I would describe the results, and as a consequence the amount of reading involved to get at the fundamentals is gargantuan. As I am writing this, hugely detailed reports are still flooding in. Because of all this and my unique position, I have decided to have a go at the story myself.

Here goes!

When I was a lad, many comics and paperbacks had published really well imagined stories about space travel. As I was growing up it transpired that these authors had underestimated or simply ignored the difficulties involved, and thus when man actually landed on the moon the whole exercise was lacking in the swashbuckling adventure themes that I was expecting.

"One small step for man. One giant leap for mankind!" Even that was rather boring the way it was presented. Not at all like the fictitious space stories involving future history, massive colonization and rip roaring adventures of a million fertile imaginations, but the stories all had a common factor, and that was that space travel was so easily possible that it was taken for granted. In real life it was to prove much more difficult to really get going than that.

During my earlier years the name of Albert Einstein figured high not only in intellectual circles, but in the sort of circles that I inhabited. I gather he was trying to work out a relationship between magnetic forces, electrostatic forces, and gravitational forces. I don't think he completed this work before he died. Others no doubt took hold of this baton and ran with it, and as you will see, a positive result eventually emerged. Of the various cosmic forces, gravity is considered to be the weakest one, *but it never gives up. Gravitational effects are all that get out of a black hole, not even light can do that.*

Over a number of years, with probes sent to various places, a host of factual discoveries were made, and logged. Looking on the internet, there are pictorial diagrams and some interesting facts about the average density of each place, and in the case of solar system planets, how much you would weigh on each of them. Other facts include the extremes of temperatures endured on some planets, the chemical compositions of the gas giants, but most of all the lack of running water and free oxygen.

Some moons did have water and or an atmosphere, though the water was frozen hard due to the unimaginable cold, and the travel distances involved to get to them are unbelievably large, so that with the rocket technology available in the twentieth and early twenty first centuries, the distances involved precluded most manned space adventure. It had been noted that comets travel to and from the outer reaches of the solar system, so if a bundle of ice particles could do it, why not man? Well man only lives for a short time so travel involving a 50 years or more journey time was not an option.

Something else was needed. Time travel was a nice idea but that is all it was- an idea. Einstein had reasoned that mass, energy and time were all somehow interrelated, but it appeared that you couldn't actually go *through* time, there is no short cut. Scientists were all striving to conceive a rocket engine (for want of a better description) that would power a craft through space with enough fuel to last for a very long time. Now engineering is quite truly the illegitimate but poetic son of science, so it was perhaps no surprise when an engineer arrived at a beautifully elegant notion, reasoning that space already had a web of gravitational forces spread throughout it, and theses forces controlled the orbits of comets and other fast moving items as well as planetary travels. So that all you had to do was to use the forces already there, exactly as a comet did and therefore the emphasis of designing an engine should be based on that fact. This idea was like a shaft of light. The emphasis of engine research was irrevocably changed.

The actual breakthrough came with the invention of the gravity shield motor. The basic notion had I believe, come from the fantastic science fiction author HG Wells two centuries ago, but the real fruit bearing research doesn't seem to be attributable to any one man. The gravity shield motor enabled engineers to design a vessel with a modulatable central core. This heavy metal core had a magnetic and electrostatic shield round it, completely hiding the core from gravitational forces. But by suitably controlling the surrounding magnetic and electrostatic fields, windows allowing gravitational pull to attract the core could not only be opened but could be focused, so that the gravitational pull of some distant object could be amplified up to about 100 fold. This of course would attract the heavy core and hence any vessel that the core was mounted in, and over a large enough distance the vessel could undergo a continuous acceleration, and thus could attain exceptionally high speeds. The gentle and delicate acceleration would be almost imperceptible to the crew.

At first the established scientific and engineering world could not bring itself to accept that the system could actually work, but models were made demonstrating that not only would it work, but that production costs would be tolerably low.

As you might expect, human self interest immediately foresaw the possibilities of mining minerals and valuables from other parts of the solar system, particularly those in short supply on earth, so conventional rocket probes were dispatched from earth to every accessible point previously unexplored in the Solar System to search for venues likely to yield a reward.

Possible destination arguments raged back and forth, but some old ideas and some caution persisted so that in the end the planet Mars became the first target. Mars was relatively close, and could possibly yield sources of some of the minerals that earth's industry gobbled up insatiably. It was not thought that it would be commercially feasible to mine such things as iron due to the weights and volumes involved, but rarer metals such as platinum, germanium and silicon, which were all used in smaller quantities, may be possible.

Layman's understanding

The sun emits light and heat and all sorts of other particles described as the solar wind. The new technology collected and stored the solar wind particles to generate high electrostatic voltages and used super conducting coils to produce and maintain the high electric currents and corresponding magnetic fields required for control of the "engine". We will call it an engine though it had no moving parts at all and thus wasn't subject to wear and tear. The central core of the engine was a crystalline structured alloy of Osmium, Nickel, Tungsten, Platinum, and a host of other metals in small amounts that were put through an irradiation process. This core was unbelievably heavy until it was shielded by the control fields. It still had its inertial properties but weighed zero, once shielded. It was decided that the desired spaceship would have to be built on the moon because it would be impossible to launch a ship of the magnitude conceived, from earth.

Nothing up till then had been done at anything like this scale on this scale on the moon.

Now to give the design engineers their due, though the design features put forward took a long time to settle, settle them they did. They conceived a vast ship the size of a modern ocean liner, with complete ecosystems for the production of food, with enough stored water and oxygen, with best known means of recycling virtually everything, to last for any foreseeable emergency. Creature comforts were considered from the outset, as the comfort of the crew was seen as crucial to morale. The ship was so vast, and technologically advanced, that it took over fifteen years to complete, and the heavy metal core was gigantic. Part of the costs involved the construction on the moon of a large workshop complex with living quarters for the construction team. This was seen as a bonus because the complex could be used far into the future. The complex was so large that some nutter actually suggested holding the Olympic Games in it. Though men had visited the moon before, this was a quantum leap over anything else hitherto considered. The costs were high but spread over the 15 years or so, were sustainable.

The design engineers decided that the ship would use a store of batteries as a back up energy source to provide the small amount of energy required by the gravity motor. It was realised that the convenient solar wind may not always be available, so another source of energy was required to ensure the production of very high voltages for electrostatic control. In addition, the emergency battery power could be used to source the magnetic field current, and the freezers that guard against the superconduction system suffering a temperature rise. Remember materials only exhibit their superconducting ability when their electrical resistance is virtually zero, at very low temperatures. The ship would use a nuclear submarine reactor suitably modified to provide the heat for conversion to electricity. The steam turbines would use a closed circuit water arrangement, with armoured tubing running along the outside of the ships hull, but inside a plastic self healing skin to provide some cooling, simultaneously aiding the ship's climate control system. The issue of zero gravity conditions was solved in a most ingenious ways. Engineers used permanent magnets and wheels embedded in the soles of standard issue space boots. The walkways of the ship had sufficient iron in them to give a strong attraction to the boots. When the soles were stressed into a bend such as would happen during walking/skating, the magnetic circuit was partly broken and the effect was reduced to about 5% or 10%. The effect was similar to the sensation of wearing roller skate boots, and of course crew members could move at a good speed. The wheels only protruded a fraction of an inch below the soles. Watching a spaceman in action was strongly reminiscent of watching a child wearing "heelies", a craze that had swept the industrial world at the turn of the century. In addition to this the ship's canteen and toilet blocks rotated. They were situated in a revolving hoop, with the centrifugal forces providing some artificial gravity. In this way liquids or semi fluid substances would remain in their containers, until they were recycled! The command bridge rolled round the outside of the hoop so that it could visit any surface and expose itself or shadow itself as was seen to be best to suit prevailing circumstances.

Even the politicians, often heavily reviled for their parochial views on things, were so enamoured with the prospects of this project, they put aside their petty bickering squabbles and came together as the new engine and ship was deemed to be a world project, with full technical disclosure to all participating (financing) countries. Thus the best brains on earth were gradually conscripted into the project, and perhaps for the first time in history, every optimistic man woman and child on earth was rooting for the success of the project. It did, of course attract its share of doom and gloom pessimists and religious extremists, though these were in a surprisingly small minority.

The space travel calculations were frighteningly complex, and the situation was rendered even more complex than usual as the ship would travel in an orbit that was stretched tight by use of the gravity motor. However in layman's terms the ship was projected to take off from the moon using rocket technology; and then open its gravity window to get a gravitational pull from earth, close the window again, but still use the rocket motors to gain speed. This would give a slingshot effect as the ship was pulled into an arc by earth's gravity and this would hurl the ship towards the sun. The rocket motors would then be shut down, until they were needed for a course adjustment to ensure that the ship didn't collide with the sun. The gravity window would finally be controlled to allow the sun to pull the ship and accelerate it. Subsequent reclosure of the gravity window on approach to the sun, in conjunction with the rocket motor course adjustment ensured that the sun would give a second slingshot effect. The ship would then streak in an arc round one side of the sun at a reasonable safe distance, and would then hurtle off into space, in a direction controlled by the angle of the arc described, which in turn was predetermined by speed and distance from the sun, and so on.

The seasonal timing of the mission being such that Mars would be in the third quadrant of its orbit, whereas the earth was in its first quadrant on the other side of the sun, and in effect the ship would be on a constrained orbit, this being a collision course with Mars. The collision time with Mars would only be three weeks from moon launch, if earth's calculations proved correct.

The tricky part was to slow down to make sure the term "collision" did not in fact occur. At the far end the ship would have to be slowed to a precise speed. The gravity window would be opened in reverse and with full amplification factor 100, would use the Sun's gravity to slow the ship down, then at the crucial moment, close the rearward gravity window and open the side gravity window to use the gravity from Mars to pull the ship into a natural orbit, which would go round Mars and at least one of its moons.

From then on it was back to conventional rocketry to land the exploration mission on Mars. The reason that one of mars' moons was part of the ships orbit was to allow the moon to take the ship to different places above mars and so give a wider choice of landing spots.

This method of space travel would save months of travel time, compared to rocket powered probe search times, and once sufficient earth presence was established on Mars, then it could possibly be a jumping off point for other adventures. To start the return journey, it was planned to open the gravity window to attract the ship to the chosen one of Mars' moons, use the slingshot effect from the moon, combined with a slingshot effect from mars itself and begin the journey back to Earth. The gravity window would be opened pointing at the sun for a long period with the amplification factor set at "N". "N" was a calculated value somewhere between zero and one hundred. This would be chosen to accelerate the ship up to a pace similar to the speed achieved by the ship as it approached the sun on the away journey.

The window would be closed to enjoy the sling shot effect from the sun again and the sun would then throw the spacecraft homeward. Many calculations were done to try to establish the timing and vectorial orientation of window openings, but the captain was told to look for the sideways 'g' forces as his measure of correctness. Observation platforms orbiting earth would be used to track the ship on its journey and the speeds that the ship attained would be demonstrated to be way above the extreme limits available to rocket technology.

This mission when tried went generally according to plan, the conventional rocket motors boosted the rocket to moon escape velocity, the sling shot effects worked exactly as predicted though the captain made minor computer aided adjustments to get the return sun slingshots exactly right. About 100 men had been left on Mars with a partly built Eden project style shelter, designed for quick assembly, and these pioneers had the shelter built and in full radio contact with Earth in only three days. The spaceship, due to its use of almost zero propulsion energy, was aptly named the "Freeloader".

I am neither a scientist nor a galactic engineer, so I don't have the knowledge to pursue the mathematics involved in the principles of the propulsion, which were daunting.

I do believe however that the general idea of the space engine is adequately conveyed above.

The space age had truly dawned.

CHAPTER 2

EXISTENCE ON MARS

We can't really call it colonization, because it wasn't really intended to put a colony on Mars at that time. The whole place was arid, though from radar mapping there were supposed to be large ice quantities buried near the poles underneath the seasonal layers of carbon dioxide dry ice. The mission base control was placed inside a large crater for two reasons. Firstly the floor of the crater was fairly flat and secondly because the steep rim walls would offer some protection against the Martian sand storms, and falling meteorites. The Eden style shelter was based on a project carried out in England years before, but suitably updated. The metal structure was a framework looking rather like a spherical honeycomb. There were triple skinned plastic windows with the space between each plastic skin filled with a fluid that would heal to a stretchy solid in the event of a puncture being suffered. Once healed into the stretchy solid the plastic took on a dim yellow tinge so that damage, when it occurred could be monitored. The plastic windows were translucent but not clear, so plenty of light was available but no direct view of the outside. This gave the occupants some protection from the sun's radiation. Remember, Mars had only a scrawny few particles and minimal gases in its atmosphere, so there was little if any natural shielding, though being much further from the sun than the earth, the sun radiation was not as potent.

To get out of the crater in order to explore the rest of mars was not easy, but after some abortive attempts a ravine like path, aided by deft use of some dynamite was constructed through the walls at one point.

The original exploration team soon settled into a routine, drove over the surface of mars prospecting for minerals and were surprised to find a small deposit of gold not more than 30 miles from the shelter. However tempting it was to mine the gold it was realised that mining it and then shipping it back to earth could possibly cause a financial meltdown, so that idea was shelved, but not of course forgotten. Some small amounts of uranium were found but again these were left to lie. Perhaps the most significant discovery was the existence of small rocky particles containing silicon. Now this would have commercial significance that could be turned to advantage in the computer industry.

One other ore was discovered in the form of black dust, and this was titanium. There appeared to be large deposits of this but how would it be transported? It wasn't as heavy as iron, only about half the weight but the volumes of the stuff were huge. Ok, let the engineers back on earth worry about how to get it back home, for the moment it would simply be transported to a dump near the base complex.

The diamond mining fraternity on earth, held its breath, because they knew that a sudden influx of extra terrestrial stones could blow their cosy little existence apart. No doubt diamonds will be found one day, but it hasn't happened yet.

A small amount of water was discovered frozen hard at the bottom of another crater, about 200 hundred miles from the shelter. This was probably the result of a collision with an asteroid or comet.

Initially the water was tested for signs of life, viruses, bacteria, fungus and just about anything else that the pioneers could think of. It turned out to be free of these though it did need boiling and condensing before it was potable.

This though meant that a vital source of a life sustaining element had been found.

Experiments were carried out with glass mirrors and lenses to focus the weak sunlight onto rocks to see if oxygen could be released. There are ongoing experiments doing this but all with no major success so far. The visual impact of the planet was strange; it was very mountainous being covered in volcano like craters, and yet in spite of the massive variety of these it was considered a monotonous view.

With humans in the exploration team conflicts of ideas and interests soon arose, and yet the oldest member of the team, a rather learned guy that everyone referred to as "the Prof" seemed to have that invaluable skill that was able to quell arguments almost before they arose.

The exploration team consisted of a well chosen 50/50 mix of men and women, and so it was not long before the mission doctor was able to confirm the first pregnancy. The child when born would actually be a Martian.

The team excitedly relayed the information back to mission control on Earth. Some old stick in the muds immediately wanted to recall the parents. However fate took a hand, as the father was suddenly stricken down with a strange illness and so Earth did not recall them in case of initiating a massive pandemic. The team requested and got enough materials on the next freighter mission to build a sizeable crèche.

The team also knew that soon there could soon be a number of fresh inhabitants, because nature will have its way.

CHAPTER 3

THE SUBSEQUENT RUNS.

Due to mars having a year approximately equal to 1.88 earth years, thus affecting the distance between the two planets and their relative orbit quadrants, each journey required different vectors to be factored into the ships computer. All carefully logged in full detail. The point at which the two were at maximum distances was when they were on opposite sides of the sun when the slingshot effect did not need to cause much angular change and was at its best. When on the same side of the sun the travel was still possible although the sun bound slingshot effect was giving a 180 degree course shift. The total journey was shorter but it happened at much lower speed and so with careful control of speed the journey time could be managed to stay fairly much the same. The ship became a freighter, and materials were shipped back and forth on a predictably scheduled timetable. The most expensive part of the operation in terms of energy consumption was the rocket driven feeder vessels at each end of the journey.

On one trip home to earth, everyone on the ship became aware of a low pitched audible hum that had never before been noticed. Captain Johnson, cool as ever, read the sophisticated instrumentation on his ship's computors.

He raised one eyebrow and said "Ladies and Gentlemen we are experiencing a sudden increase in acceleration and we are now travelling many times faster than ever before, so I am closing down the forward vector control and opening the rearward vector control in the hope that we will slow to usual speed, and not overshoot our home planet."

The captain's computor calculated the rearward angle of his window to target mars, this being the nearest source of gravitational pull, and wound the amplification factor up to maximum.

For over an hour the ship exhibited only its expected characteristic deceleration rate, but then the strange hum reoccurred and the increased deceleration was immediately apparent. The captain had already made use of the ships computors to calculate when he should close down the rearward vector and successfully returned the ship to its normal course.

During this emergency, by chance, communication with earth had been completely lost, but now earths tracking system could see that the ship was nearing home base but staggeringly nearly five days early. The ship entered a stable earth-lunar orbit, and for safety reasons the entire crew was evacuated back to earth, and replaced with a few volunteers. There was a full medical examination and de-briefing as scientists and engineers strove to discover the cause of the phenomenon.

One young crew member making a chance remark in the base canteen sparked a sudden investigation.

He likened the humming noise to a church organ note.

One of the brighter engineers overheard this and realizing that a church organ, and indeed any old fashioned musical instrument used resonance as its means of producing noise, and further because of resonance the volume of the musical note was very loud, for quite a small stimulus. This particular engineer made an analogous connection likening the loudness of a note to the greater ship acceleration.

He was quite a gifted individual and applied his engineering maths skills to the issue, and then took his idea to the scientists who were initially very doubtful of his notion.

Some of the younger scientists though were open minded enough to give the notion some credence, and gradually the older more experienced scientists found themselves on the defensive and had to consider the idea. An explanation began to emerge. There had indeed been some resonation that had amplified the ships acceleration enormously. Fortunately, just like a church organ the effect died away as soon as the stimulus was removed. Now exactly what had resonated? What sort of stimulus could bring about the oscillations experienced?

It was some months before the painstaking research revealed that mathematically at least the behaviour could be replicated. The mathematicians cunningly factored in an unknown effect that varied the acceleration, and all the equations were found to still be valid. The journey time of the ship could be accounted for.

Laboratory experiments done on earth were unable to produce even the slightest sign of any means by which acceleration was affected, and could not verify what the mathematicians had theorised.

It was then reasoned that the earth's gravitational field may possibly have a damping effect on any oscillations or resonance, and in effect precluded them from occurring.

Space is an unusual substance. There is almost nothing there. Yes *almost* nothing.

The gravitational motor of course was aimed at a target, and in effect attached an elastic cord between the ship and the target source of gravitational pull, using the modulating function of the gravity shield control. Out in space, if anything were to disturb the spatial quiet then the "gravitational cord" could begin to oscillate, much the same as a cord down the side of a flagpole in the wind.

Again I do not have the mathematical skills to offer a full technical explanation here, and I dare say you may be grateful for that, but in effect sun spots had caused disturbances in the solar wind and had hence set the oscillation off. Why the oscillation had such a dramatic effect on the ships acceleration I cannot explain in full detail, but principally as each oscillation of the "cord" effectively tried to pull the ship ever so slightly nearer to the target and thus caused a speed increase increment, which even though small, with each half cycle of the cord twang, was additive, so that after only 10 minutes of oscillations there was a very noticeable overall increase in speed. The acceleration due to the basic gravity modulator and the cord oscillation were additive, and thus very high speeds were attainable more quickly.

With no prior knowledge of this, it was realised that the ship's captain had been fortunate in the extreme to get safely home. The captain had read his instrumentation to establish the exact amount of time that the humming had been present. He had concluded that if he could get the humming to occur again then taking the ships position, and other factors into account it could be calculated how long a deceleration was needed to return to normal conditions. He knew just how fast the ships speed was. He confided only with the ship's chief engineer, who was responsible for the programme entered into the ships computors to calculate the deceleration period. The calculation was a live one which altered as the ship proceeded, and needed the fastest digital computor to keep abreast of the continuously changing conditions. It worked well. Both men however were sweating when for the first hour or so there was no sign of the humming. When the humming did occur, the computor controlled the windows of the motor with cold logic and precision and the rest of the crew were blissfully unaware of just how near they had been to becoming a lost in space statistic.

Much to the chagrin of the commercial interests on Earth, all commuter journeys to Mars were forbidden until this effect could be side stepped or controlled but above all, understood.

CHAPTER 4

THE NEXT QUANTUM LEAP

The bulk of the scientific effort was spent in trying to negate this perceived danger, because it was thought quite reasonably that it represented instability in the control. However, one or two researchers, being hungrier for fame than their colleagues were, were more interested in trying to show how the effect could be exploited.

The answer was found, and was staggeringly simple. It was proposed that a vectorially controlled vibratory mount be installed on the heavy metal core system, and this would allow the core to be vibrated in exact anti phase to a naturally occurring oscillation.

The frequency of the natural vibration was perceived to be inversely proportional to the distance to the target gravitational source and was directly proportional to the amount of gravitational pull and amplification in use at the time, so the anti oscillation system was designed to cope with the perceived natural oscillation, and then built to handle five times these amounts. It was also hoped that the vibration system could be used to precipitate the hum effect.

A hand picked crew of very brave or perhaps foolish volunteers was placed aboard a modified American space shuttle, which had been brought out of retirement and fitted with a gravity motor and vectorial vibrator. This shuttle, used as a small ship was sent on another round trip to Mars. As soon as the ship had completed its initial slingshot round the Earth and the gravity window was focused onto the sun, a deliberate oscillatory vibration at a pre-calculated frequency was introduced. The ship immediately began to suffer the increased acceleration. The oscillation control was immediately swapped to anti phase and the acceleration immediately began to fall as the vibration died away, to values experienced on most of the previous space flights.

So in a nutshell, the world had discovered a means to really get into space travel.

This system of control was explored quite freely by the shuttle's crew. The tracking stations on earth were staggered at the speeds achieved. Within a matter of hours the ship's speed could reach levels far outside that which a rocket could hope to achieve, and more important far more quickly than what the plain gravity motor could achieve. Whereas the mark 1 gravity motor could accelerate a ship up to near the speed of light it would take days to achieve it, whereas the mark 2 version could do it in a matter of hours.

Thus the mark 2 gravity motor was quietly hailed as a triumph. The space shuttle re-entered earth's atmosphere in the normal way, and landed at its chosen point without incident, and without the information reaching the world's press.

After a few minor delays caused by design refinements, the vibratory control was fitted to the "Freeloader"; commercial flights back to Mars resumed and these were now done in about 5 days. More important was the fact that neither the ship, nor crew, suffered any substantial stress or discomfort, and still the energy used for propulsion was absolutely minimal. At this time the full extent of the resonance effect on the Freeloader's top speed was not known, but it was abundantly clear that the whole of the solar system could now well be within grasp of spaceships with this system of propulsion. I still find myself using the word propulsion, though of course the real accelerative effort now came from external attraction.

Developments of this system would be made over the next few years, as the full extent of the propulsion system parameters, were explored. It was found that by carefully controlling the geometric shape of the ships heavy metal core, the sharpness of the gravity focus windows was vastly enhanced so that amplification factors went from 100 or so, on the original ship to over 100,000 on later designs. The windows were then perceived as lenses rather than windows. This enabled best use to be made of very distant targets. The central core was given a servo system to position it so that the best gravity attraction amplification could be garnered in any direction. The ship would slowly align itself by rotating around the core until acceleration was dead ahead

Finally the use of harmonic oscillations was discovered, and this was just as easy to control as the fundamental oscillations, and gave an even greater increase in acceleration. For example a third harmonic gave three times the acceleration of the fundamental.

CHAPTER 5

LIFE ON MARS

When we last took account of life on mars, mars was expecting the birth of its first citizen (planetzen?)

The stock of building materials and supplies was gradually being built up, and the exploration team had spent some time trying to improve their outside clothing to cope with the cold. They succeeded in this, managing to weave a gas tight fabric that permitted good freedom of movement but that also kept the inside temperature up without resorting to electric heating. True at times the outside temperature got positive up as high as 20 degrees Celsius, but mostly it stayed at sub arctic levels.

The black titanium dust was found in reasonable abundance and now the team had great mining style trucks to shovel it up and carry it to within the protective crater where the mission base had been built. The original ravine pass had been widened into a true road.

The first child born on Mars was a girl, who was named Venus would you believe? The mystery illness suffered by the father had all been an act, as he had successfully hoodwinked the authorities on earth, to ensure that he stayed on mars. Possibly due to the lower gravity (40%) on mars she grew very tall very quickly, and was universally known by her nickname, "Queenie."

One day Queenie picked up a piece of lead, noticed how heavy it was, and asked what it was. When she was told what it was she had asked if there was any more "out there". Nobody knew but a search mission was started and after months of searching a rich vein of lead bearing ore was found. As one of the heavier elements it was unlikely to be shipped back to earth but the mission engineers had another idea in mind.

Using the mirror lens kit to heat the ore, the ore was reduced and processed into lead sheets. The maintenance engineers soon made a vast lead-acid battery system to provide emergency power. The sun was not as powerful as on earth, but using considerable ingenuity, the pioneers used mirrors and lenses and a spare satellite photovoltaic array, and constructed a battery charger. This arrangement gave the team a certain independence from earth as now they were no longer wholly dependent on the mother planet for their energy supplies. The room where this power generation was sited was known as the "Queen Venus Suite", after the girl who sparked off the moves to make it. The suite contained a large distribution circuit breaker set and invertors to convert the basic battery dc voltage into ac. The planet now had its first beginnings of a "power station."

The sand and dust storms were frightening when in progress and could last for many days. After numerous failed designs, earth came up with a wind power generator, sturdy enough to resist the phenomenal erosion caused by the storms, yet still efficient enough to produce usable power. That gave yet another source of energy to the Martian team. Even under the protection of their accommodation roof, energy was required for heat and now with the improved energy sources, at last temperatures could be sustained at a pleasant level so much so that inside the shelter it was possible to wear ordinary earth type clothes for the first time. The wind turbines were used to charge the battery system which had been quadrupled in size to maximise energy storage.

The experiments to make oxygen had been successful in so far as a small amount could be released from certain mineral deposits, and enough could be made to supplement the precious air supply that kept the mission supplied. Gradually the chemists had been able to obtain some nitrogen and some helium, which when mixed with the oxygen gave a breathable mixture. This was particularly useful when exploration missions were undertaken, because it meant that the natural earth air supply in the base camp would not be diminished.

The team made up what was effectively an allotment. In this they grew potatoes and runner beans initially followed by carrots and peas and even grass, all using Martian soil. For meat the pioneers had to rely on supply from earth and a good big freezer.

Queenie had been joined by another little girl called Astra and a boy called Robert.

The three children were educated by the pioneer team, and they played in the garden tending their favourite plants, which of course were flowers, and generally larking about. The adults could see that all three children were severely restricted in where they could go and so it was decided that they and their parents would be sent on indefinite leave to earth. The six adults involved were replaced by recruits from earth.

Earth ran a television campaign to select suitable individuals.

CHAPTER 6

BACK ON EARTH

Earth's thirst for minerals and adventure was still only in its foetal stage. After the experimental space shuttle had proved so successful, five other shuttle craft were made available; two new ones and three old ones brought out of retirement and were fitted with the latest gravity motors and test flights were done to evaluate the limits of possibilities. The astronauts could confidently approach the speed of light, but not exceed it. It seemed that Einstein had been right and that nothing would ever exceed this speed, and during my lifetime this dream has remained just a dream. Anyway, the speeds available now were so immense that missions to the outer reaches of the solar system were feasible from a time consumed point of view, and just had to wait their turn in the queue for financing.

A dead straight shuttle carrying railway was constructed. Being dead straight it did not follow the curvature of the earth, and in effect it appeared to slowly rise as it went along. This "ramp" as it became known was fitted with a trolley operated by powerful linear electric motors, which was effective enough to impart great speed to the shuttle as it went along the track. In effect this track replaced the earlier solid fuel boost rockets so that the shuttle got into space using the linear motor and its own liquid fuel rocket motors. This made the launch of moon or orbit bound objects far less wasteful of earth energy supplies and materials and less stressful on the shuttle's structure.

Earth was pleased with the progress made on the Mars mission and decided that Jupiter and its moons would be the next target. This meant that the spaceship would have to traverse the dangerous asteroid belt, but the Freeloader was now fully committed to freight duties. Another ship generally similar in concept to the "Freeloader" freighter was built and this only took 8 years. The hull of this ship was a triple skinned polished alloy affair, between skins filled similar to the Eden shelter skin and for the same reason.

As the most experienced spaceman, Captain Johnson of the "Freeloader" was given command. The new ship was named "Solar Orbiter." The ship was like an extreme stretched limo and so about nine times larger in terms of volume than the "Freeloader", but was of course much faster in terms of acceleration, and having a hull that would give some protection against leaks in the event of a meteor strike suddenly seemed important when considering the planned traverse of the asteroid belt. Purely as a precaution it was fitted with weaponry, some long range lasers, and there was a section in its stores with a number of side arms and ammunition. Earth had developed some larger shuttle style short range rocket ships that ran on the ramp and these were used to get material up into orbit. This ship was built in earth orbit due to its size, and though it was never intended to make a planetary landing it was equipped with large rocket motors and enough fuel for several hours at full thrust. The ship carried twelve enlarged shuttle style rocket ships equipped with the latest gravity control motors as well as rockets, and these were to serve as landing craft and if necessary as "life boats". Well we didn't want another disaster like that of the unfortunate Titanic.

During the 8 years that it took to put the ship together, great attention was paid to the safety of the construction workers, as they had to work in the "junk belt" that surrounded the earth. Some bits of space junk were harvested and recycled and the total content in the junk belt was reduced by over half, which was a good thing.

Further studies of the asteroid belt were undertaken. It was already known that a number of asteroids shared Jupiter's orbit, but Jupiter itself no doubt due to its gravitational pull seemed to have hoovered many of them up leaving Jupiter itself in a relatively clean space. The biggest asteroid namely Ceres was to be avoided as its gravitational pull was thought to risk pulling any ship near it off course. It was a big asteroid about the same ratio to the moon as the moon is to earth. Of course there were also the main belt comets to think of. These peculiar inhabitants of the asteroid belt, contained large amounts of ice that on occasions became detached and were displayed as comet like tails.

CHAPTER 7

GANYMEDE IS THE TARGET

Now the launch date approached and Captain Johnson had rehearsed his crew through every conceivable exercise so that it was expected that the whole enterprise would go like a well oiled machine.

On the launch day every man knew what he had to do, and every key man had an understudy. In the event the captain ordered the ships rocket motors to 15% thrust and the ship accelerated up from orbital to escape velocity. As the ship escaped earth's gravitational pull, the captain orientated it to point at the moon and tried his first gravity motor operation. The rocket motors were shut down, and the ship slowly accelerated towards the moon. The captain was also well rehearsed in his duties and skillfully checked and monitored the ship's computor as the gravity window was closed to permit the first sling shot round the moon. The whole thing went very smoothly and then the target was changed to the sun.

Whether by a sense of humour or a belief in comic books it was never established, but the engineer in charge of the gravity motor function sang out "Warp factor 0.5 Captain?"

The captain raised his one eyebrow and with the ghost of a smile agreed to the target speed.

The engineer then set his vibration frequency and the hum characteristic of the move began. After about half an hour the hum suddenly reduced as the engineer confirmed "warp factor 0.5 attained sir." Only a short while later the sling shot effect was felt as the ship felt the gravity of the sun, and described a gentle arc while still a million miles or so from it. After this the captain aligned his next target as mars.

The journey was aimed so that mars would provide a sling shot effect to put the ship into the asteroid belt and the ships speed would be controlled to achieve the average speed of known asteroids. The speed of the ship would be reduced to this relatively slow rate and the ship was expected to stay inside the asteroid belt for several days. In this way observations would be kept and logged. This method would minimize risks from collisions with asteroids. The general risk of collision was considered low as many small space probes had already traversed the asteroid belt with no problem, but of course the Solar Orbiter was large enough to possess a small but noticeable gravitational pull of its own and was itself thousands of time bigger than probes previously sent through the asteroid region. So the captain kept the rocket motors on dribble feed so that he could accelerate or steer the ship suddenly if he had to. On the fifth day he had to. A jagged piece of rock or ice was detected and seen to be approaching from the rear and may have collided with the back end of the ship, but the captain used his motors to widen his orbit and avoided the collision by a fairly narrow margin. He took this opportunity of testing his laser guns as it went by. With a sustained burst of about 10 seconds the asteroid split first into two and then burst into many fragments as the heat from the laser penetrated the initial cracks in it. This was a fantastic event when viewed from the bridge and the captain had it relayed along the ship communication video channel. Shortly after this, the bridge lookout warned of another group of small asteroids that were heading directly at the ship. A careful watch was kept on these and as the ship altered course, so did the asteroid particles. There was no doubt about it; the asteroidals were being attracted to the ship. The captain ordered the gravity motors to be closed down and yet the particles still followed the ships course deviations. The Prof who had graduated from the mars mission to the space service commented that perhaps the ships immense mass still attracted these particles even though technically the heavy core should have been invisible. The captain used his resourcefulness to resolve the issue. He used a more sudden maneuver to position a larger asteroid between the ship and the nuisance asteroidals. These still tried to follow the ship but were overcome by the asteroids gravitational pull and collided with it. The captain made due entries in the ship's log, and sent off a report to earth, for their consideration. The following morning the ship was clear of the known asteroids and aligned itself with the gas giant Jupiter.

The gravity motor system was brought into full effect and the ship was hurtling through space at warp factor 0.8. This was not flat out but was quick. In old money the speed was just below 149,000 miles per second.

I've never really got on with this kilometers per second lark!

I've been unable to find the flight log data for the first manned flight to the Jupiter system, so I only know what crew members told me down in our local pubs, and that was some time ago, so bear with me if it doesn't quite add up!

They already knew that Jupiter had 63 moons though some of them were just irregular asteroid-like chunks of rock or ice. It was planned to land on Ganymede, the largest moon in the solar system. Other moons would of course be within easy reach, as would Jupiter itself. There was no plan to land on Jupiter largely because the nature of the planet meant that there was loads of gas, possibly some liquid, but no known solid large enough to actually land on, and anyway its gravitational force was a lot higher than earth's, 2.5 times as much.

The captain used his skills to perform a watching brief over the ship's computor, and was delighted at how the ship entered an orbit which looped the ship around Jupiter and Ganymede. He further knew that other moons may affect the safety of his ship and was well aware of when to move orbit and where to move it to. He knew that they would have just over 36 days to find and secure the mission on a suitable landing place on the chosen moon before any maneuvers were required.

The vast visual appearance of Jupiter seen this close to, was awe inspiring to say the least, its rings only visible from earth with the most advanced telescopes, were a spectacular colourful sight.

The moon landing rockets were already fully prepared but even so a rigorous checking system was followed. They found a flat bottomed crater and landed their equipment much as had been done on the Mars mission. In this case the away team excelled themselves and had their Eden type structure up and running within 48 hours, but unlike on mars had sited it in a large protective cave. Every man of the crew wanted to get down onto the surface including the captain but he knew that the safety of the Solar Orbiter was of paramount importance and ensured that at all times a fully competent crew were kept on board.

Ganymede is bigger than Mercury but less dense and a fully space suited man would weigh about 20% of his earth weight on it or perhaps a little less.

The away team soon acclimatized to this level of gravity and set about planning their primary exploration tasks. Ganymede is largely covered by ice, but the team had chosen well and established themselves on one of the tallest mountains on it. Even this mountain when examined closely was composed of ice and black dust, but it was solid enough to form a stable base under the Eden canopy. The cave had about fifty feet of headroom and was about 200 feet in length so that the Eden shelter was well protected, and its design was such that the overall shape was modified to suit the cave.

All vehicular activity was done at a slow pace. Drillings were taken to see if running water could be found.

After three weeks, drilling had gone down about 800 metres (2700 feet in old money), when suddenly just like striking oil, up came the fluid. Samples showed it contained a fair amount of acid, but that didn't matter, neutralizing the acid would not mean an insurmountable problem. Water was there, and it was warm enough to flow!

The fountain froze over again in a very short space of time. Checks on the atmosphere revealed a low gas pressure containing some oxygen but not enough for breathing.

The system was some 500,000,000 miles from the sun, and there was very little in the way of solar power to be tapped for human survival, the sun appeared as a large star and was about a fifth of the size as seen on earth. A source of heat was desperately required.

Over the next year or so the team constructed a heat pump using a pipe system buried some 2500 feet below the surface to source heat. Neutralized water was pumped round a closed system to fetch what little heat was there up to the surface. But the primary source of heat was a double helix pipe that spiraled round the closed system with unpurified acidulated natural moon water. The water came from the deep drillings but was captured and pumped down the spiral and back out again. Heat was transferred into the closed pipe system. As the water exhausted from the second half of the double helix it was allowed to flow out onto the surface of the moon and allowed to refreeze. The net result of this was that the closed system of water ran at a temperature of some 28 degrees Celsius.

Well for all the engineering involved this was a poor return because it took energy to operate the pumps, but at least it was there, and would help sustain temperatures inside the Eden shelter at a livable level. This mission was proving more daunting than the Mars mission. No significant winds had occurred yet and anyway the atmosphere was so thin that a wind turbine was a waste of effort. The mother ship had sufficient reserve of materials and did provide a good lead acid cell system capable of providing some back up power but the primary sources of energy so far discovered were well below what was needed. The atmosphere was that thin it equated to the earths atmosphere at about 200,000 feet. That is to say, virtually non existent.

A large photovoltaic array was erected to try to garner what ever sunlight it could and this did manage to provide a trickle charge for the newly installed battery system. So this represented a minor advancement. It was found that the charge into the batteries was just sufficient to allow the water pumps to run in short bursts and as such meant that the system was just about self sustaining.

Due to the frustration involved in trying and failing to find life prolonging sources of energy, tempers of the guys and girls of the away team became strained. All squabbles were settled by the Prof. He really was in the evening of his career now but his skills in such matters were staggeringly good. It was a real miracle that he managed to defuse even the bitterest squabble in a matter of minutes. How did he do it? I don't know, but do it he did. After another month of unrewarding toil he suggested that the away team return to the mother ship for rest and recuperation. A huge cheer went up and the idea was put into practice.

CHAPTER 8

BRAINSTORMING ABOARD THE SOLAR ORBITER

Captain Johnson realised that a mood of depression had settled over almost the entire crew, and so he assembled every one of the operational crew in the canteen and declared an open discussion. Ideas were bandied around and most people offered ideas that had already been tried. The Prof however suddenly interjected "perhaps if you listen to your granddad, you may learn something!"

The captain raised his customary eyebrow and said "well, er Prof, you have the floor!"

The Prof warmed to his task. "On the mars mission we used every available source of energy that we could. Now these were reasonably easy to tap into. Here on Ganymede, you have done incredibly well to tap any sources of energy because none of them is easy to get at. In my view heat is what you want, because heat can be used to warm you, to drive generators, and so to make electricity etc, etc" he paused and looked round the room. He had the avid attention of the entire crew.

He went on "in so far as my education allows me to think, there is only a small amount of sunlight, insufficient to use lenses and mirrors to melt rocks like we did on mars, so at best, such energy will only be a small but perhaps vital link in the chain required. The on moon energy trapped in the core could be got at with a system such as you already have as up and running, but time and costs really rule this out as we would have to drill very deep, perhaps thousands of feet. There is only one source of energy on this moon that we can use and that is nuclear power!"

He waited for the hubbub to die down.

"We must ask earth for proposals, and we must build a nuclear reactor power station here. Only a small one, capable of, perhaps, half a megawatt output.

Now I have given this matter some thought over the last month, and I am chucking this into the melting pot for discussion. Everyone here knows that I am not an engineer or scientist so I may well be wide of the mark. We could build the station say 200 miles or more away for safety reasons. The copper cables required to carry the electricity to base camp could be laid generally on the surface. The temperature is so cold that resistance of the cables and therefore power losses in transmission would be minimal. When operational, the reactor would make heat. Some of the heat would be used to free up a fair amount of water, and this water could be stored in an artificial lake. Lake water could then be used to keep the reactor cool, and this would also keep the water temperature above freezing so the lake would remain liquid. The residue of the heat would then be used to convert some water into steam which would drive our half megawatt turbine generator. The cooling water exhaust would of course go into the lake. The lake would expand in size until the energy lost due to radiation and conduction into surrounding ice exactly balanced the heat input from our reactor. There is no known life on Ganymede and so pollution would not be an issue. The turbine generator would have to have purified water to stop corrosion of the turbine, but it could be a closed system. I have seen a system like this on earth and it was used to power the Royal Yacht Brittania. This was the personal ship of the Queen of England.

Now this would not be an overnight thing, and it would cost money but it could be done!"

Again he waited for the ideas to percolate through his audience. "The other alternative is to stock up the Eden shelter with a reasonable amount of resources and leave it as a staging post or sanctuary for other missions or until some bright spark has a better idea!"

He paused and was astounded as the crew burst into spontaneous applause.

The Captain strode thoughtfully out and said. "Well, everybody, the Prof has given us some solid food for thought; the Prof doesn't know perhaps that this ship itself relies on a nuclear reactor for light and heat so it wouldn't be the first such venture using closed circuit technology! I suggest that we all sleep on it". The crew dispersed to their quarters, and there was a noticeable excitement in the babble as they went.

"Prof, I am ashamed to say I don't know your real name" said the captain.

"Oh, Prof will do, I've been stuck with that ever since I was a lad. Just every so often I come up with an idea, and that ability has caused my nickname. Quite honestly I actually prefer that now, and I know that when anyone refers to me in a conversation they call me 'The Prof', and that has a ring to it that is almost as good as The Captain!"

Both men chuckled and went off to their quarters.

CHAPTER 9

FURTHER THOUGHTS ON THE NUCLEAR STATION

The next day senior crew assembled on the bridge.

The captain barked "I never gave orders for this assembly!"

Some of the crew looked uncomfortable, but the captain grinned and added "However, the Prof's ideas need urgent discussion, so good morning to you all!"

The first to speak was the senior ship's engineer. "Erm, Prof, you may be glad to know that very few of us got any sleep last night! In my view the idea is not only sound, it is brilliant. The type of reactor he is thinking of is basically the same as our on board electric energy support system. There is though a problem that I could not see an easy solution to and that is that Ganymede is covered in ice, and if we melt it our power station would have to float or sink. And I don't think we have a ready made solution at hand."

The prof stood up "I think I remember mentioning asking for earth's help. Perhaps we could simply offload that problem to them for the moment. I did think though that the design would have to be a three legged bridge with the span wide enough to be on dry land so to speak, don't forget with a low force of gravity the weight of the suspended power station may well be handleable. In the meantime if we conduct a wide ranging geological survey, using the instruments at our disposal, and analyzing results ourselves, then we would send the data back home, and ask earth's opinion on whether or not there is anywhere at all where rock is close enough to the surface to provide a foundation!"

The captain then took the floor "It is incumbent upon me to ensure the safety of this mission, and I have listened to the ideas proposed. Frankly I think that we should follow all of the Prof's advice as follows:-

Firstly, the only chance of establishing a long term mission on Ganymede rests on nuclear power but that is for the future. I will not land a permanent mission on Ganymede at this juncture. Over the next few days we will carry out the geological survey and send all data with our ideas back to earth. Secondly we will restock the Eden shelter with a good supply of stores and medical items so that we would not have to put anything else on it when and if we return to it. Thirdly we can just take a look at the other big moons, Europa, Io and Callisto. I don't think that Io can sustain life because it is too volcanic and hostile. Ganymede, Europa and Callisto are all too cold but we may find means to provide heat so we will survey them all, while we are here so to speak. We will complete all our surveying work before we submit any proposals back to earth. There was a body of opinion on earth that suggested that Europa really should have been our target and not Ganymede. Our surveys may help to either sustain or dispel that notion.

Now should all of these avenues remain closed to us, then it will be off to Saturn and her interesting moon, Titan.

Questions anybody?"

The Captain knew that the morale of the crew had been reinvigorated and noticed how everyone now went about their duties with a particular crispness to their attitudes.

"Restock the Eden shelter first captain?"

"Agreed, please proceed with all possible speed."

The Captain assembled those crew members with geological knowledge, on the bridge and asked for a plan of action to be drawn up. There were in all some twenty good men assigned to this task. The Eden stocking procedure plan went ahead at the same time.

The Captain offered the Prof an overseeing role. He realised that the Prof had an innate wisdom, and his ability to quell squabbles was already legendary.

"I am giving the Prof an overwatching brief on these plans and he will only be answerable to me" He ordered.

The Prof, mildly surprised by this turn of events, smiled as a he said "Now get to work, you idle good for nothing scroungers!"

Such a remark coming from anyone else, even the captain, may have been met with some hostility as it was bound to ruffle a few professional pride feathers, but somehow it only provoked a good hearty laugh when the Prof said it.

The captain's one eyebrow rose as he heard the words but settled as soon as he saw the response and knew that he had made an inspired choice. Two shuttle trips were required to take the supplies down to the Eden shelter, but that part of the Captain's orders had been completed before the geological survey of Ganymede was even half done. Ganymede was a large moon and was comparable to Mercury in size, so it took almost a month to complete the survey.

Meanwhile the flight engineers had been tracking the other large moons to decide which one would be visited first. This changed every few days, but finally the ship headed for Europa.

They passed close to Io and could see that it was literally a boiling cauldron of volcanic and chemical activity, and in addition the radiation and magnetic detectors registered lethally high readings. Details of the flypast were of course relayed to earth for their digestion. Io looked so hostile that it would take a remarkable leap in protection against heat, chemicals, radiation, and magnetic fields, before if ever it was to suffer a visitor from earth.

I must say I can't imagine why any mission now or future would be sent to Io.

Another month was spent surveying Europa, but no landings were attempted. Next came Callisto and again a month was spent surveying. Finally when all of the information was collated a full report was sent back to earth. Callisto had been chosen as the last moon because it was the outer moon of the four big ones, and would position the ship at its best point for departure.

Surprisingly earth already knew about the surveying data and admitted that there was an auto relay of all such information going back to earth.

To the captain this represented a breach of trust, and he felt very aggrieved that no-one had seen fit to tell him.

The Prof however counseled him that it was basically nautical pessimism, and that members of the crew may have felt that they had a Jonah on board, which would not have been good for morale.

The captain accepted this only in part, but he asked earth that if there was anything else they would like to come clean about because he was going to give full disclosure to the crew. This after all being late 21st century space travel, and not Jason and the Argonauts.

He awaited a response from earth. Earth was dutifully penitent and assured him that there was nothing else to say on such matters.

True to his word he made full disclosure to the crew and asked if any member knew of anything that was not easily accounted for. They didn't, except one engineer in charge of the digital transmissions back to earth, who commented that it would explain one little thing that had mildly intrigued him for some time and that was that the standby power consumption of the transmitting system was an edge higher than he was expecting. This was explained if data was being transmitted at all times. Generally the transmissions were just for analysis.

The captain sent a further transmission back to earth, stating that the data transmission was an excellent idea, one which he would have fully endorsed if he had known about it. He also made it abundantly plain that as captain he should have been informed and that he would hunt down those responsible for keeping him in the dark upon his return to the home planet. Such things were an unacceptable breach of trust and it was down to him as the only really experienced spaceman to set the standards for future space adventure. The job, he told them was unbelievably lonely with the permanent prospect of imminent danger and he doubted that earth and desk bound wallahs would swap places with him, and they should have had more respect.

The Prof chortled when he learnt of this last transmission and said "that told them!"

After a few moments the Prof quietly told the captain who he thought may have been responsible.

"What!!!! That little weasel" exclaimed the captain.

The Prof said "Yes, and "the weasel" is his nickname but he thinks he has the best interests of the mission in mind. I know him, and he would have been worried that you may have gone off your rails or whatever, so he reasoned that earth needed to know what was going on, on board this ship, so that earth could do something about it in that unfortunate event! I think all data has been relayed back to earth and that would include all medical records."

A grim smile slowly spread across the captain's face as he said. "Well when I get back to earth I will chase this up just to see how close you are, in the meantime let's get on with the projects in hand."

CHAPTER 10

SATURN HERE WE COME

The captain decided that the mission should explore the Saturnian system and in particular Titan because this moon alone was known to have a dense atmosphere. The journey was accomplished swiftly with absolutely no fuss of any kind.

As the ship neared Saturn there was an urgent transmission from earth demanding to know the reason he had stopped the auto data being transmitted.

The captain was astounded, as he knew nothing of this and summoned his transmission engineers to the bridge.

"We don't even know where the transmitter is!" he was told.

The captain sent back a blunt message to earth saying as much and in return he demanded full disclosure of the design or he would abort the mission and return to earth.

There was a long delay from earth, (it was night time) before a reply was sent. Full details of the design and location of the transmission system were sent to the ship.

The captain immediately sent two crew members on a space walk to examine the transmitter aerial, which was located on the outside of the hull. Each crew member had a digital camera strapped to his helmet and the captain insisted that the detailed view as seen on the bridge was sent back to earth via the main transmitter.

When the auto transmitter aerial was located, two thirds of it was missing, with evidence of a meteor strike as the culprit. The captain asked the crew to make a more suitable transmitter aerial up and ensured that a second channel on the main transmitter was made available, thus providing earth with clearer information, and dual circuit capability. This was a resounding success, and the images received back on earth were brilliant after some computor processing.

"Just what would you have said if we hadn't discovered the covert transmission system- would you have allowed the ship to travel on with increased jeopardy?" the captain said, "and I insist that you reply to that!"

Earth capitulated and admitted to him that with events such as they were, a serious error of judgment had been made, and offered a full apology.

The captain had no time to feed on the satisfaction this gave him because the ship was just entering orbit round Titan.

CHAPTER 11

Moon landing

Titan is second in size only to Ganymede. Titan has an atmosphere about 50% denser than earth's. Titan also has a volcanic spot near one of its poles, and the captain was anxious to get a closer look at it. All data of course was relayed back to earth.

Earth showed a solid interest in the views of this moon and had noticed that there appeared to be a shelf on the rocky surface near to the hot spot.

An away team was sent to explore the possibilities. Earth had been correct, there was indeed a shelf and what's more it was a rock shelf. The away team reported that there appeared to be a flaming gas eruption continuously in operation from the top of a very tall volcano. This eruption was probably 50 miles distant from the shelf and even at that distance the noise was deafening.

The gas emissions were not steady but came in huge gusts every few seconds. This turned out to be due to the natural frequency of the escape hole, similar to the geysers on Iceland back on earth. Transmission of noise was just about audible on mars, non existent on Ganymede but damned loud on Titan. However the shelf rock proved soft enough to allow swift tunneling and could provide shelter and protection. After four hours the away team returned to the Solar Orbiter.

The geologists digested the information and four days later a full scale landing was attempted. One shuttle took the men; the second shuttle took an Eden style shelter, and digging equipment.

Using hand held powered rock pulverisers, a tunnel was started. Because of the low force of gravity the men found they could easily carry large chunks of loosened rock, so they did all that manually. The tunnel was deliberately made in a curved shape, with its entrance on the lee side in the hope that it would shield the occupants from the noise of the volcano. The team had tunneled in about 40 yards when the pulverisers broke through into a massive internal cavern. A rush of escaping gas blasted past the drillers as they broke through. The cavern was easily big enough to contain an Eden shelter, though the floor was uneven, and was covered in stalagmite like growths. There were no matching stalactites hanging from the roof. Broad chisel tools were fitted to the power rock pulverisers; a flat floor area of some size was quickly completed and the floor resembled a sand pit in its texture. The mission team then managed to transport the component pieces of the Eden shelter into the cavern though the entrance tunnel required more excavating to get the largest piece through. Both shuttles returned to the mother ship. Some crew members were photographing the sky view which was absolutely unique. Saturn filled the sky and the rings were as large and colourful as to defy apt description.

During the debriefing session the temperature inside the cave was stated to be 25 degrees Celsius, though cooling as heat escaped through the newly hewn entrance tunnel.

The Prof declared that the discovery of this cave if repeated on Ganymede would throw a whole new prospective on the question of tapping in to planetary resources.

The shuttles made several more visits taking rover vehicles and geological surveying equipment. The rock pulverisers were used to provide shelters for the vehicles instantly known as "garages."

The garages gave protection from atmospheric storms and helped to keep the temperature of the vehicles somewhat higher. They were still cold enough to freeze flesh from hands in the unlikely event of anyone touching them. The space suits worn at this time owed much to the research done on mars, but suits comprised a double layer of Martian fabric. This was effective but a man could only stay outside with this protection for about half an hour.

Inside the Eden shelter it was warm and fairly quiet as the sound of the erupting volcano was lost in the cavern. No transmissions from the cavern were possible due it was supposed to the nature of the rock, so a transmission aerial was set up outside on the wall of the rock face and communications were re-established.

The captain was now reasonably confident that his away team was in no immediate danger and so arranged for a further delivery of food water and medical supplies, along with a number of tasks for the team to do. He proposed that the mother ship and all shuttles would remain in orbit while the away team conducted a survey and carried out certain required experiments. Just as a precautionary measure the shuttles would reside inside the Solar Orbiter. These could be at the cave within the hour if needs be.

The rotation of Titan is synchronous that is to say the same surface always faces Saturn.

Saturn takes about 11 hours to rotate, and Titan takes about 16 days to orbit Saturn. Saturn takes about 30 years to orbit the Sun. Ok, ok, this makes it far too difficult for me to decide about summer and winter or day and night so I won't try. The mission had landed on the back half of Titan that is to say on the back with regard to the orbit direction. The adventurers' main task was to get to the front of the moon. Now the choice was to go inboard, that is facing Saturn, or to go outboard, that is to say on its dark side opposite to Saturn. On the outboard side of Saturn, the weak daylight from the sun would last about 8 days, followed by a similar night period. In the event they chose inboard because light reflected from Saturn at that time would give them a better chance to see what was going on. They requested the use of a shuttle, due to the distances involved. They used the shuttle to go 180 degrees round the moon and drop them on a suitable site with a rover vehicle.

Some hours into this mission they had landed and made about 100 miles progress back towards camp when the on board instrumentation recorded a sudden rise in radio activity. This was not at lethal or even danger levels, but was unexpected and rather worrying. It was not easy to establish whether the radiation source was on Titan or Saturn. They moved onwards with caution and the level fell again. From this they reasoned that it emanated from Titan itself. Thus possibly uranium or some radio active isotope was there for the taking.

There were hills to be seen but the moon was strikingly flat in general and the rover vehicle managed to touch speeds of almost 50 mph, and maintained an average speed of some 35 mph over an extended period. The denseness of the atmosphere had a marked effect on the performance of the rover vehicle, as it was a 200mph design in principle. After an extended period, on board instruments indicated that they were on the equator, from here on the moon surface took on a different aspect. There were small craters that were already self filling though the outside temperature was so low it was difficult to imagine any substance being liquid enough to move let alone fill a crater. Then came the rain. The crew had no time to analyse the contents, of the rain. Survival was suddenly not a foregone conclusion. They looked for and found a hilly region and managed to get the rover vehicle up onto it. This was about 200 feet up. A massive lake formed effectively marooning them in their position. All radio and video link contacts were ominously absent, but their plight had been spotted by observation from the Solar Orbiter. As the weather moderated they were amazed to see the lake disappearing almost as quickly as it had arrived. They walked outside and got a small sample of it. Soon the ground became hard enough to tread on without sinking into it and after about another 4 hours the rover vehicle was driven onwards. A shining pool that they had noticed from the hill top did not sink below the surface and upon investigation this was found to be mercury. The driver had a gold ring belonging to his mother in his pocket he dipped the ring into the pool and was rewarded as when it came out; the ring appeared to be silver. Mercury has an affinity for gold and here was definitive proof that it was indeed mercury.

The drivers mate said "that ring will be worth indescribable amounts of money back home!"

"I dare say but it won't be for sale!" came the reply. One of the primary duties of their mission was to gather small samples from the lunar surface, and the rover was fitted with a small scoop which they operated every 100 miles or so. The rover sampling system was fully automated, and each sample was bagged and provided with a label giving time date location and weight of each sample. The weight was a calculated value bearing a relationship to the actual weight on Titan and its forecast weight on earth.

There were no further incidents and the rover finally got back, was garaged and the crew parceled up the samples ready for full analysis.

Two days later the entire mission away team was back aboard the Solar Orbiter.

The rain sample was of course not water; it was far too cold for that. It proved to be some complex form of weak acidified methane. The boots used by the away team were not the wheelie boots used in the solar orbiter; they were made from some other substance. I don't know what the substance was, but the weak acidified methane, (This would usually have been gaseous on earth but was liquid on Titan due to the low temperatures), had eaten half the thickness of the soles away! Worrying or what!

This weird acid compound remained liquid! Also there was something else to consider. The mercury should have been solid at the temperature it was found at, but it too had remained liquid.

"You need some of that stuff in the water then", quipped one young chemist, "and it could be used as antifreeze!"

In so far as I know, this notion is still on the "to do" list. The young chemist's idea may never succeed, but it was food for thought.

Now samples of rock taken from the tunneling residue were interesting. Though the rock was soft it was highly magnetic and proved to contain both iron and nickel. Titan itself did not have a magnetic field, yet the necessary elements to support a magnetic field were clearly available.

Analyzing the other samples taken would prove a long drawn out procedure because of the shear quantity.

From samples taken from the high radiation region, there was uranium in small quantities but there were also minute traces of plutonium. Now back on earth, plutonium was man made, so this was a revelation, but may explain the radiation readings seen. Plutonium is a very dangerous element, so greater care would have to be taken on subsequent visits. The other samples taken proved very interesting to geologists but were of less import to the layman. When the captain assembled his information and sent it back to earth, the earth scientists compared it to the data that was being auto transmitted. The two sources of information were similar, but not identical. The one complemented the other. Due to the distances involved and the fact that space noise occasionally drowned out the transmissions, the second bite at the cherry really filled in some of the gaps.

The captain called another general all senior hands bridge conference.

"Gentlemen please confirm the state of the Titan Eden shelter."

His away team commander confirmed that the Eden shelter had been stocked to the same level as the Ganymede shelter.

"Geologists report please!"

The head geologists looked carefully at the information in his folder. "Captain, it will take some time to analyse and collate all that we have collected. We are proceeding with all possible speed with due deference to our duty of care."

"Propulsion engineers, your report please!"

"Captain, there is no sign of any undue stress on the gravity motor or its control functions, rocket motors are A1 and we still have fuel reserves of 92%. We have sent our junior engineers out on the hull after the transmitter failure but though there are other small signs of damage the self sealing internal plastics are fully effective in their purpose"

"Junior engineers outside?" questioned the captain.

"Privilege of rank and training Captain!" The eyebrow half raised.

"Life support engineers, your report please."

A full investigation was finished yesterday sir, and we have still got 98% air supply compared to our voyage beginning. The battery charging system is operating with full efficiency, there is water still at 87% of voyage beginning value, all internal heating and lighting systems are still fully operational and the weapons system is ready for testing." The nuclear electric generating system is fully functioning, all parameters within their required boundaries.

"Is there any increase in carbon dioxide in the ship air supply?"

"Minimal sirs, the figure is 6.2%, and for good measure the carbon monoxide value is less than one third of the value in earth's atmosphere."

"Prof, how is morale amongst the crew?"

"As good as I have ever seen it captain!"

The captain drew a deep breath and said "well with this deplorable state of affairs, I intend to head back to earth!"

A still silence pervaded the entire bridge but less than half a second later there was a roar of approval.

"Be professional gentlemen!" grinned the captain.

"Ok to your stations every one" ordered the Prof, then diplomatically deferring to the captain. "Prof, you have the bridge, me I'm going for a little shut eye!"

CHAPTER 12

THE SHIP PAUSES AT MARS

The Captain had every one on full alert as the ship reached the outer layers of the asteroid belt. Again the ships speed was synchronised to the average speed of the orbiting rubble, and managed to traverse the danger zone without incident. The captain decided to chase an asteroid and he selected a medium sized chunk of asteroid that was travelling a little faster than the average speed and gave it a 20 second blast with the laser gun. This blast forced the asteroid into a spin but it didn't split. It gathered a little speed, and was deviated slightly. As the ship tracked this asteroid it was soon obvious that it would collide with an even bigger one. Those on the bridge watched on the long distance scanner as an almighty explosion took place some 5000 miles away, and were amazed when the intensity of the light far from fading, shone brilliantly for a few seconds and then sustained itself at a steady lower but bright level.

The Prof arrived on the bridge just at the critical moment, and said, "We may just have solved the nuclear reactor issue!"

"Yes a nuclear reaction is the only form of reaction that could sustain itself in space," mused the Captain.

Over the next few hours although the "new asteroid" went further and further away it seemed to get bigger and bigger. Its gravity increased as it sucked other asteroidal space dust in and finally was big enough to attract itself to anything in its proximity. The force of the supposed nuclear reaction had given the resulting asteroid a new slower speed and a new course, and suddenly it began to noticeably respond to the gravitational pull of mars.

The captain saw a sudden immense danger for those on mars and demanded an urgent opinion from earth as to land fall on mars if that was going to happen.

Earth's scientists could now see what was happening on telescopes and concluded that the new moon, for that is what had formed, would enter a stable orbit somewhere between Phobos and Deimos, but going the opposite way round.

The Solar Orbiter was put into a synchronised orbit on the opposite side of Mars for safety reasons and the shuttle craft were hastily prepared for a landing.

The mars mission team was delighted to welcome them into their Eden shelter. As yet, the mission was unaware of the drama that had unfolded above them. However after about 6 hours or so the new moon rose and it was immediately obvious that there was a new source of heat. It could be plainly felt through the roof of the Eden shelter.

The moon mission was made aware that the reaction on the new moon was nuclear and in earths view it was fusion not fission so radiation was not quite such a worrying factor, but they would need to use suitable protective clothing. The orbit of this new moon was such that it soon disappeared from view, below the horizon.

The mars mission engineers and scientists had just about reached the end of development of mars with the power sources formerly at their disposal, but this new mini-sun could make a considerable difference.

"How long will it last?" they asked.

No one knew- it was a new phenomenon.

CHAPTER 13

BACK TO EARTH

THE WEASEL.

Captain Johnson made it his primary task to search for the weasel. He found him sitting behind his desk smiling weakly.

"Ok, ok a poor decision" he admitted.

The captain asked him if he could ever justify such a decision.

The weasel, otherwise known as head of space administration looked the captain straight in the eye and said bluntly "No!"

This eased some of the wind out of Captain Johnson's sails. Quite against his expectation he suddenly warmed to the man.

The weasel suddenly exploded with excitement. "Captain Johnson, I believe that you left fully provisioned Eden shelters on Ganymede and Titan?"

"That I did!"

"Well something has happened on Titan or Ganymede, actually the identification isn't possible but it happened since you left!"

"What would that be, exactly?"

"One of your technicians left a camera running, and that has sent these pictures back to us here!" he spun and hit the enter button on his keyboard.

"Christ, it looks like a sort of pig!" ejaculated the captain, "But there was no sign of life at all while we were there, not on either moon!"

"In so far as we can tell, there was a minor eruption in the vicinity of the Eden shelter and a medical supplies cabinet was tipped over. Within the cabinet was a small container of stem cells to be used in extreme cases by your ship's surgeon. We think that these have leaked out and somehow precipitated a life form."

"But on Titan the atmosphere is largely nitrogen, and on Ganymede the atmosphere is very thin, so how could it breathe, and what on earth can it feed on?"

"That is a matter for some conjecture. Your next mission will be to return there and I am afraid you will have to be put up with me, and a few other scientists. Look I am aware that everyone calls me "the weasel", but I am made of sterner stuff than that. My actual name is James Whistler, and you can see from that how easy it was to brand me as the weasel."

"James, welcome to my crew. I am due a few weeks leave but after that I will be at your disposal."

"James Whistler smiled and said, "Take your time I have a massive amount of work to do before I will be ready."

They shook hands and the captain went out into the corridor.

"How close was I" said the Prof, who happened to be passing just at that moment.

"Bang on!"

The captain then paused and said "listen, I have a few things to do in the next couple of hours, but principally the formal adoption of you as my second in command!"

The Prof's face suffused a delightful pink as he glowed with the shear pleasure at this show of confidence in him. The captain continued "As my second in command, you will be privy to the fact that we seem to have planted life onto Ganymede or Titan! See you after our leaves are up. And I think the weasel wants to see you!"

The Prof digested what he had just heard and then saw on screen the evidence as James Whistler demonstrated on his computor. "The whistler" as we shall now affectionately call him for expediency, brought the Prof up to speed. So that when he left the office one hour later he was buzzing with excitement as he knew that he would be part of real history. Strangely although it was me that started to refer to James

Whistler as 'the whistler', that nickname somehow percolated into the space service and he suddenly became known universally as "The Whistler."

After very deep discussions about mars' new moon, the realization came that the event could have happened naturally at any time, and the Solar Orbiter had merely altered the time frame slightly. The blast of the laser had knocked the first asteroid but had only increased the speed slightly, so the collision had been virtually inevitable, and probably such things happen all the time. In this case the laser seemed to precipitate a nuclear reaction, but even that may have occurred naturally.

The best explanation put forward was that the asteroid that was lasered in fact contained two lumps of uranium held apart by a piece of ice perhaps 1000 feet thick. The laser had upset the stability of this particular piece of space debris and with it spinning it caused severe friction and stress inside it. So much so, that the ice became water, allowing the two lumps of uranium to come closer together. There must have been more than the critical mass of uranium and the result was a nuclear fission bomb. Just about the time this bomb was about to explode the asteroid collided with another larger chunk consisting of an outer crust and an inner core of water. The explosion was so violent when it happened that the water temperature was driven so high that it split into hydrogen and oxygen with the oxygen causing simple burning and this accounted for the high initial brightness, but the hydrogen may be part of a nuclear fusion reaction. The nuclear blast was on a point on the larger asteroid that caused it to slow down and hence lose it place in asteroid orbit. As all this was happening the new moon gathered other heavy particles in the proximity so that after about a week the size had grown to that of a small moon and the orbit around mars stabilized. Now this idea was stretching the imagination a bit but it did describe what had gone on in principle. The new moon had carried on gaining mass from other objects right until it broke out of the asteroid belt and took up its new orbit.

This was all conjecture but if true it was calculated that the new moon would burn only for about 5000 years. Then it would run out of energy and simply cool off. The orbit was expected to change slightly as the moon stabilized to its new conditions. Its orbital time was such that, some times it was seen during the Martian day and at others during the Martian night. This would give rise to mini summer and winter effects. During the "summer" period its heat was additive to the sun's. During the "winter" period it lit up mars on its own. The nights on mars suddenly had a very different aspect. A natural Martian day was similar to an earth day being about 2.6% longer.

Earth's scientists and engineers hoped that the temperature of mars would increase and that means would be found to release oxygen trapped in the various rock formations. This would provide protection from the gamma rays and other harmful emissions from the new moon. The new moon was referred to as "sonny", and of course the ultimate hope that a breathable atmosphere would be produced or rather reproduced, with cloud formations allowing a greenhouse effect to help keep mars warm. There was evidence that mars had once had mighty oceans and rivers but these had simply evaporated into outer space for as yet unknown reasons and the planets water supply became depleted.

The whistler was hoping that this nuclear moon trick could be repeated near to Ganymede and we would then have a moon going round a moon. If it was possible to do this, the nuclear power would be provided without building a power station on Ganymede.

CHAPTER 14

THE NEXT BIG MISSION

The Solar Orbiter was revictualled with enough to account for additional members in the crew. The whistler took three other top scientists with him and the captain assigned some simple duties just to include them in the general running of the ship. This was a good move because the scientists soon realised just what slick crew ran the ship and without exception they would obey the orders of the Prof and the Captain.

The trip out to mars was accomplished without fuss. It started at almost the same time as the latest run by the "Freeloader", but they got there a couple of days sooner. The Captain organized a brief visit to the mars mission and the four scientists were sent down to look at progress. To a man they were impressed by the ingenuity of the mars team and when back on board the Solar Orbiter they were animated in their discussions about mars' progress for several days. The scientists took a myriad of readings from sonny. It was a lot bigger than they had expected and indeed it seemed to the captain to have swollen since the last time he had seen it.

The Prof called the scientists to the bridge as the captain slept and gave them a pre-agreed lecture on the technique for getting through the asteroid belt.

"While we traverse this belt the ship will be going fairly slowly so we need you lads to tell us if there is any likelihood that we could repeat the trick that brought "sonny" into existence. There will be literally thousands of asteroids for you to view, but they can be millions of miles apart. Look for close groups. If you find suitable candidates we have a system of electronic marker buoys to deploy, and we would plant them on the asteroids as we go by. They have a radio transmitter that will remain dormant until we send an initiating signal and then the batteries will last for a week. We should be able to find them again, even if they are on the opposite side of their orbit. Now we only have a limited number of these so use them sparingly! I suggest that you leave it until we are in the outer reaches of the asteroid belt before you use the markers because they are more likely to be steerable to where we want them!

The Whistler made a mental note that the Prof was truly no fool and agreed to the ideas put before them.

Suddenly the Whistler was galvanised into action.

"Prof, we need the laser now" he yelled.

The laser gunner was called to the bridge and the Whistler gave very precise instructions on what to do. The gunner aimed at the asteroids in question, and hit them with 60 second sustained blasts. All in all the Whistler blasted five asteroids over a period of a couple of hours, and once this done his animated face resumed its normal glacial calm.

He turned to the Prof and said "well you said to look for close groups and just as you said that a close group came onto the viewer. I know they are still hundreds of thousands of miles away, but I also know that the laser beam does not diverge and would be just as effective at any distance!"

The Captain returned to the bridge just at that moment and the Prof indicated what had been done.

The captain took the Prof and the Whistler to one side and demanded an explanation.

James Whistler said "following your accidental creation of a new moon, I have thought along a similar line but for a very different reason. Mars is never going to be a green planet like earth; it simply does not have enough water. It did have water once and of course may have been a fertile place. Possibly due to its atmosphere being burnt away by large meteorites and other spatial debris the atmospheric pressure would have dropped to the point where the water would simply have evaporated and then formed mars atmosphere. This in its turn could easily have been removed by the transition of spatial debris after massive uncontrolled chemical reactions. There are millions of tons of rock up here in the asteroid belt, and a small amount of water and I wondered if we could get some of it down onto mars. I have done calculations on my computor until I was dizzy from the effort but suddenly right in front of me on the long range viewer was the key to this jigsaw. A large enough chunk of asteroid ice, close enough for us to influence with the laser gun. I think I yelled at the Prof, for which I am sorry, but I would have yelled the same at you if you had been on the bridge.

The five asteroids that we hit were all water bearing ones, and have all been slowed down in orbit with the first one the slowest of the lot. With a little help from us, the others will collide with it and thus build up the bulk. At their new orbit speed the asteroid will firstly be pulled out of asteroid belt by the sun. This moment in history may have been quite unique, which is why I was so animated. Mars is just about exactly where I needed it to be to finish my jigsaw. The targeted asteroid group will find itself losing the influence of the sun as it gets nearer to mars and mars will become the dominant force so it will go into a new orbit round mars, but will not have sufficient velocity to maintain the orbit. In a short time, the asteroid will get caught by mars' thin atmosphere but will not make landfall and should evaporate on entry. After that it will refreeze in mars cold atmosphere, and then mars will suffer a hailstorm but the bulk of this will fall in and around large craters centered about 200 miles from the mission, and with any luck we'll have some large lakes there!"

"My god" exploded the captain, "inform mars immediately with your predictions!"

"Before I do that captain I have another prediction for you to consider. The asteroids will inject a considerable amount of gaseous matter into the atmosphere and if we can get enough of it in there it would help mars to protect its new found water supply. So perhaps with a little ingenuity we really could provide mars with the basis of an eco system!"

The captain opened communications with the galley. "Double rations for the entire crew today, make sure all functions are on auto, because I want the entire crew to know what I have to say!"

The meeting was held in the canteen. The captain broke the news that it was beginning to look as if mars could be colonized after all. "With our accidental atomic moon circulating providing heat and the water supply suddenly increased a million fold, or even more, the only thing missing is oxygen, and that could be supplied by electrolyzing the water!

The man responsible for this is none other than The Whistler. James, perhaps you would like to fill in some blanks for the crew?"

James Whistler stood in front of his audience; he was not comfortable when speaking to such a large gathering. He pressed on, nevertheless.

"Ladies and gentlemen, we will know within a matter of days just how successful or otherwise this enterprise is. The lessons we learn now are vital. We of course will try to repeat this success for Ganymede and Titan, though it may not be quite so easy.

Titan, however, has already beaten us to the punch" he glanced at the captain who nodded approval. "Titan already has some form of life on it! Well we think it is Titan but it may be Ganymede" the canteen was silent. The Whistler opened his laptop, and established communications with the on board computer and display screens. There were audible gasps as the crew looked at the pig like creatures.

"Where have they come from?" said one voice. The Whistler told them of his suspicions regarding stem cells.

"The thing is they are basically human so we won't be able to consider them a source of food!"

A more cynical voice rang out "I bet they are more likely to consider us a source of food!"

The Prof interjected "we don't know what actually precipitated this life form. It cannot breathe oxygen because there isn't enough so human it is not, but of course they could be our cousins."

One wag then chortled "It is all clear to me that we have been barking up the wrong tree. We never descended from apes, we descended from pigs!!!" the laughter died down as the Whistler took the floor again. "You may be closer than you realise. Pig parts have been used in experimental transplant surgery with partial and increasing success. We are more closely related to pigs than you may have imagined, there are striking similarities in our respective DNA chains. Any way, whoever is selected for the away team, *be careful*. We don't know if they carry fatal diseases, if they are ferocious predators, what they feed on, how they breathe, whether they make droppings or indeed, where they actually live. What we do know was that the growth rate was extraordinary, and they may now be of dinosaur proportions."

The captain stepped forward. "The Prof has had another brainstorm"! The faces in the audience were agape with expectation.

"Instead of blasting asteroids with our lasers, which uses precious energy and is a crude tool, he has postulated the idea that, as we will be on the outer edge of the asteroid belt we will need to accelerate the asteroids not slow them down. He therefore wants me to use the gravity motor to pull them into a desired direction and speed. We are pretty sure that this will work, because we have already had an example of small asteroidal particles being noticeably attracted to this ship. James Whistler and his team are working on this idea in principle but they will only be able to finalise calculations once the asteroids have been chosen. As you know we plan to mark certain ones already so I ask you all to give full co-operation. Please now return to your duties."

Again the departing babble showed the crew to be in fine fettle. The operational crew of the Solar Orbiter is about 1000 souls. The other 17000 or so people on board, the undercrew, are responsible for the well running of the on board facilities, nevertheless within minutes of the canteen meeting closure, every man jack aboard the solar orbiter new of the pig issue.

Quietly the captain asked the Whistler for his thoughts on the asteroid control issue. "Captain, the Prof is simply brilliant. If we can't do this then our mission will not get the accolades it deserves, I have all four of us scientists working on different aspects of the problem dynamics. As soon as I can I will be into your quarters with a result!"

The Whistler deep in thought added "you know we can try the Prof's idea here and now. Phobos is a doomed moon because it does not quite have sufficient orbital velocity to sustain its present orbit. We must try to enhance the velocity somewhat to guard against it crashing into mars, to protect our investment so to speak."

Using his laptop he calculated the position of the ship and how to situate themselves between the Sun and Phobos, and the vectorial alignment of widow opening etc, etc. the captain agreed to the maneuver and the idea was tried out. It would be a while before the effect could be seen or if indeed the maneuver had been successful at all, because the change required was minimal.

The crew had been chosen to represent all interests. There were Christians, Muslims, Hindus, Buddhists, Atheists and a good proportion of free thinkers. No one had made even the slightest objection to the asteroid control; no-one thought that the ship was interfering in God's work. Perhaps, the captain mused they all saw themselves as instruments of god or history or whatever, but right now they were united. The captain knew that James Whistler was a cautious man, and would not rush into action without first having solved the mathematics involved. He was glad to have him aboard and deep in his mind he decided to probe the Whistler to find out what had really prompted the spy transmitter. Originally the captain, fired by anger had tracked the Whistler down; but know he knew just what a valuable man the Whistler was, his motive had become overbearing curiosity. His simple desire was to know.

CHAPTER 15

MESSAGES FROM MARS

The Whistler had been right. There had been a hailstorm on mars. That had left a legacy of strange colours in the sky. But in a crater within three hours drive from the base a sizeable lake had been formed, this did freeze over but the ice was only three or four inches thick. Sonny shone brilliantly and helped keep the surface temperature of the lake water just below freezing.

The mars mission technicians were keeping a close eye on the water level in the lake and noticed that it was dropping slowly as water soaked into the parched Martian soil.

They estimated that it would be about 25 years before the lake dried up. The mars mission engineers set up an electrolysis plant, that produced oxygen and after filling every available bottle with it, allowed the rest to escape into the atmosphere.

They also noted some chemical activity at one end of the lake. This was under observation for the moment to establish exactly what was happening, but early indications were that the oxygen levels at that end of the lake were higher than expected.

The message ended with the hopeful note asking that on the way back from its present mission could the Solar Orbiter give them a few more hailstorms. No mention was made of Phobos.

The normally glacial face of the Whistler absolutely beamed, revealing a warm side to his personality.

"James" said the captain, "I formally ask you to consider that request."

The Whistlers face slowly returned to its normal cold expression as he began to slowly nod in the affirmative.

The captain knew that he was already deep in the thoughts that such a request entailed. He further warmed to the man and suddenly realised that he actually liked him.

He mentioned this just casually and was rewarded when a slight pink glow appeared on the Whistler's face. His eyes said it all and the two men glanced at each other and could see that each held the other in high regard.

CHAPTER 16

ON THE OUTER REACHES OF THE ASTEROID BELT

What can we do about Ganymede and Titan?

Markers were dropped onto about 20 asteroids, all to suit parameters as laid down by the Whistler and his men. The vast bulk of asteroids were as predicted by earth. Basically they were composed of rock and metals, but fortunately there were a number that still contained water ice.

The captain chose a small unmarked asteroid and orientated his ship to be between the asteroid and Ganymede; he opened both forward and rearward gravity motor windows simultaneously. This was only the second time that this had been done, the first being the attempt at modifying Phobos' orbit. His notion in this case was to use Jupiter as an anchor while attracting the asteroid.

This worked brilliantly, the asteroid responded with a gradual increase in speed and changed course exactly as planned. The captain then closed the gravity motor down and used rocket control to get out of the way of the rapidly approaching asteroid. The asteroid passed within visual range, and although it was classified as a small one it looked vast compared to the ship. However it hurtled on towards its target. The captain took the ship outside the asteroid belt and then kept station with it while observations were done.

The grinning Prof said "Told you!" the captain then informed the Prof of what they had done to Phobos.

The Prof said "well if this one worked the Phobos one should have worked too!"

The asteroid temporarily became another moon of Jupiter, but then on its second orbit it was unable to escape the attraction to Ganymede. It skimmed Ganymede but stayed in orbit. On its third orbit it hurtled towards Ganymede. It hit Ganymede and made a sizeable impact crater. As they observed, the crater soon lost the sharpness and it was realised that somehow or other it had begun to fill itself, or the wall produced had begun to sink.

There was an urgent message from earth requesting close monitoring of Phobos when they made the return trip. Earth was worried that Phobos had increased its orbital velocity and so may escape into the asteroid belt. The captain, the Whistler and the Prof exchanged guilty glances.

The captain asked the Whistler "well what do we do James, come clean or leave our actions covert?"

"Touché, captain I see we must come clean!" a full explanation was beamed to earth with a request to allow Phobos about a month to settle and check again to see if earth's fears were upheld.

The next move in this technological enterprise was to use the gravity motor to collect several asteroids and get them to follow the pilot. Asteroids of metals and rock; that is chunks of heavy metal, were gradually shepherded together until finally they were close enough to be treated as a single entity, and the ship used its gravity motor to send them towards Jupiter.

There was some tension on board the bridge of the solar orbiter, but quiet calm remained.

The calculations of the Whistler proved spot on even though he had had to estimate the true mass of each one, and the new moon bits hurtled around Jupiter. During their orbit they became slightly separated as the gravity and outer atmosphere drag from Jupiter affected them all slightly differently. As they were drawn down towards Ganymede there was a slight glow just detectable on the ship's instruments. They ascribed this to dust left in the atmosphere from their pilot shot, giving friction heating of the asteroidal bits.

The captain ordered the crew to stand down to normal after all parts were seen to have made landfall. The Prof thought they should leave it about a week to allow the affects of the asteroid collisions die away and said as much. The whistler said tersely "three weeks!"

The Prof dipped his head in acknowledgement and grinned saying "I'm glad somebody round here knows what they are talking about!"

In a rare show of friendliness the Whistler said "fancy a beer?"

The two men went off to sample the brewed on board stuff. This really wasn't bad and some wag had dreamed the name as "kick up the asteroids" they used a laser printer to make the labels which proudly declared "4.2% free of customs and excise duty, brewed by the mad hatter". The name that stuck to the beer was 'mad hatter', and this was what everyone asked for. Strictly enforced rules prevented consumption of more than two pints at any one time. Back on earth, virtually every measure was in kilograms and kilometers. Out in space we still had pints, feet and inches. Hooray!

The Whistler was disappointed that there was no sign of a nuclear warming moon, and realised that Ganymede may simply require a nuclear station for heat. Too much heat would simply have flooded the place anyway.

Now of course Titan was one hell of a long way from the asteroid belts, and the Whistler found the calculations much more difficult to do but finally he took them to the captain's quarters to aquaint the captain with the needs of that part of the project.

The captain read the recommendations, and then raised both eyebrows. This was a rare event and the Whistler asked "can we do it?"

The captain leaned right back in his chair and clasped both hands behind his head, before saying "we would have to go half way to Saturn in order to impart sufficient speed to the asteroids and I don't think we can simply turn the ship round and come back. So, we would have to go the whole way, we would release the asteroids from our tow at some calculated point on the journey, use the sling shot effect to go round Saturn and come back along a very different flight path to avoid colliding with the asteroids. The asteroids would take about another month to enter orbit round Saturn. And would probably," he paused scanning his laptop, "enter Titan's atmosphere when Titan was on the blind side of Saturn so we could not directly observe!"

"We could try to get the camera in the cave out to take a peek" said the Prof suddenly. "I have been playing with its remote control functions recently and they are still operational" he added.

"Well it looks like the answer is yes, but I must sleep on it to see if there is something else to fret about" said Captain Johnson.

"Very well, I now have to select the asteroids".

The Prof said "captain, I have just heard from mars and they are saying that there is definitely a massive increase in oxygen emanating from one end of the lake and they say the rate of oxygen production is slowly increasing! The orbit of Phobos should avoid the possible mars crash scenario, and it will not escape from mars."

"Thanks Prof; as usual you have found something to put me in a positive frame of mind".

CHAPTER 17

THE FLYING VISIT ROUND SATURN.

The ship successfully shepherded the chosen asteroids and even sent shuttles out to retrieve the previously dropped markers, taking readings to confirm the asteroid compositions, since this necessitated putting a man on the surface of each asteroid great care was taken. This mini mission was done with the usual professionalism and went without incident. The on board instruments of the shuttle relayed information back to solar orbiter about the composition of each asteroid.

The whistler evaluated the data and said with surprise, "these things are 95% rock but there are traces of iron and uranium on the three largest ones"

"Problems?" enquired the captain

"No, just surprises" said the Whistler while his intellect was furiously engaged in further calculations. "No, but I have been given more food for thought, though it will be touch and go as to whether there is enough uranium to spark off a nuclear reaction"

In the event the mission went exactly according to plan with the asteroid group being released to orbit freely while under the influence of Saturn.

The captain decided to send a shuttle exploration to the cave on Titan at the earliest opportunity, and see if there really was evidence of life. The away team was under strict orders to return long before the asteroids were due to strike Titan. However the away team was stood down as the camera information being received on the Solar Orbiter needed more analysis.

To the excitement of the entire ships crew the pig like creatures really were there but were really quite small, but at least we now knew that it was Titan not Ganymede that had this miracle of life on it. There had been several camera sightings of the creatures.

The Prof burst out laughing. "You know, we really are a bunch of idiots! When that creature appeared, somehow it must have been very close to the lens and thus appeared very large, so when we put the system to auto focus it has used the previous image to base it on. It must have been even closer for the second image. Dinosaur sized indeed!"

The captain then intervened "the Prof is usually right, but in this instance we have to presume that he is wrong. Sorry Prof. Safety first please." The other exciting thing was that it may breathe oxygen and it appeared from the running gas monitors left outside the Eden shelter that there was a layer of oxygen close to ground, and this had not been spotted by the original mission.

The men of the mission were a little disgruntled when they heard of this as it impinged on their professionalism.

The Prof was quick to point out that there had been a minor eruption and who knew what chemicals might have released, and anyway it was their foresight in leaving the gas monitors running that had given us a new swathe of information.

The away team leader, able spaceman Keith Windridge capitulated, and even felt slightly ashamed that he had allowed personal pride to cloud his judgment, and was man enough to admit that leaving the gas monitor on had been an oversight.

"We were fortunate in the extreme to create a new mini-sun for mars and maybe that is not the end of our good fortune. Everybody needs luck from time to time," smiled the Prof.

The Prof postulated that perhaps the pig thing had not been created by stem cells, but was a native of Titan that only came out when there was oxygen to breathe. He likened it to the existence of lungfish on earth. These creatures are fish, but when the water supply dries up they bury themselves in the soil leaving their mouths at the top for breathing and stay there for months at a time until the rains come.

"Prof, if that is true it could be the best piece of theorizing on the trip so far" said the Whistler whilst sucking his breath in sharply, thinking that the Prof was almost certainly right.

Even though the ship's communications video had not been on, every man jack of the crew knew about the Prof's notion within 10 minutes. Possibly we would never achieve the speed of light but the jungle telegraph was close!

Perhaps as a result of this, one of the women crew members went straight to the Captain and volunteered for away team duty, as soon as Titan was revisited. When questioned as to why, her reply was "Why not? After all, my husband can be a bit of a pig sometimes and I want to see where he comes from!"

The Captain always thought that one volunteer really is worth a ten pressed men, and accepted her offer. He later checked into her personnel file and found that she was better qualified than many men, and so asked her to his quarters.

"Come in" he mumbled halfway through a sandwich as she knocked. She rather diffidently came inside and the captain went straight to the point. "May I call you Jane?" and as she nodded he went on "I see from your record that you are a very well qualified young lady, are you in fact married?"

"No she replied, certainly not, I am only 23!"

"Children?"

"Absolutely not!"

"Well you evidently have a well developed sense of humour! These away missions do involve personal danger, after all we are existing right at the forefront of technology and knowledge, and so if you had children I probably would only consider you in an emergency, but as you do not I will consider you as an able bodied spaceman and you would then be subject to normal away team regulations and controls. There is one small issue. You are a stunningly beautiful woman, and so I feel I must offer my full personal protection to you. This fact would be known to your away commander and yourself only, and I would swear you both to full secrecy!"

"I can look after myself!" she retorted slightly stung by his attitude.

"Under 99% of circumstances, I do not doubt that you can, but I will not be the commander accused of throwing a young woman to the wolves!"

She suddenly felt the power of plain chivalry and rather liked it. "Captain your every wish is my command!"

He in his turn felt a sudden rush of attraction, quite against anything that he would have expected. He had always rather liked women, but had remained a bachelor.

Bringing his mind back to its professional status he said "Jane, your status is henceforth changed. You are now a member of the away team; you will replace Brian Edmondson who has just become a father. Now if you please your new station is situated on level four, Corridor J. Please proceed there immediately. All other formalities will be taken care of by myself or the Prof!"

"Clothes?!" she mumbled.

"All in hand" said the Captain "dismissed".

Jane walked/skated the not inconsiderable distance to corridor J on level 4, and when she got there she was welcomed by her new superior officer.

He was of German stock and of course spoke impeccable English. "Welcome Jane, I am Heinrich."

"Hello Heinrich, so pleased to be on the team!"

"Ok, I understand from the captain that you have a certain protection while you are here. I understand what the captain wants. However I cannot offer any protection from the ribald humour that even embarrasses me occasionally!"

"I dare say you think of me as a delicate slip of a girl, but I have six brothers and I defended myself against them. I do not need special consideration sir".

"Reserve that "sir" discipline for the senior crew, I am Heinrich, got it!"

"Jane" she grinned, offering her hand. This was more like it!

On the return leg from Saturn, the ship behaved perfectly and they managed to check the orbit of the asteroids just before Saturn blindsided them. So far, so good. The ship continued until they reached Jupiter. Christ the planet was colossal! The ship used the slingshot effect with the utmost precision, and entered its desired orbit. A quick visit to Ganymede in the Jovian system revealed that there were no significant changes to report, the rock asteroids had been gobbled up and frozen, so immediately after that, Titan was what the mission focused on. The Solar Orbiter returned to Titan and the Saturnian system.

When all shuttle systems had been thoroughly checked, the away team was assembled.

CHAPTER 18

THE SECOND VISIT TO TITAN

It was known that the rock asteroids had crashed into each other and then fallen on Titan, but there was no noticeable general change to conditions, no nuclear reactions.

The away team again used two shuttles, the second one carrying guns would you believe. Their on board computors maneuvered the shuttles with consummate ease, and they described graceful parabolic arcs on their way to the landing place. Upon entering the cave and then the Eden shelter, there was no sign of life. Jane however said "look, I am by far the lightest member of the crew here, and I think these things may be cave inhabitants and they are sensitive to earth movements and vibrations".

"Heinrich thought and then spoke "ok, Jane here is a revolver, use it if you have to and leave your communication channel open. Don't worry about battery life. There is plenty for the rest of us to do outside, but we won't be far away".

Jane settled down to wait, and after a good hour there was a small disturbance from the sandy floor. A flat nose appeared followed by a body with a large number of legs. There were groups of shiny spots on the head, and Jane realised they might be eyes.

The creature was about the size of a guinea pig, and it scuttled slowly across in front of her. Then another disturbance and a similar creature about the size of a small dog heaved itself into view. Jane hardly dared breathe. She was in the history books now as the first person to see an extra terrestrial form of life in the flesh on its own turf so to speak. She carefully opened her digital camera, and switched the flash off but put the camera into movie mode.

Suddenly the large one froze in its tracks and she knew it had sensed her. It wagged its head from side to side and then cautiously approached. It had no mouth that she could discern. She waited for it to breathe. It didn't but then again it didn't move either. It must have finally decided she presented no threat and began to move. Its flat snout seemed to draw sand in without there being a sign of breathing from the main body area. She smiled at her own humanity as her mind wondered whether or not you could eat them. The small one suddenly retreated and as it went by the large one, (mother and child?) it received a sudden whack from the tail of the big one. This was a substantial blow and it rolled the small one onto its back. Suddenly Jane could see there were many legs like a millipede, and that the underneath had a sort of armour like an armadillo. The little one suddenly twisted its body and as soon as the rear legs were on the sand it somehow found purchase and twisted the rest of itself upright.

She wondered whether they were hermaphrodites or whether they had male and female sexes. As the thought came into her head a third one heaved itself into view and it was half again as big as the large one. It shuffled up to the large one turned it on its back and began doing something. Jane knew they were breeding, and recalling how hard it was to get some zoo animals to breed, knew she was privileged to see it, although she could not really see anything going on. Suddenly all three disappeared under the sand as quickly as disturbed cockroaches disappear from inside a kitchen. Jane switched her camera off.

Heinrich suddenly reappeared and said this visit was over as they had retrieved all of the data requested.

Jane then turned her helmet camera off, and returned with the others to the shuttle.

Back on board the solar orbiter, she hurriedly made out her report and first showed it to Heinrich.

Heinrich immediately took her to the Captain, who was in conference with the Prof and the Whistler, and signaled that he did not want to be disturbed. With typical Prussian directness, Heinrich simply ignored this and held up his hands in surrender, whilst barging straight in.

"Ok, ok Heinrich what is it?"

Jane turned on her laptop and hooked into the captain's personal cabin screen. She then played her report.

"I'll have this over the ships communications system in 10 minutes" breathed the captain.

He looked at Jane and she gave him her run down of events.

"Cave dwelling creatures" said the Prof. "it all fits. Remember the drilling guys saying that there was a blast of gas as they broke through, it could have been oxygen trapped in there.

Heinrich then said, "Well there does appear to be oxygen on the floor to a depth of about 6 inches. What's more the oxygen is oozing up through the soft rock. It soon mixes in with the nitrogen that is there, and effectively disappears into the atmosphere".

"Far from introducing life to this planet we could have killed it off" said the Prof, thinking that the stalagmites they had hurriedly shoveled away may somehow be crucial to survival, "unless there are other caves!"

The captain stood up "it is unlikely that we stumbled across the only cave on the moon. I think that we will have to take soundings and if we do find a hollow place, drill carefully and check oxygen levels before re-sealing our drilling.

Jane said "well I watched these creatures close to. I mean they were within just a couple of feet of me. That flat snout may enable them to venture out if there is oxygen low on the ground. I watched and it just seemed to hoover the dust up without any sign of breathing. I looked for and saw no flanks swelling and reducing".

"When you saw the armoured underside was there any sign of a dust exhaust" asked the Prof.

"Well there was a rather dirty bit at the back I just thought ah, backside" said Jane.

The Prof sucked his teeth for a second as the thought formed in his mind. "Well you know how a snake walks on its ribs, could it be that their breathing is like that where they contract moving groups of muscles and simply propel gas through their body from one end to the other?"

"Heh, well what a cracking idea, you could be right, but there is something else that struck me", said Jane. "Back on earth life sustains itself by living on other life, it can't exist on minerals alone, so what do they feed on, our little moon pigs?"

"Prepare another mission for 3 days time; in the meantime get some sleep you have all earned it!"

The Prof was still mulling things over in his mind. "You know, we new the sandy floor was not likely to be impervious to gas but we expected the pressure inside the Eden shelter to reach a sort of status quo with the atmospheric pressure of the planet and thus stop gas interchange. Now if oxygen is oozing up through this soft rock there is a chance that the atmosphere inside the Eden shelter has been oxygen enriched. If that is the case it could happen in caves and could be the primary reason for attracting the life forms to it, and more than that it may attract other life forms if there are any! Interestingly, we might find it breathable!"

"Prof, considering you're not a scientist or engineer, you have a better grasp of fundamentals than many university quality top men." The Captain then mulled things over in his mind.

CHAPTER 19

PREPARING FOR A THIRD VISIT TO TITAN

Down in the canteen the following morning the Captain gave out some fresh orders.

"Following a line of reasoning begun by the Prof last night, I have now realised that we are rushing headlong into this and I now urge more caution. I want to see the away team in my quarters immediately after breakfast, but those of you in preparing the shuttles, reduce your activity from level one to level two."

The whole ship knew something was afoot, but having full trust in the captain, were not worried at all only curious.

The away team assembled as ordered.

"Ok let's get to it" began the captain, "you are all aware that there is oxygen oozing up through this soft rock on Titan's surface. It has been put to me that the atmosphere inside the Eden shelter could be oxygen enriched. We don't know that as you all stayed fully suited up the other day. But, assuming it is true, the Prof and you Jane have put dangerous information before me.

You Jane wondered what these animals feed on; on the basis that life exists only on other life. It cannot feed itself on minerals only and survive. Now within the sphere of our own existence that is true and may be true here also. The Prof reasoned that if oxygen enrichment is going on in the Eden shelter, it may well be an attraction for life forms, and if there are other life forms they may not be so benign as those figuring in Jane's report. I don't think I need to say more, but so far we have had no fatal accidents, and this is not the place to have them is it?"

The Captain thought for a few seconds longer, then just before dismissing them spoke slowly and deliberately. "I am captaining this, the greatest enterprise to date from our home planet. Though I can do virtually any small and dirty job as well as any junior member of the crew, I cannot be more expert than all of you in everything. I now caution you officially but at the same time I cede to you the powers of a field commander. Such powers are only to be used when absolutely necessary.

Heinrich, this responsibility will fall onto your shoulders, and though I trust you will not experience severe danger, you may do. Thus you are free to use weaponry to defend this mission. Do not use this power in a cavalier fashion. There are those on earth who will dissect your every move in a courtroom if they deem it necessary. Good luck, don't give the lawyers back on earth any ammunition, dismissed."

CHAPTER 20

TITAN GETS REALLY INTERESTING

The away team reached the cave area without incident. The shelf that had been designated as their preferred landing position was only the flat bit at the top of an escarpment, so access to and from the rest of the moon was unimpaired.

The team first tried to establish if there was any oxygen enrichment within the Eden shelter. Indeed there was. It had been left with an oxygen level of about 19%, generally as earth's atmospheres. Gas analysers showed that the oxygen percentage was almost up to 30%. Enrichment had been suspected but the amount exceeded all predictions. Traces of helium and other gases were also found.

This time they took simple spades as a means of deciding just how soft the moons crust was. Outside the cave it was fairly hard. It could be dug but gave severe jarring to the wrists. Inside the cave however not only was it soft, but a spade could easily be driven in to a depth of two feet.

When the team checked into the medical cabinet, it had been tipped over but there was no sign of leakage from any of the jars and containers. Stem cells were thus in no way linked into the life form found.

A simple experiment was left running. Firstly a wide angle lens camera was set up and an infra red detector was set to start the camera, which would run on a timer for 15 minutes, then shut down. The results of this would be relayed direct to the Solar Orbiter.

Heinrich gave orders to each member of his team. The team set up seismic recorders with a transmitter to send data back to the solar orbiter. They used the shuttle to take them about 200 miles away and searched for another cave. Sonic echo lances were used to listen for hollows and after the best part of 8 hours without result, another cave was found. This cave had a very thin outer crust so the good old spade was used to dig in, as they broke through there was the unmistakable sound of escaping gas, so they quickly shoveled Titan soil over the small opening. The gas escape stopped. A gas analyser was inserted through the soft soil and oxygen levels of nearly thirty percent registered.

They twisted the probe to try to raise it above floor level and still the oxygen level was high. They had been surprised at just how good a gas seal the few inches of titan soil had been. The soil when analysed contained enough water to keep it damp, and mysteriously it hadn't frozen. There must be some property possessed by the soil that stopped the water content from freezing. Ok they were getting somewhere.

The team returned to the Solar Orbiter and each member made out their own report. This way every point of view was studied.

Heinrich noted that Jane seemed to have an analytical thread in her report that was far better than other crew members. Other crew members were proficient but Jane was unbelievably deductive.

The ship went about its daily routine and the away team watched as their experiments began to show signs of activity.

In the Eden shelter one of the larger moon pigs suddenly surfaced and swinging its head from side to side, seemed to sample the atmosphere. One of the slightly smaller ones presumed at this stage to be female, shortly surface as well. The two shuffled warily round each other for a while, then the camera's 15 minutes was up. The team was expecting the camera to shut down, but Jane had used the 15 minute timer to trigger another event. A spring loaded arm suddenly extended as its latch was released by the timer and pushed a tin of baked beans from a table onto the floor, with a resulting thud. The two moon pigs buried themselves much as a crab does on earth, but far more quickly. All this was caught on camera and only then did the camera shut down.

"Nice one Jane!" said Heinrich," any chance of a repeat?"

Jane replied at once. "I set the infra red detector to trigger the camera on the basis that the moon pigs are warm blooded. I don't believe that a cold blooded creature as we know them can exist in this environment. Anyway the set up is such that it will rest for a quarter of an hour then will trigger new filming if the infra red unit fires off!"

No other life forms appeared for several days, but a newcomer eventually found its way inside the Eden shelter. It could only be described as a sort of worm. Unlike an earth worm it was dry, more like a small snake, but it had no problem moving through the soft titan soil.

The Solar Orbiter kept watching for several days, and Jane watched avidly.

"Heinrich enquired why she watched with such concentration, but before Jane could reply, the reason was shown on a transmission. One of the moon pigs was seen to be somehow consuming a worm.

"That's why, I was sure that they formed part of the diet of the moon pigs and I was right!"

"But what do the worms live on?" wondered Heinrich.

Over the next few days it was established that there were oxygen rich pockets about 10 feet below the surface and inside these were stalagmite like growths that the worms fed on.

"Those growths must be some sort of fungus" Jane reasoned. From reports of the original away team Jane read how these floor growths were basically shoveled away to get a flat floor for the Eden shelter.

Reports of all these findings were relayed back to earth and studied with ferocious urgency. So far there had been no sign of other life and the moon pigs were top of the food chain, with the worms being at the bottom.

An away mission trapped and brought back to the ship two moon pigs and several worms. These were kept in a sterile chamber in an oxygen enriched atmosphere, but the crew introduced an earth mouse into the environment. The mouse tried a couple of bites on a worm, and this provoked a severe pain reaction in the worm. One hour later there were about a hundred little worms but the original one was completely inert and presumed dead. The moon pig devoured the dead worm. So they were a form of natural scavenging cleaner.

The captain expressed the opinion that he did not wish to leave a manned mission on Titan, though he thought that Eden shelters, fully stocked of course, should be placed at other chosen locations ready to facilitate later missions. The infra red triggered camera system would be left set up in each shelter, and after that the homeward run could begin.

Morale in the ship was high and this news was greeted with shear delight, though the homeward run would take them via Jupiter. No further visits were planned for Ganymede, because cameras and experiments were still running and being used to gather data. These experiments had been initiated by remote control from the Solar Orbiter, and another visit to Ganymede was not required yet. Titan was the focal point of the mission. It was cold, covered in ice but in places only thin ice. Where the ice was thin the soil could be exposed fairly easily. Pegging a simple thing such as a sheet of polythene to the soil soon produced an oxygen enriched environment. The moon worms were attracted to these oxygen tents.

CHAPTER 21

ANOTHER VISIT TO MARS

The first part of the return journey seemed to be over almost as soon as it was begun. The ship carefully negotiated its way through the asteroid belt, and the Whistler put in certain requests to the captain. Suffice it to say more of the rare ice asteroids were sought out and they were fortunate to come across a huge one. The gravity motor was aligned with mars as the anchor and the target asteroid as the other half of the project. All in all about twenty asteroids were garnered over a few days and when they were so close as to be almost a single entity, the final gravity motor action sent them on their way to fry up in mars atmosphere.

The Solar Orbiter assumed a safe geostationary orbit above mars and was left with only a skeleton operational crew. The shuttles took every one else of the operational crew down onto mars.

The Whistler informed the mars mission that they could expect more hail. There was a tense expectation. This was not the stuff of comic books. There was massive danger, if the contents of the asteroids chosen were substantially different from the instrument details carried in the Solar Orbiter's computors. Everyone remained fully suited with their helmets at hand.

The Martian sky lit only by sonny at this time suddenly took on a northern lights appearance. Stunningly beautiful, but as the asteroids got nearer to the surface the colours changed from blues and greens to fiery red. The Martian atmosphere had increased more than any one knew, and this was affecting the rate of descent of the asteroids, and had not been factored on the correct scale into the calculations.

Suddenly the individual asteroids could be made out, and gasps went round the Eden shelter as the mission realised just how big one of them was. The asteroids hurtled past glowing brightly and leaving a trail of particles like the tail of a comet. Landfall when it came for the large asteroid was within visual distance of the Eden shelter and was displayed on the internal information screen, and boy did that asteroid bounce. Seconds later that earthquake thump was felt in the shelter. After that though it was out of visual range, the asteroid broke into many small fragments and peppered down some 300 miles away. The lighter smaller asteroids effectively burnt and fragmented as they came in. Two hours later it rained, and how it rained. Everyone had expected hail but the precipitate fell as rain. The Martian soil thirstily consumed the rain for the first two hours but after that pools then ponds and then lakes began to form.

Communications from earth enquired whether everything was ok as the red planet had suddenly changed, showing areas of a bluish green. At that time on earth, it was not possible to observe sonny, and the pessimists there had imagined that sonny had exploded with dire consequences for the mars mission.

It took over a week before the skies cleared, but now instead of sand storm clouds there were water vapour clouds. And mars now had enough water to sustain life in abundance. Far from mining minerals on it, the idea that it may be possible to farm it took hold. This idea was in vogue on earth for months and many imaginative ideas were put forward. None of these ideas contained enough information with regard to the atmosphere on mars, and were thus bound to founder.

Altogether 39 lakes had formed and the temperature outside had risen for another reason than the existence of sonny. The impact of the large asteroid had so upset the internal structure of the planet so that earth quakes and volcano eruptions were seen in three regions, including the previously extinct giant volcano Olympus Mons, which became very active. Olympus Mons an 80,000 feet giant was already a known volcano before man arrived on the planet, but had been inert for centuries. Now this release of internal energy warmed the atmosphere up so much so that most of the surface was now above freezing. The two poles were still frozen solid, much as on earth, but relatively larger.

Mars being much further from the sun than earth did not receive enough sunlight to ever become warm enough to permit human life. But with the additive nature of sunlight, sonny light, eruption power and clouds forming a greenhouse top, it was evident that only oxygen was missing and this would be the only stumbling block to colonization.

Much of the oxygen on earth comes from the life cycle itself, namely treelife, which breathes in carbon dioxide and gives out oxygen The production of carbon dioxide from living things making for a living cycle, as trees re-released oxygen and the carbon dioxide producers such as man, cows, cars etc, etc used oxygen to produce carbon dioxide.

The farm experiments began by transplanting some of the items grown inside the Eden shelter. These really struggled but somehow survived. Earth scientists produced gm modified crops. These had been outlawed, on earth. These plants spread across mars like weeds in a lawn. The whole planet began to control its own ecosystem, and slowly the oxygen levels began to head to the desired level.

About five years later some hardy madmen who deliberately ventured outside with no space suit found them selves under the same duress as mountain climbers on Mount Everest on earth.

They found you could survive in it but couldn't really live in it.

No one really would admit to how dragon flies of all things came to be on mars, but they were there and survived. They did not increase in numbers rapidly but their larvae found something to live on in the Martian waters, even if it was each other, and thus became part of the planet's eco system.

Perhaps if Charles Darwin had been alive he would have been able to explain how the plant life on the planet suddenly produced reeds. These were found in some of the lakes, but would not grow in other lakes when they were tried.

Man was witnessing the proliferation of life, and this made a pleasant change from the extinction that some people had forecast, based on earth's experience.

The Solar Orbiter meanwhile had returned to earth and awaited instructions for another mission.

Earth drew breath because of the costs involved, and their desire to see the final outcome of life on mars.

Various larvae were introduced to the lakes, and then Fish were tried. The larvae produced flies, and the flies survived long enough to lay eggs. Fish ate the eggs and slowly life began fill the lakes. The fish were caught and eaten and tasted rather bland, but were an invaluable source of protein.

Though it was possible to repeat the water asteroid trick, to date it has not been done as by now there was too much at stake to risk another major impact. The whistler however made plans to try and drop more asteroids on the other side of the planet, though his thoughts centered on smaller ones. So far he has not obtained finances for such an expedition.

Without several more asteroids there would never be an ocean on mars but regular rain fall came and spread the water supply far more evenly than happened on earth, so no one was willing to rock the boat, so to speak.

To date the Freeloader has dropped off 185,000 souls on mars, Queenie has gone back to live there, both earth and mars have benefitted. To the best of my knowledge mars population is unlikely to exceed about 400,000, for the planet to be self sufficient, there is simply not a large enough eco system due to the still pressing shortage of water.

DNA modified cows were scheduled to go out there, and were duly sent. It was hoped that they would be able to cope with the rare atmosphere. This could well work as the cow has been artificially interbred with the high altitude yaks from earth. This was a full success. The cows devoured the GM crops with gusto, and no observed side effects. Their milk was nutritious.

CHAPTER 22

BACK ON EARTH

When the dust has settled on the early colonization of Mars, Ganymede and Titan, much will be seen to be owed to Captain Johnson, and The Prof, who has now retired and the Whistler who is now a famous and much respected man.

The Prof thinks that the Whistler put the spy transmitter on board the Solar Orbiter in case some unknown space disease struck the ship, like happened in the first TV space adventure that you may remember- you know the one it was called "The Quatermass Experiment."

Captain Johnson never found out the reason why the Whistler had put a spy transmitter on the solar orbiter, partly because the Whistler would admit nothing, but the captain lost no sleep over that. He has been seen out and about with Jane, and I think if children appear as they well might, space exploration will have lost, temporarily at least, two very able teamsters.

If the Prof was right about the space disease it would be impossible for the Whistler to admit it. The Whistler being a man who believed himself driven by pure logic only, could never admit that it was a simple fear of the fate of his comrades that had driven him to his decision. Did the Prof get this wrong? Somehow I doubt it!

The one thing that sticks in my mind and didn't come from researching the space reports was the shipping to earth of Martian steaks. (I told you the cow issue was a success) They did nothing for my palate but they were undeniably popular, making loads of money as the novelty of eating extra terrestrial food had and still has general appeal, and the meat was undeniably lean.

I don't expect to live long enough to see the results from Ganymede and Titan but signs are encouraging. I am still healthy and active but at 94, I think I have a good future well and truly behind me.

It is fortunate that the least impressive of all space bodies, i.e. the asteroids would figure so largely in the future of Mars, Ganymede and Titan. It was a major feat of space engineering that asteroids could have been used in this way. After all they are just unwieldy lumps of space debris although there are literally millions of asteroids in orbit, they are spread far and wide, and Captain Johnson made it look so easy to seek one out and then harness its properties. I consider that to be spacemanship of the highest order. Opinion on earth is divided on their origin. Some think that various bits of junk from various sources merely collected in this belt, and didn't coalesce into a planet because Jupiter's gravity was too powerful an influence, others think that another planet may have suffered a cataclysmic collision with something else, well, who knows? Whether or not this asteroid technology could be used to explore even further into space remains to be seen. The largest known asteroid chunk was "Ceres" although this is now in doubt as someone in the scientific community has challenged the notion. Ceres is classified as a dwarf planet and is large enough to form a ball shape due to its own gravity. This asteroid was never seen during any of the crossings of the belt so far, the belt after all is astronomically big. No pun intended. Personally I think that Ganymede requires the ground based nuclear generator before it will realise any potential that it may have, but that remains for others to decide.

From the Hubble telescope, earth scientists have observed that Mars' new satellite universally known now as the rather unscientific name of "sonny" was a peculiar mix of fission and fusion. This process is unique, and still not understood. Phobos settled into a rejuvenated orbit and is not now predicted to either crash onto Mars or escape to the asteroid belt. So the Whistler once again got it spot on. Those of a religious persuasion credit their God with sonny's creation. This I suppose is fair enough, because although mankind had a hand in precipitating its creation, some other force that some may decide to call "lady luck" was definitely involved. The life of this satellite originally estimated as 5000 years, is now in some doubt. Some calculations predict less than 100 years others predict 200000years. We will have to wait and see.

The Titanese moon pigs and worms, have been bred in captivity on earth, the zoos that now have them have provided very large secure environments to protect us from them and them from us. Both species seem to thrive in the richer earth environment, and gradually their diet has been changed with no ill effects seen as yet. This is a fascinating legacy of the Titan mission. The worms like earth grown fungus in their diet, and the moon pigs enjoy meat, slugs and snails, and even earth worms in theirs. Earths greater gravity and lower oxygen level was expected to seriously affect the Titanese creatures, but no affects of discomfiture were seen. In fact it appeared that the moon pigs simply operated their legs in threes instead of singly and thus found a simple way to adapt their strength to the new environment. Many tests have been devised for the moon pigs and it was established that they possess rudimentary intelligence. One character took an ordinary pig into the viewing chamber, and the two species simply stood stock still watching each other. It would have been interesting to know what was going on in pig minds! Their existence has really fired up the imagination of Sci-Fi authors who have in turn fired up the imaginations of the younger folk on earth. For me fact will always be stranger than fiction. When the first moon pig died after about 5 years on earth, its body was studied in detail. The findings were that they had vision, poor vision but it was there. They had hearing and smell. Their digestive tract was unlike anything yet imagined, and was integral with their method of breathing and is still under study. Their hearing was unlike our hearing as it was most sensitive to very low frequencies, presumed to aid their subterranean activities. The moon pigs have a voracious appetite for the Titanese worms and have so far defeated all efforts to get a dead worm onto the laboratory table. Thus far we know very little about the worms.

The moon pigs breathing system did turn out to be in one end and out the other. So I have decided to visit our local zoo where I know they have a viewing house. These creatures do not like direct sunlight, but love a sandy floor where they can bury themselves if they wish. With my luck I'll probably never see one up and about!

All I've got to do now is to find some publisher for this historical account. Wish me luck, because I will need it.

If I'm still alive when any progress is made on Titan or Ganymede, I will write an addendum to the yarn. Whether or not this lot ever gets published, I still have the satisfaction of writing it. This has been surprisingly enjoyable.

CHAPTER 23

ADDENDA ABOUT TITAN

THE NEXT BIG MISSION AND I DO MEAN BIG

Captain Johnson was by this time a married man, but was asked to command the next mission to Titan. Jane stayed at home as she was expecting her firstborn.

It was considered that Titan being the harbourer of life obviously had more potential than Ganymede.

Titan's soil supported the presumed fungal growth, which supported the worms at the bottom of the simple food chain. The soil also remained damp when by rights it should have frozen solid. It was known that the presence of ammonia with water, would keep water liquid, down to about minus 19 degrees Celsius, but there was some other additional catalyst presumed to be in titanese soil.

The Prof though gave the scientific community something to chew on. He had declared that on earth it had been established that water could be cooled way, way, down below freezing point and could be proven to remain liquid. However the slightest movement in the fluid triggered the freezing mechanism. He postulated that something in the Titanese soil simply precluded the freezing mechanism from operating. There was plenty of ice on titan but the soil was somehow staying damp, and therefore his idea was valid. The scientists will eventually figure out just what is happening, but I would bet that the Prof is right. I really would like to meet him, he is an interesting man.

Titan's surface was easy to burrow into for protection and there was the massive continuous gas eruption geyser belting out heat all the time, albeit at temperatures very little above freezing.

Oxygen generated from within the moons innards was only about a six inch layer at the bottom of the atmosphere and yet the layer never seemed to get any thicker, so what happened to the oxygen?

Were there any more life forms, plant, animal, viral or fungal?

The only way to find out was another full scale expedition. The space authorities asked the Prof if he would come out of retirement for this one last junket. He agreed on the notion that this time he would be along as an advisor or observer—less stress.

The Solar Orbiter was fully refueled and revictualled, and amongst the cargo were the piecemeal parts of a nuclear reactor steam plant and steam turbine driven electric generator. Earth's engineers had been busy!

The Prof was both surprised and delighted when he found that his idea of a three legged support structure had been considered almost the best option. A Five legs design was finally considered the best and that is how the design was drawn up.

Captain Johnson was soon running things his way and proceeded with rehearsals as if it was the very first mission. He was as usual particularly thorough.

We can fast forward now to the actual landing on Titan. The first thing to be done was to get the electricity supply system working. The captain sent his most experienced away team with Heinrich at the head. The parts of the structure were partly assembled in orbit and then ferried down to the "building site", as it became known.

The away team set about their task with gusto. The first thing done using small excavators was to level five slots on the ice top. The site for this had been selected carefully because the five slots looked like a giant asterisk in the ice and clear and smooth progress had to be available along each line of the asterisk. The five legged bridge structure was put together from the centre outwards. A screw jack was adjusted to slide each leg out, with the foot of each leg sliding like an ice skate and the next section was then fitted in the centre and the whole process was repeated until, the whole structure was about half diameter. At that point another support leg and foot was attached to each main leg, to take the slowly increasing weight. The structure continued to take shape. Finally the whole thing was at designed width. A circular wheel rim for want of a better word was attached to the inside edges of the feet at the extremes of the legs; a circular hub was attached into the central region. Steel cables about a half inch thick were then threaded in basically as spokes, and the entire structure was tensioned. The spokes pulled the wheel rim and hence the legs together and the structural weight tried to force the legs apart. The tension was set to balance the weight and was adjusted as weight was added to the structure during manufacture, and the wheel rim added enormously to the integrity of the structure stiffening it considerably. The steam turbine and electric generators complete inside their respective rooms was hung from the structure and the tensioning spokes were adjusted. The additional support legs were taken from their initial support role and were re-bolted onto the outer feet, with their sliding feet now at right angles to the main feet. This meant that the outer feet could not now slide at all and added to the structural integrity of the system. The central boss of this structure carried a full size turntable controlled jib crane. The crane could reach anywhere within the effective radius of the structure.

Next a central tube was sunk into the ice extending down to about 500 feet, that is, 100 feet below where the reactor itself would be positioned. This tube would surround the reactor and was to prevent lake water from flooding it. The tube was built in sections and the first section had an electrically heated bottom edge, so it would sink into the ice with minimal persuasion from the team. A fairly deep rectangular hole was then excavated in the ice inside the central tube, about 400 feet down and the nuclear reactor in its lead lined housing room was lowered to the bottom and secured to the walls of the pit. All of the electrical connections for the control system were of heavy industrial connectors (plugs and sockets to you and me), with triple points for every connection. All connections were made to the surface control room. Electric pumps were installed. Their job was to keep the reactor supplied with cooling water. They were all dry at the moment. All pipework was connected and checked and double then triple checked. The constructional electrical supply was provided by a good old fashioned gas powered internal combustion engined three phase generator, the only difference between it and its earth cousins was the oxygen cylinder as well as the gas cylinder. This had auto changeover to spare cylinders when levels ran low, so there was never a break in the electricity supply. Empty cylinders would then be replaced as necessary.

Pilot holes were drilled down through the ice until they were almost at penetration depth, these all being sited at or near the pump inlet points. Finally the pilot holes were plugged near the bottom with a small amount of explosive. Secondary pilot holes, very close to the primaries were drilled and "U" shaped copper tubes were inserted these being piped to the nuclear reactor unit. Liquid warm water was to be pumped down the u tubes and re-circulated to and from the reactor system, their primary function being to ensure that the water supply holes did not re-freeze.

The scene was set. Engineers carefully began the rod withdrawal and the nuclear pile began to give out some heat. The heat first reached the internal closed steam circuit which began to send steam to the turbine. This was a tense time for the away team. A mistake now and a nuclear explosion was indeed possible. The explosive charges were set off and the explosions blew the ice core from the bottoms of the pilot holes and up shot the "fresh" water. At the top of the pilot holes, there were pipes connected to the pump inlets. The pumps were started and began to circulate the water before it had chance to refreeze. These pumps had heated pipe work just in case. There was an immediate reduction in the steam produced as the reactor was cooled, so the chief electrical engineer ordered further withdrawal of the nuclear control rods. The steam returned to then surpassed the previous value, and to the great delight of the whole team (and no doubt relief), cooling water was seen to flow out of the exhaust points as it returned from the reactor and began to flow a few feet away then refreeze. Significantly the water near the cooling pumps outlets remained liquid, and gradually the reactor was allowed greater withdrawal of the rods. Every one was ready to hit an emergency stop to shut the whole thing down. The reactor temperature stabilized and the heat generated was pumped via a secondary pipe system to circulate down along the "U" tubes near the pilot holes. The pilot holes thus could not re-freeze. The electric generators were then brought on line, and every one stood tense as the characteristic whine of the generators could be heard to increase. The whine reached normal pitch signifying that the system was up to speed. Inside the control room many more checks were made and finally the system was synchronised to the electricity generated by the three phase internal combustion generator and the system was switched on. Right then the various lights and heaters of the mini power station all came on but in a preordained sequence.

Cautiously the three phase generator was turned off. The system remained active. The life support systems back at the caves and the construction site complex were all switched over to the nuclear generator and the whole thing operated. The cooling pumps water got warmer and warmer so that a mini lake began to appear around the area. This slowly grew then stabilized just as the Prof had predicted. The bridge structure was well sized and was in no danger of sinking with things as they stood. The nuclear station could not now be shut down other wise it would freeze over and so a permanent manning rota was set up.

The Prof had watched from aboard the Solar Orbiter, and though he was not responsible in any way for what went on he found the tension draining, then rewarding. Captain Johnson said "easy peasy Prof or what!"

The sweat on the Prof's forehead showed that he had been down there in mind and spirit if not in body.

One clever design feature of this system was the reduced power operating level. Once an unfrozen lake was available the water supply from the internals of the moon could be switched off and the lake water could be re-circulated as cooling water. The pilot hole heating system remained in operation so that there was no chance of the fresh water supply freezing. This effect was two fold; it helped keep the lake liquid when very low power consumption was wanted, a vital consideration. When the reactor power was low it did not need the continuous supply of fresh cold water and so the lake was big enough for the job. The design allowed for a big enough lake to operate continuously at full power using the recirculating method, though it was not planned to do that unless the fresh water supply was to fail. The water temperature would be somewhat higher and the lake would expand as a result, but so what, the legs were wide enough spaced to cater for it. The lake was radioactively contaminated of course but most radioactivity was trapped in the ice and was not anywhere near danger levels. A great amount of heartache and skill had gone into the station design, so it was gratifying to see it all in operation. If the lake was used as cooling source continuously it would slowly become more contaminated with radio activity, thus the decision to use the freshwater supply as much as possible. The problem of where to store excess water once the lake had reached its optimum size was solved in an ingenious way.

A circle of drain points had been constructed around the perimeter of the lake just inside the liquid zone. These fed an outgoing feeder that took the excess water about five miles. This outgoing pipe was heated but also very well insulated so it didn't take too much heat to keep its contents liquid. A flat area designated as the 'overflow pond' had a central rotating nozzle. This sprayed the water away. On earth the gravity would have brought the stream down after fifty yards but on Titan the distance obtained was several hundred yards. As the water froze again it formed a ring wall. The nozzle in the centre floated on a gas filled slewing ring, which in turn floated on the water produced as soon as the water reached back as far as the nozzle point. As some of the water seeped back towards the middle before freezing, it eventually raised the nozzle slewing ring. The net result was a slowly deepening lake of part water and part ice, self constructing its own container. Some of the sprayed water evaporated into the atmosphere and was carried away by prevailing winds. The rest formed the overflow pond. As the overflow pond grew in size the perimeter ice walls grew upwards. At a particular depth there was a sudden increase in the amount of evaporation and the overflow pond size stabilized. This was an unforeseen benefit. Not only that but the worrying amount of acid in the cooling water acted as a scourer and kept the cooling and supply pipes clean without damaging the integrity of the pipes. Beggars can't be choosers so these advantages were accepted gracefully but were studied ferociously to gain a full understanding of just what was going on. The studies taxed some of the best brains on earth.

The walls and underneath of the control room had lead linings. Radiation levels were as low as earth standards required, but crews did a week on and six weeks off to minimize exposure even more.

Earth had originally considered designing a thorium based nuclear system due to the much cleaner operating record of thorium stations over uranium stations. However uranium stations were simpler and not quite so high technology so as pollution was not considered to be a stumbling block the older system was used.

CHAPTER 24

CAN WE FARM ON TITAN? AND WHAT THE HELL IS THAT?

A long string of Eden shelters was erected between the original cave and the power station, stopping about a mile short of the station for safety reasons.

The path from the power station back to the original Eden shelter was chosen to cover a part of Titan found to only have a thin covering of ice, and this was shoveled to one side. The Titanese soil exposed was added to by soil that was usually excavated from convenient caves. Simple protecting polythene tent covers were spaced in long lines and a number of earth plants were tried much as on mars. The greenhouse results were not quite what were expected as plant growth was almost non existent, until some bright spark enclosed the root area of the plants within a metal mesh, and then the plants grew strongly. The polythene covers ensured a rich supply of oxygen. Prior to the inclusion of mesh root protectors, very little growth occurred, and the guy responsible for the solution found that something was attacking the roots. He had heard about the Titanese worms and thought they might be responsible. He turned out to be correct. There were a number of varieties of subterranean creatures about to be discovered.

The farmer for want of a better description erected what amounted to a large tent and tried growing an earth type banana plant. Now all earth's bananas come from some botanist's efforts a couple of hundred years before, and staggeringly these grew well, but his larger tent attracted the local moon pigs. These were not the same as the species previously studied, so a few were caught and ferried up to the mother ship.

Why is there always a madman who throws caution to the wind?

Perhaps he was related to the guys who did this on mars, or perhaps it was a stupid bet.

Inside the confines of the farm tent four men hatched a plan. Two of them would open their space visors and the other two would do what was necessary if something went wrong. The visors were opened and the men felt the sudden increase in atmospheric pressure. Absolutely nothing happened until somebody said something and that started the laughter, peals, of uncontrollable laughter. The two men who had remained fully suited suddenly twigged that there must be a fair amount of nitrous oxide floating about and quickly shut their colleagues visors. Recovery was quick, and they knew they would have to come clean to their senior officers.

The Prof, when he heard of this simply said "well there is always somebody isn't there? Still I suppose it tells us something of what is happening to the oxygen".

The away team though had the idea that it could be used to give a new lease of life to the standby three phase generators, by ditching the oxygen bottle and replacing it with a butane one, and then using the moons nitrous oxide to work the engine. It was tried and it worked, though it had to be done inside a tent.

This was not the end of the matter as one of the other technicians found use for a single cylinder gas engine. In addition a use was found for the local methane gas; this could be shoveled up in crystal form. Gas bottles were designed that split and had a screw top. The crystals of methane were placed inside and then the tops were screwed tightly back on. Inside the warmer confines of the tent the methane re-liquefied, and would gasify when released into the tent atmosphere. It was used to help run engines, so even the requirement for butane was reduced.

The first the captain knew of any prank going on was when the Prof suddenly said "Christ, look at this, on the viewer screen!"

The technician was down on the surface of Titan tearing along on a crude motorcycle!

"Get that man back here to explain himself" barked the captain.

One and a half hours later, a contrite looking crewmember stood before the Captain.

"You are not alone in this project!" groused the captain; you have five minutes to bring all others associated with your project up to the bridge. Who issued you with a space suit? How did you stow your self and this motorized bicycle on board a shuttle? Where did you source the components from?"

The young crewmember disconsolately turned to the ships communication system and pressed very few keys, stood up and said "they will be here directly sir!"

When the group was assembled, they each felt the dentists drill effect as the captains glittering eyes bored through theirs.

"As you know this enterprise has a captain" he began speaking in measured and clipped tones. "This captain must indeed be of little value to our enterprise as he is not worth a request even for projects that you have in mind. SILENCE!" He roared and the words died in the throats of the miscreants.

They all looked at the captains glittering eyes and none had seen him so angry at any point before.

"What do you think of them Prof?" he glowered.

"Well I can see a fairly able team of young men who have gone behind the back of their Captain. A pathetic and stupid thing to do. I also see that they have misappropriated supplies to aid them in their escapade. I further see that there has been collusion between them all, again completely covert collusion, and they have broken all codes of discipline and worse still behaved unprofessionally. In this instance I do not consider the mission itself to have been compromised, but this sort of behaviour only just falls short of dishonourable, is a disgrace and cannot go unpunished!"

The faces now looked even glummer if that were possible.

"You will all report to the officer in charge of the brig, and volunteer to stop inside it. I will decide the length of your stay at my leisure. DISMISS!" With this command from the captain they filed away disconsolately.

The Prof then mused "they knew they would be caught and had already made plans to take their punishment. After all it took only minutes to assemble the whole group here."

The Captain then grinned and gave new orders. "Bridge to brig, bridge to brig" he intoned.

"Aye, aye captain, brig here. Your fourteen men are all inside, looking a bit down I might say!"

"Number X27 was the designer behind their escapade; make sure that he has a laptop computor. And let it be known that the captain thought the design of their motorized bicycle was of very low standards. In fact any of them who can contribute to that project may have a laptop, and then I will be down. Others who were not directly involved in the design must produce a hand written dissertation telling how their idea may have been brought properly to the attention of the captain. Bridge out."

"That will give them something to think about!" chortled the prof.

"Prof, I know that you are on this mission as an observer, but I must say in all candour that your words stung them a lot more than mine did!"

"Aye, well they were expecting me to use my quelling skills and get them off, so I think the bottom fell out of their world when they found out I was 100 percent behind you."

"Ok the away team is doing well, and for the moment the mission is running itself. I will let them stew in the brig for 28 days."

The group was stood before the Captain once again. "Well?" barked the captain X27 whose name was Eric Whistler, stepped forward.

"Captain I am contrite. I fear I have let both you and these men down. They have all served in the brig with me, and we are agreed that nothing like this will ever be contemplated again. We all bear our share of guilt but mine is greater than anyone else's. I offer unreserved apologies for my actions and for my colleagues here"

"Are you related to the Whistler?" barked the captain.

"Grandson, sir!"

"Well what else have you to say for yourself?"

A slight murmur broke out from the others that died as soon as the captain glanced across.

Eric Whistler said "well sir we hope that we have done something to atone for our stupidity. Whilst inside the brig we have designed a proper moon cycle, and trust that it can be considered as a positive contribution. I know that earth is always looking to reduce energy consumption, and I believe that the latest design would fill that bill!"

"Dismiss, I will consider your comments as a design request!"

Some relieved men turned to go to their quarters, but Eric Whistler stood his ground. "Return to normal duty sir?"

"Agreed" nodded the captain.

The Prof observed "Captain I think you way well have forged a team there, complete with a leader!"

"He is like his Grandad, the covert transmitter and the covert motor bike have a certain similarity don't you think?" grinned the captain, "and by the way I heard about your Quatermass Experiment theory, and I think you could well be right—again!"

The captain then turned his attention to the hand written dissertations before him and read each one carefully.

Not one man had attempted to justify his actions, but every detail about borrowing a space suit, and where the engine had been procured from—all details were fully disclosed, including how the design broke down into component parts suitable for reassembly on Titan. Each man had also written how he thought the project should have been approached

After two hours the captain requested that all the miscreants return to the bridge.

The group of men stood before him and he barked "I have now read your dissertations, and I know how and why you all played the part that you played. The only person not to have explained himself is you Whistler. What have you got to say for yourself?"

Eric Whistler could not explain why he did what he did. "Captain I cannot explain this. I have sat for hours in the brig contemplating what made me do such a thing. If I had an explanation I would offer it now!"

To his surprise and relief the Captain grinned "that's alright son, I think it is just in the blood, but don't ever give me cause to worry about it again!"

"DISMISS!"

Over the coming weeks Eric Whistler's designs for both a two wheel and three wheel motorized cycle was formally adopted. And work began. The air intake again for want of a better description was low on the floor, like the moon pig's mouth, but trailing behind the machine. The gas bottle used butane from the mother ship or methane from Titan and a second bottle of Titan produced nitrous oxide was used to supplement the total gas intake of the machine. On the surface of titan this gave a powerful yet economic engine capable of 40 mph on the flat. This was quite quick as due to the thick atmosphere on titan, it felt more like 80 mph. A number of these were produced and were left ready fuelled in case of emergency evacuation at the nuclear station.

The captain kept a careful eye on Eric Whistler, and generally liked what he saw.

Several men who had ridden the cycles were surprised by the effect of the wheels on Titan's surface. The surface sand seemed to scatter to one side but slightly before the bike got there. Upon investigation more excitement ensued. It was another life form. These creatures had a crab like top and small wings, and could fly about as far as a grasshopper on earth. As they sensed the approach of a motor cycle they got out of the way. Clearly another avenue of study had opened up. How many more secrets would Titan reveal?

Eric Whistler requested a visit to the surface of Titan, and asked the captain to trust that his visit was a serious one without revealing its purpose. The captain agreed provided he could watch all experiments done down on the surface.

When Eric whistler stepped in front of the camera on Titan, he had on what can only be described as a Batman outfit. In spite of himself the captain grinned widely and murmured "what the hell is he up to now?"

He soon found out. Eric Whistler cast off the cloak and hung it on a framework down by his feet; this revealed some bat like wings fixed to his arms. He flapped his wings and took off. He performed a clumsy looking flight and landed rather heavily in a heap.

Back on the bridge, the Prof said "Christ he can fly, in fact anyone could on Titan. Your natural weight is only about 14% of your earth weight perhaps 20% when suited up and the air is thicker. Why didn't I think of that? It could solve the problem associated with weightlessness too; the exercise is just what the doctor ordered."

Eric Whistler reported to the bridge as soon as he got back and was out of his space suit.

Captain Johnson was nearly doubled with laughter. "Son that was the most inept example of flying I have ever seen, but you proved your point I think!"

"Yes captain, you are right, and I did land rather heavily," said Eric whistler rubbing his one hip. "I think we need aeronautics chaps to fashion a proper design. When I saw how small the wings were on those funny little crab things it started me thinking, but instead of going off at half cock I asked your permission first. I knew if the aeronautics chaps were given first shot at a design we could have been halfway home before they produced anything, and I only wanted to establish the principle!"

"Good and you have succeeded" laughed the captain.

CHAPTER 25

ANOTHER IDEA BRINGS AN UNEXPECTED BONUS

The farmers amongst the ground crew were keen to try out a large tent/marquee design that could be arranged to cover several acres or hectares as the new men called it. A suitable area was flattened and the tents which had closed walls at the ends but individual close fitting bands along the roofs and sides were erected.

All major earth crops were tried except rice, which needs enough water to drown it, and this would never be the case on Titan. Most grew better than expected and it was found that inside the tent it was warmer than expected, considerably warmer. Some investigation was carried out and the heat source was established as Saturn itself. The infra red radiation from Saturn was only mild but the nature of the material of the tents trapped it, also due to the nature of their construction, did not re-radiate it, or allow it to convect out. The result was a temperature of about 18 degrees Celsius in the tents, without the need for supplementary heat. The supplementary heat came from the nuclear station and thus the tents were kept at 25 degrees Celsius, but again at reduced electrical power. This was ideal for many plants. The roof not being gas tight allowed some of the oxygen enrichment to escape and almost provided ideal conditions for mankind, except for the nitrous oxide. Many men had tried the atmosphere by now and all with the laughter creasing them up after a few minutes.

Probes previously sent to Titan had not revealed the existence of nitrous oxide, and it was down the experts in the field to establish why.

There had been some conjecture that back on earth with so many animals, men and cars producing carbon dioxide, the plants were missing a major item in the life cycle. Eric Whistler, with full permission simply left one of his three wheeler cycles ticking over in one tent and allowed its exhaust fumes to circulate within. The fumes became part of the atmosphere and the plants in that tent advanced more quickly than in the other tents. Here was another avenue of thought for the botanical scientists to consider.

After 4 months the first fruits of production arrived. The captain invited the top men in his crew to try a Titanese salad. It comprised tomatoes, lettuce, radishes and potatoes.

The medical crew was on standby in close proximity to the diners. Some stomach aches occurred, but they turned out to be psychological. The taste of the products was not bad, and even the captain tried some. Eric Whistler opened his mouth to advise against it, but in the event said nothing. The captain said "Mr. Whistler, I suspect I know what was in your mind and you really should have spoken up, after all I am the captain and you cannot afford to lose me!"

"Any one else but you, and I would have spoken up!" he rejoined, "However, captain as there appears to be no harm done by your rashness, may I invite you to take a beer with me?"

A wide grin appeared on the captain's face and the two men went off to sink the permitted two pints.

CHAPTER 26

THE HANDOVER OF POWER.

Two days after the comradely drink the captain ordered Eric Whistler to the bridge.

He reported to the captain and then wondered why he had been summoned there. He soon found out.

"Mr. Whistler you have the bridge, please proceed"

"Any particular last orders, captain?"

"None, sir. You have the bridge" and with that Captain Johnson turned to stride away.

"Just one moment Captain Johnson, where do you think you are going?"

"An excellent response Mr. Whistler, with your permission I am going for some shut eye. And I have just become the father of a baby son."

The cheer that rang out was quite spontaneous. "Proceed, Captain Johnson"

Eric Whistler took to command as to the manner born. He had studied Captain Johnson's methods on advice from his grandfather, the Whistler. He would never be Captain Johnson, but he was his own man with that streak of originality sometimes essential for a commander.

Captain Johnson returned to duty after seven days. He had kept a watching brief using surreptitious methods and verbal chats with the Prof. When he got back to earth he would recommend the ship's captaincy be handed over to the younger man.

When he returned to the bridge, he barked "Issues, Mr. Whistler?"

"None that have come to my attention sir, and then almost regretfully, you wish for the bridge sir?"

"Indeed I do!"

"Then you have the bridge sir. Permission to discuss my experience of command, sir?"

"Aye Mr. Whistler, but first bring me up to speed."

Twenty minutes later both topics had been covered and Eric Whistler enquired as to the Captain's new found family.

The Captain said ruefully "I shall be earth bound from now on, that is why I threw you in at the deep end! I shall recommend you for immediate promotion as soon as we are back home. Of the various personnel on this ship, there are several that I have been considering for promotion to captain, all of whom would do a decent job. You however have shown the independence of spirit in greater amounts than anyone else, so bad luck, the job is yours!"

After a few moments the captain asked again why the motorbike project had been started.

Eric Whistler admitted "sir I am still trying to guess that myself. I know the idea filled my conscious mind as soon as I thought of it. What I did went against all my training in discipline. I knew that we would need an emergency evacuation procedure from our nuclear plant, and that most of the electric vehicles available would be too slow, or may have flat batteries. I remember the really hot motorcycles on earth used nitrous oxide as a performance boost similar to what German aircraft did in World War 2, and once the idea took hold I simply could not put it down!"

Captain Johnson then told the story of the covert transmitter and how the Whistler had been responsible for deciding to put it in place.

"I guess it really is in the blood then!" laughed Eric. "I have learnt though that once one assumes the role of Captain there is simply no room for undisciplined acts such as that".

Captain Johnson nodded in agreement, and sent a communiqué back to earth with his decision.

"Eric, that crazy decision showed me something. There will rarely be times when the logic of a situation is not going to yield the result that you know that you need. When it does not you must have the single mindedness to drive the situation along, and that really is why I have offered you this promotion above every one else. You aren't going to turn it down are you?"

"TURN IT *DOWN*! I AINT THAT CRAZY!"

The Whistler was one of the first to read the transmission, and smiled with pure delight, and then smiled again at the thought of taking orders from his grandson whenever he ever got into space again.

So what are we going to do with Titan? We can use it to farm on. There seems to be a vast amount of hydrocarbons that earth could plunder. We could establish a penal colony as part of the general expansion plans, using penal discipline to show the prisoners that they were full members of an away team and fully valued as such. When back on earth it was foreseen that prisoners would brag incessantly of their escapades, but would not want a second visit. Earth would benefit from and use the skills of prisoners to further both earth's and the prisoners' desires.

We could improve the design of the Eden shelters by increasing their size, using them as homesteads, so that humans could live without discomfort. Titan could then become an extra terrestrial trading post. With one nuclear station in operation there could of course be others. For the moment the Eden shelters could be home to advance colonists, but means needed to be found to control the oxygen enrichment and to exclude Titanese life forms from entry. Earth had not yet given up on Jupiter but may transfer attention from Ganymede to Europa. There was still much to think about. I am getting a bit crotchety now, but at 97 this is to be expected. I wonder if my life span will permit more jottings yet. Fortunately when I am gone my work may yet carry on.

CHAPTER 27

CONTINUATION?

My Grandad really is on the final downward slope now and perhaps it will be down to me as the only family member to have taken an interest in his scribblings, to carry on. He is still able to raise his game on occasions but is tired most of the time. I am his granddaughter. I have read his notes in preparation of his historical story and have checked some of them from notes made in the margins, and the facts do check out with the archive files. He was right about the archives themselves being daunting. The shear volume of reports is mind numbing.

I have written to the World Office of Space Travel, and offered my services. As yet I haven't had a reply. Grandad is still their employee and he still receives a handsome payment each month. I really think that they haven't realised just how old he is yet.

The logic that Grandad brought to bear on the reports in terms of archiving them is in my view quite substantial, and as I am now fully conversant with it, having spent the last five years preparing myself. I really want to carry on with his work, so I am expecting to hear from the authorities shortly. Looking through Grandad's work I notice that he calls anything to do with Titan as Titanese, and actually he should have used the adjective "titanian." When I dared one day to mention this he brushed it aside simply saying "well they are just wrong!" That's Grandad!

Today I am entertaining the second most famous space captain, namely Eric Whistler, for lunch. He and I have been going out for the last year or so though I must say his duties have taken him away for much of the time. Tomorrow is my 28th birthday, and I am praying that Eric and I will be able to celebrate quietly.

Ah! I can hear the doorbell.

Of all the unexpected things, I find that Grandad has beaten me to the front door! What a grand old man he is!

"Come on in Eric! She will be down in a jiffy!"

I have made an effort and as Eric turns to look, I am pleased to see that his eyes gleam with delight. It was all worth the effort.

Eric smiles at me. "Sorry I'm a bit late but I've just been to the christening of Captain Johnson's latest son, and you know how these things can go on."

CHAPTER 28

EARTH CHANGES THE REGULATIONS

Eric later confided in me that he had been to see Captain Johnson on another matter as well as the christening. He had considered the latest proposals from the World Office of Space Travel. In a nutshell married couples were being considered as crewmembers. Both he and Captain Johnson thought there could be no real grounds for complaint apart from pregnancy. Earth was not willing to risk possible deformation of children, brought through a full term pregnancy in space. This seemed fair enough to me I must say. It also seemed fair enough to Eric as he asked me to accompany him as his wife and librarian on his next and imminent space flight.

"Librarian?" I enquired.

Eric reached inside his jacket and gave me an envelope. I looked at the unmistakable, official envelope, from the World Office of Space Travel. With trembling fingers I opened it.

I had been accepted as the archivist! Grandad could retire!

I found Grandad snoozing in a chair in the conservatory. I suddenly felt very selfish about what I wanted to say.

97 or whatever, he was already ahead of the game! He roused himself and chuckled. "That last e-mail I sent them must have woken somebody up! I told them I was 104 and just how long did they expect me to continue especially when they had a ready made replacement!"

"Oh Grandad", I had to fight the tears that welled in my eyes.

"Get yourself down to that registry office then" he chuckled again. "I've known you carried a torch for Eric for quite a while now. I know about the married couple rule change, so get yourself aloft, and do something that I dare say I've left too late. Write a report from out in space and I will archive it as my last act in this saga!"

CHAPTER 29

I MAKE IT INTO SPACE!

I made it both as the captain's wife and as librarian. The mission this time was destined to go to Europa in the Jovian group.

I kept well away from the bridge except when the captain called a general meeting there. I must say it felt odd to call my husband "captain" instead of Eric, but there you go.

I had read of the vast size of the Solar Orbiter, but once on board I really appreciated it. It was a flying city with shopping malls and factories. Not only did it have shopping malls just like on earth but it also had a whole host of barbers shops, boutiques, cinemas, roller skating and ice skating complexes and even a good size foot ball pitch and all the other paraphernalia found in an inner city. Football was just about impossible under zero gravity conditions. I believe that the full complement of crew members on this flight was around 18420 all told including me. All of grandad's jottings referring to the crew in effect mean the operational space crew. The vast majority of personnel are the undercrew, involved in the function of the space ship, the canteen, the shops, factories and the entertainment complex and so on. These folk never set foot off the ship, save to go on leave back on earth. The major costs of going out to the planets were thus revealed as wages for the crew rather than the capital cost of the ship.

That's a lot of folk to provide living arrangements for. There were signs everywhere extolling the virtues of recycling and the minimal amount of rubbish produced was compacted and crushed into small handleable cubes for disposal back on earth. The captain could at his discretion eject scrap into space, but he chose to take it to whence it came.

The captain was a year younger than me and I marveled at the easy way that he kept command; any dissent expressed was usually only a joke.

One day I was summoned to the bridge. I was well up to date with my tasks so I wondered what on earth I was wanted for.

"Ah! Catherine, I would like to introduce you to this gentleman here on my right"

I looked and found my open gaze returned with a quizzical look through twinkling grey eyes and I said "The Prof, unless I'm much mistaken!"

The Prof because it was indeed he, nodded and smiled. In all my life I had never met a more charming man. He even outdid Grandad, and that is saying something!

"I am delighted to meet you Catherine. I believe your grandfather is still responsible for the space archives, even though he is 104!"

"Gosh, his last E-Mail really did go to the right people! He did say that but actually he is just coming up 98. He asked me to come into space, because he never did, he left it too late. He said if I would transmit the various reports my job entails, he would archive them up and retire, leaving me to carry on the family tradition. Any way, Prof you are no spring chicken so how do you manage with space flight?" I asked.

"About the same as your Grandad did!"

"Oh very funny, but I'm sure he would have liked to come just the same!" I said as I turned to see Grandad smiling serenely standing behind me.

The captain said "remember professionalism!"

"Sod the professionalism" I wept, and fell into Grandad's open arms. Just at that moment I saw a rather imposing figure with his wife clinging to his arm.

"I suppose you have got to be ex captain, now Mr. and Mrs. Johnson" I said only half believing my own mouth, and furiously blinking back the tears.

"Hello Catherine" said Jane, "our kids are either in school or nursery just now and space travel is like motorcycling, once in the blood it is a disease with no known cure. So here we are!"

I noticed Eric give a sudden furtive glance as the word motorcycle came out and recalled from Grandad's accounts just why this was.

"Gentlemen, I'm sure you will excuse us, but I think we ladies have a few girlie things to discuss. Buy you a coffee Jane?" I smiled.

Jane had the sort of personality that encouraged talk and I wasn't going to miss this! She in her turn must have liked what she saw in me because we linked arms and strolled away to the coffee shop. I saw Grandad sit down out of the corner of my eye as we were leaving. Jane commented on what a game old guy he was, and she said he might be over a hundred by the time this mission was over"

We talked of this and that and nothing in particular, and Jane smiled again and said how refreshing it was to have someone of her generation to chatter to, without having to be mindful of all the protocols of space travel.

I knew that we would form a strong friendship. Real friends are hard to come by, so I was delighted to have met her.

"You merited a mention in Grandad's story you know "I chattered.

"Story?" she questioned.

"Oh yes, Grandad invented the archiving system for all the reports that go back to earth, and he decided to pick the bones of it and write the true history, the real story of real space travel before he died. You are in it. You were the first person to see extra terrestrial life with your own eyes."

"You know, I've got three kids now and all that seems so long ago that I pay it very little heed!"

I said "well I liked the bit where the captain was chivalrous to you and you liked it!"

"Actually I remember that vividly. I was expecting nothing of the sort, but surely that cannot have come from the dry reports that get written?"

"Probably not, but Grandad often met with guys who had been on missions; and he made deductions from what Americans used to call scuttlebutt!"

"Oh my god, walls have ears!"

I said then "my Grandad has been an inspiration to many and to me in particular, and I reckon from making correct deductions based on zero information he is second only to the Prof!"

CHAPTER 30

DOWN TO BUSINESS

Since Grandad's most recent entry, there were a lot of discussions about return on investment. After all it was money that drove any enterprise. Mars had given a fair return, and as it was slowly becoming more oxygenated, the returns were improving. There was a sizeable holiday camp there but for those who signed up it was always a working holiday. Mars was farmed and mined. A means had been found to reduce the titanium ore, and when overall costs were calculated it was compatible with costs on earth and of course it would always be there if earth's own supply ran out. Perhaps even it would be used locally as mars began to provide for itself with the beginnings of its own industry.

There was a trade in the rare minerals, Platinum, palladium, silicon, arsenic, germanium, and even an odd alloy comprising copper and something else which didn't occur naturally on earth.

Sonny still shone brilliantly with no sign of dimming and earth's best brains still had not coughed up an agreed theory on exactly what was going on to sustain the reaction. There was another member of the crew that I was just about to meet, and this was none other than the Whistler himself.

When I did meet him, he being my grand father-in-law, gave me a welcome, and he was almost as surprised to see me as I him.

Eric was a highly intelligent man but James was a full blown intellectual. The reason that he was on board was due to his galactic skill in using asteroids for humanities purposes. All of the mars colonists were at or around the site of the original encampment, but he wanted to encourage exploration of much more of the planet.

This point in history seemed again to be a unique moment. If his plans went according to his predictions he was going to re-water the other side of the planet.

In a very short space of time the Solar Orbiter was into geo stationary orbit above Mars.

Quite a number of the crew got off the Solar Orbiter at this point and were ferried down to the encampment. The grand father-in-law, no it's no good I shall have to refer to him as the Whistler or no-one will know whom I mean. He studied the planet's surface and then went to the captain saying, "Captain I have selected the impact site, all we need to do now is to find some suitable asteroids".

The captain gave orders and the ship eased away from Mars, and headed to the asteroid belt. Soon a huge round one came into view. That I think is Ceres, itself so large as being classified as a dwarf planet. The ship cruised on. The whistler suddenly grunted. "Yep ok there are about four suitable comet asteroids slightly to port, and I think we are still close enough to Mars to harvest them. This was the first time Eric Whistler had tried the dual attraction method, though he had of course read extensively about it from the ship's log. He carefully positioned the ship to point nose first at the asteroids and tail towards Mars. He focused on the farthest one first and then the next and so on. He handled this with such aplomb that the collisions between the asteroids were hardly noticeable. Captain Johnson silently applauded the efforts. The Whistler then asked the Captain if he could decelerate the entire group to a new velocity. The Captain found this rather tricky because of the relative closeness of other unwanted asteroids, but he finally said "ok Grandad how about that!"

The Whistler's face was glacial for a few moments. But he exploded, "ok Eric that is truly as close as I dared hope at this stage!" the asteroids were hurtling through space at a newly imparted speed, and as mars was approached, still far, far away, the asteroids' course began to change under the influence of mars' gravity. The changing course was plotted and new calculations done. Then the calculations were left running permanently, and new information as to the projected landing points and entry points in Mars' atmosphere were continuously calculated.

The Whistler stood up from viewing his lap top. Ok nothing to do now but wait. However Eric pointed out that there was another asteroid on a very similar course. The Whistler stared at the ship's main screen for a while before saying slowly; "It is as though another giant hand has guided that one. Captain, point your analysers at it please." The captain did exactly that and the Whistler summoned his men to the bridge for a consultation. After a few minutes the Whistler suddenly relaxed. "That rogue asteroid for want of a better name will collide with our selected group just about the time when the group will hit mars upper atmosphere. In effect it will pulverise both itself and the damn things we have selected!"

"Well is it good news?" asked the captain.

"I have spent weeks with my team here trying to ensure that the water bearing asteroids would not disturb the planet's equanimity too much. We don't want hundreds of volcano's to occur do we? The pulveriseation act will ensure that only small particles will make landfall, and so we will simply have tripled the planets water supply, please inform mars."

I was scribbling furiously because this direct information would take weeks to filter out of the reports, which I would read, honestly!

The result of the collision was two fold, firstly the pulverised bits behaved as the Whistler predicted. But a large fragment of the rogue shot off in a different direction altogether. It was observed to be on a close encounter course with sonny. The encounter was so close it was a collision. The entire crew held its breath as it waited for sonny to react. Extinction was the fear but the scientific members worried that the intensity of the reaction may cause a catastrophic explosion. There was an odd sort of visual distortion, and the rogue piece was already glowing before it hit sonny. Sonny simply kept shining though its orbit was pushed a little further out, so much so that its orbit time increased giving better periods of exposure on mars to sonny's heat. Though its orbit had changed it was still within the parameters of maintained orbit, and thus would stay as a moon of mars. Sonny was still giving scientists back on earth something to chew on. It was far too small to sustain a nuclear fusion reaction, and yet the particles emitted were not those of a fission reaction. No answer is forthcoming just yet.

In the event the disturbance to mars weather patterns was bad enough. A vast amount of water vapour eventually condensed as rain though some fell as snow on the poles and higher ground. It took 6 weeks for the weather to settle down, and the cloud cover seriously impeded the arrival of heat from the sun and from sonny. Mars had a sort of mini winter. The weather did settle and the original 39 lakes which had dried out to 37 lakes had now increased to about 140. The water was flowing across the land now and it was evident that when it had finally stopped there would be a very large lake on the uninhabited side of the planet. In fact it never stopped because the planets weather patterns re-circulated the water so that Mars now had flowing water on it. As the clouds cleared, evidence of the new water was clearly viewable from the ship, and earth. There still wasn't enough water for a real ocean but the lakes were quite sizeable. It suddenly occurred to me that I didn't know the difference between a small ocean and a large lake. Is there one?

My Grandad was enthralled. The zero gravity conditions seemed to have allowed him a new lease of life and he didn't get so tired. So he wasn't finished yet!

I could suddenly understand why so many people believed in God. The actions taken by man were perhaps instrumental but puny. The intervention of some other force had ensured that not only would Mars be wet, it would be warm. The hydrolysers as they were called were already splitting the water into hydrogen and oxygen. These gases both had commercial uses but the quantities made were such that the atmosphere was slowly being re-invigorated. There was an increasing life cycle in operation and I gather that some of the flies living there became so much of a nuisance that spiders were introduced to help control them. This apparently worked brilliantly.

Following the success of earth's high altitude cow, goats and sheep were given their chance and they are slowly acclimatizing to the Martian conditions.

From my Grandad's story I know that fish were doing ok and I have found out that there were plans afoot to introduce predatory fish such as pike. I have read no reports confirming this just yet.

The farming side has seen the introduction of a few more species of trees, which were planted in chosen locations. They are growing!

I remember Grandad theorising that the population of mars would never exceed about 400,000 due to lack of water. I must ask him what he thinks now!

Many folk on earth simply want to live their life and don't give a fig what is going on elsewhere. Me, I'm in the other school, exciting or what!

That evening as we retired for the night, Eric brought out two glasses and poured one each. Alcohol was never my greatest love, but it had been a momentous time. I took a mouthful and was pleasantly surprised by the taste.

"I see by your face that you like it, I'm glad because you are the first fresher ever to drink wine produced from Martian grapes."

"Martian grapes" I said incredulously.

"Yep, derived by a botanist on duty on mars and genetically modified to suit Martian conditions."

"GM grapes" I said as the nice taste was replaced by fear.

"No one has even had the slightest problem with this wine and it is now being shipped back to earth in huge amounts. Earth does not want GM crops or anything like them that could upset the earth's eco system. But it is a different story with the wine. I may as well come clean about this; I have invested over half my savings in this venture so I really don't want it to fail, I am the major shareholder in the enterprise."

"Well, I admit that it does have a lovely taste, so with all that chunk of our future tied up in it, I hope you have backed the right horse!"

He relaxed and smiled.

CHAPTER 31

BACK TO BUSINESS

The ships orders were to look in on Ganymede and report on any observational changes, but earth's interest had shifted to Europa.

Reading through the technicians reports from Ganymede, there did not appear to be anything worthy of note. The captain however ordered a skeleton away team to stay behind, and observe, while the main mission went to Europa.

I kept well away from the action and let the crew go about their daily routines, after only three more days, an away team was prepared for the visit to Europa.

Due I understand to previous mapping of this moon, a good landing place had already been selected. The ice was very thin at this point, but there was deep ice only five miles away and the team's first job was to establish the correctness of the geology.

The original survey was very detailed and was confirmed as correct, at several points where tests were done. The team ferried parts of a nuclear reactor down to the new building site as they called it and construction of the power station went ahead simultaneously with the latest Eden shelter. The Eden shelter was erected with almost indecent haste as it provided base camp facilities. It provided eating, sleeping, and some recreation.

From the observation platform and the ships main screen, I watched as the five legged construction took place. I marveled at how the cranage required was built in to the hub function at the centre. The central anti-flood tube was first to be sunk in, then the deep rectangular pit was finished and the reactor room was lowered and fixed in place. The construction of the first nuclear station on Titan was covered in fair detail. Suffice it to say that the new one on Europa was completed more quickly due in part to design improvements. The supply of fresh water for cooling purposes was available in much the same way, but the bore holes were required to go down much further to find liquid water. The away team surmounted all these issues and the station coughed out its first welcome kilowatts just about on schedule.

Europa unlike Titan does not have a substantial atmosphere. It does though suffer from enormous amounts of radiation. The away team had to use full protective gear which is heavy and cumbersome. The improved versions of the Eden shelters could now be heated up to 25 degrees Celsius, and so it was possible to doff the space suits and use normal clothing. The plastic self healing compound filling the gaps between the four layer outer skins of the shelter contained lead particles that filtered out much of the radiation from Jupiter.

Earth did wish for a permanently manned station on Europa, so the away team leader, non other than Heinrich, decided that a cave needed to be found or dug. Nothing suitable was found, indeed the surface of Europa was very flat with only slight inclines here and there. Finally a suitable piece of ice presented it self and the rock pulverisers were used to hollow out a cave; it took some weeks to achieve a great enough volume. A new Eden shelter was erected inside it and the radiation levels were finally at a low enough level to be considered absolutely safe. There was no oxygen enrichment on this moon.

From probes sent from earth a few years before, criss-cross lines and striations had been seen. From the ground these were huge but the colours were almost nonexistent, nothing as bold as was expected. Chemical analysis though was to prove interesting. Long amino acid strings were found, these being the building blocks of protein. The temperature of this biological key was so low as to render reaction almost impossible, *almost*.

Further samples taken from deep fresh water showed other active proteins. No life was found but the building blocks were all there.

Unfortunately for our mission, insufficient care was taken in handling the europan samples and aided by the rich biology on board the ship, a new virus emerged.

The first sign of it was when I found myself feeling rather groggy. The captain ordered me to isolation immediately. A full investigation was carried out; when a crew member suddenly realizing that it was he that had broken procedure was man enough to own up. The captain was enraged, and realizing that his judgment was impaired asked the Prof to handle the issue.

I felt worse and worse, and suddenly I doubted that I would get better at all and just might die.

The ships medical team was on full alert, and needed a blood sample. Grandad immediately volunteered as he knew he had the same blood group as me. The blood sample was infected with the virus taken from my blood. As I grew weaker and weaker, in common with most viruses it caused me to sweat, and then some, and as I was getting increasingly despondent, I had a visitor. It was the Captain. He had a very drawn look and I knew from that he was expecting me to die.

"Drink this" he cajoled me.

I drank it. "It tastes like Martian wine I said"

He did his best to smile. "That is because it is Martian wine!"

I polished the glass off and strangely felt better for it.

Research into my condition was continuing and over the next few days I began to feel just a little stronger, so I requested an audience with the Captain.

He came directly and seeing the slight improvement in me asked if I wanted anything.

"More wine" I said.

He brought me a full glass and I drank it. I felt immediately a little better.

Now the medical team was still on my case and they analysed the wine but could find nothing to link it with my recovery.

I took a little food and some more wine. Psychological or not it worked for me.

They took another blood sample then half an hour after my next drink of wine they took another. The analysis showed a sudden reduction in the viral activity. Over the next two days they took samples at different times and admitted that they could find no anti-viral properties in the wine.

"It must act as a catalyst to something else" said the Prof.

I was now taking decent amounts of food again and was out of bed the following day.

When Eric came down to see me again his relief was obvious and he smiled rather wanly and said "Catherine I have ordered the labels for our Martian wine to stipulate that the wine was a proven cure for the first galactic disease known.

I grinned saying "you opportunistic rat!"

The medics could still find no link to the disease.

Grandad though, suddenly became a little bit ill. A quick blood test revealed he had contracted the disease, which we termed "europan flu". I gave him a glass of our wine from a fresh bottle, and he went to bed, taking the bottle with him. Six hours later he declared himself fit for another 100 years.

I chided the medics for their tardiness, as to me there was no other explanation. I fully endorsed the addition to the wine label, but I also suggested that the wine be named "Martian Elixir"

You might already have bought yourself a bottle; it's been on earth's supermarkets for a while now and it really is a refreshing drink, and only slightly alcoholic.

The Whistler had watched the disease progress, and he realised that when something like this occurred, survival was down to the human body's ability to cure itself. I don't think he knew that I knew about his surreptitious data transmissions all those years ago. He was not the most effusive of men, but gave me a very warm smile when he could see I was recovering. Because it was such a rare event, I found his smile rewarding.

CHAPTER 32

CONCLUSIONS DRAWN

On earth, there was a lust to find other life, and this had been fuelled by the results of the Titan missions. The captain though could see another worrying possibility that could even be a likely probability. He reasoned that life itself was rather dangerous and cited my experience as proof of this. A number of amino acids from Europa with a little help from us humans had suddenly fused themselves into a virus that was new and thus harmful to humans. His notion, inspired by the Prof was that humans themselves had been instrumental in the gestation of the virus, and of course there was no way of knowing if or when something else may occur.

Perhaps it had been the hand of the almighty that gave us the cure, or perhaps the virus had just run its course, and I had simply recovered. I do not subscribe to this latter idea. Grandad was given the wine when he was only in the early stages and yet recovered overnight.

The Captain spoke.

"It is of course incumbent upon me to ensure the safety of the mission in so far as that is possible. Therefore I do not want to see any harebrained schemes being tried. I will have a bridge committee comprising myself, Captain Johnson, The Prof, The Whistler and a selection of top men who will be charged with finding an answer to how this virus came into being and how in the end it was defeated. The away team is for the moment isolated on Europa and must stay there until our committee is in total agreement on the answers to our quest. Questions anyone?"

There were a number of technical questions raised but the captain had his responses ready. No one was in any doubt as to the seriousness of the quest.

As from this point I was not involved on the bridge and had to rely on reading the reports as I archived them.

Grandad was a frequent visitor and conceded that I really had got the hang of his beloved archive system.

One day when I was in the midst of a rather awkward piece, his visit wasn't really welcome just at that moment and I suggested that he and the Prof should get their heads together and see if they could come up with an answer to the virus question. This question was still vexing the best brains on the ship.

Grandad went quiet, but as I glanced at him he wasn't upset, just deep in thought.

He stalked off presumably to search out the Prof.

CHAPTER 33

THE OLD MEN FIND A LINK

Grandad and the Prof entered a discussion about the qualities of the wine. Due to their seniority and the fact that they were not directly part of the mission the alcohol consumption rule didn't apply to them.

They rattled about this and that, and sipped from wine glasses.

"Is this elixir red or white do you think?" mumbled Grandad.

"That's a good question" slurred the Prof, "the grapes are about half and half, you know!"

"Well I thought they harvested them young when they are white!"

"Yes but they found that using a few old ones in the brew, gave the distinctive flavour, and they are virtually black by that stage!"

"You are very well informed on the matter" grinned Grandad.

"Shareholder, you know" replied the Prof.

"Well the other night when I was feeling a bit seedy my granddaughter gave me a fresh bottle, and I drank the lot. I thought if I was going to die I would have a smile on my face" chuckled Grandad.

"The only thing that I thought of as odd was the temperature, because it wasn't chilled but it certainly wasn't chambre." Said Grandad

Both men exploded simultaneously "surely that can't be it, can it?"

A check with the laboratory soon established that as a matter of course all substances were chilled unless there was a procedure ruling that out.

Grandad fished in his pocket, and gave the lab technician a half empty bottle that he and the prof had been imbibing.

"Quick lad, do some anti viral checks on it, as it is now!" urged the Prof. The checking soon showed that the virus died within seconds of coming into touch with the wine. The technician was a meticulous lad and conducted several other tests while our two old guys stood watching.

"If you chill it to lower than about 18 degrees Celsius the effect disappears, but it you warm it past about 27 degrees Celsius, the virus mutates, and god only knows what that might do!" he grimaced as he said the words.

Ok, we three are going to the bridge right now" commanded the Prof.

The captain noticed the unsteady gate of the two older men and demanded an explanation, a good explanation.

The Prof nodded acknowledgment of their clear breach of protocol but said "Captain this simply could not wait!"

The Captain nodded curtly, anyone else would have been in the brig in a trice.

The Prof outlined their discovery and offered their inebriated state as the key to the whole affair.

"Ok Prof; get all the senior lab technicians to the lab as a matter of urgency". Then remembering the Prof's status as an observer, gave the orders himself.

The requisitioned men stood before the captain. The captain outlined the discovery, and was told that the general disciplines would have ground through the system and within 48 hours the whole system would have been on the right track. The temperature checks were already programmed into the research.

"Good" barked the Captain, may I suggest that you leap frog the low temperature issues and get on with the higher temperature ones.

CHAPTER 34

A NEW FORM OF THE DISEASE ARRIVES

The Whistler then intervened. "Captain, I agree with your general attitude here but I think just for thoroughness we cannot and must not abandon the low temperature research."

The Captain acquiesced.

The Whistler then indicated that he did not feel at all well. The medical staff quickly established that he had contracted a mutated version of europan flu. Just how the mutation had occurred was not known, but I thought that somehow it had escaped from the lab just as the discovery of the properties of our Martian elixir was made.

"Ok, it is all hands to the pumps. I want the corridors that the Whistler traverses during his existence on this ship to be isolated, I do not want this virus to spread, but I fear we may already be too late".

The Martian wine was given to the Whistler, but in this case there was no discernible difference in his condition.

The captain spoke privately to the chief medical officer. "James Whistler is of prime importance to this mission. He may recover on his own, but I fear we will not be so lucky and he will not. He already has symptoms of pneumonia/ legionnaires disease. And so I expect you to give him the antibiotics for this. Any change in his condition, I must be notified immediately. As you know, he is my grandfather, and I must afford him every chance. Do I make myself clear?"

"Aye, aye Captain, rest assured no stone will remain unturned."

CHAPTER 35

THE WHISTLER NEARS THE END

I was allowed to see the Whistler, but only through glass windows. He could see me there and weakly raised an arm as acknowledgment.

I realised with dismay, that the virus was weakening him far more quickly than had happened to me. I really feared for his life.

The chief medical officer asked for a private audience with the captain, and this was granted.

"Captain, I have no good news to report, only bad. James Whistler gets weaker by the hour, and I feel he must have a blood transfusion immediately. We have no stock of his blood group and there is only one person aboard the Solar Orbiter who has the same group, and that is you, sir. I must point out however that there is a risk of cross contamination, no matter how careful we are. We do not know for certain whether this virus is contagious or infectious, but indications are that it is infectious.

The captain agreed to give blood but first drank a glass of his beloved Martian Elixir.

The blood was screened and a proportion of it was duly given to the Whistler. He rallied but was not yet out of the woods.

He was given the Martian Elixir again but without any effect.

The captain showed no sign of a virus, but had taken the step to ensure that Captain Johnson would step in if needs be.

One of the gifted medical technicians had isolated this latest virus for the purposes of study. He found that the virus could not live if the body temperature was allowed to rise. The snag was that the body temperature would have to be so high that the patient would die as a result. The Whistler was fading. As a last resort the Whistler's blood was circulated via a heater, then cooled before being re-introduced to his body, and was then mixed with the remains of the captain's transfusion blood.

This technique allowed the blood to go a few degrees over the survival level of the mutated virus, and then brought it down to below the delirious level, so it could be given to the patient. A simple microwave oven was used as the blood heater, and a decent refrigerator was used for cooling. The Whistler began to recover slowly.

The captain ordered that all samples of blood and the virus be brought inside full isolation boxes and left on the bridge. The researchers grumbled because they knew the captain would eject them from the ship.

"Problems, gentlemen? As you have no doubt guessed, I have decided to get rid of these europan viruses before the ship suffers any more infections. I understand that having worked so far and so well to find answers, you will not wish to see the samples go to destruction. Your records of your work must be kept for future reference, but I have another overriding responsibility. The safety of the ship and crew is my major concern here, and so with out further ado, we will eject these containers into space. None of the technicians knew a better solution and some were frankly relieved to be shot of these dangerous virus cultures. The crew members assigned to the actual ejection task, placed the boxes inside the ejection chute, closed the air lock a quiet hiss and then that was that.

The Whistler recovered slowly, and speaking to Captain Johnson, ruefully commented that data transmissions back to earth overt or covert, were of no value in a situation such as they had endured. Captain Johnson allowed himself a half smile. This was the nearest that the Whistler ever got to revealing his motive for the covert data transmissions on the first Solar Orbiter mission.

After a further 6 weeks the Captain was able to declare that the ship was safe, and he could then recall his away team. The consensus of opinion was that Europa itself posed no problems, but extreme care was needed to avoid contamination with europan partial viruses, which could then develop into other unknown ones, as soon as they came into contact with earth life forms. The entire away team went through a thorough hose down, and then all of their clothing was ejected, including the space suits. After a few more days they were deemed clean.

Earth had invested a lot of money in this project and was anxious that it continue.

The captain refused point blank to leave a manned station on Europa. In his reports back to earth he mentioned that the illness seen could end up being a planetwide, uncontrollable pandemic, and that in itself might cause further viral mutations. Earth went rather quiet.

The nuclear station was set to low output with lake water used to cool the reactor. Eden shelter and roadway heating and lighting were left switched on to provide a load for the power station. In effect the power station was put into semi hibernation. All of the away teams were finally recalled to the ship, and were carefully screened for diseases. None were found to the relief of the entire crew. No member of the undercrew reported any symptoms at all, and as they only had minimal contact with the operational crew it was reasoned that the viruses were contagious not infectious.

The captain decided to head for home going via Jupiter and Mars. The cheers rang and reverberated throughout the ship. The captain's intention was to pick up a few remaining away teamers that had been left on Ganymede, then to ship me, Grandad and the Whistler down to mars so that their medical teams could examine us thoroughly and provide a second opinion on our condition. I must say I felt quite well again and expected no complications. Our blood would be screened for unusual antibodies and a supply of these would be manufactured in their laboratories, and made available in case the diseases somehow were to spread.

CHAPTER 36

MARS REVISITED

GRANDAD SPENDS SOME TIME ON MARS

As the ship approached mars, the Prof advised Grandad to spend some time there to reacquaint his body with the force of gravity. The idea being to provide a lower gravity as a stage in aiding re-acclimatisation, before returning to earth. Normally anyone desiring to leave the ship had to endure several days in the giddy room. The giddy room was in the rotating section of the ship but went at a fair rate, creating about 30 percent of earth's gravity. Everybody was aware that grandad's 100th birthday was imminent, and no one wanted to see him simply collapse back on earth. He spent half a day in the giddy room just before being shipped down to mars.

The mars colonists had been busy. The atmosphere was still re-oxygenating, and one bonus from the last asteroid plant had been the appearance of some nitrogen. The atmosphere was still inhospitable, but the madmen who tried to exist in it unaided, were against all expectations slowly succeeding. There was sufficient oxygen for survival now, but the general shortage of nitrogen, and mars' smaller size kept the atmospheric pressure low.

At the end of the lake where the chemical reactions had been noted, it was discovered that a new and useful product was available. The ground there had properties similar to clay and had been successfully baked and made into bricks. A powdered version of this clay was found to be similar to cement on earth. It was obvious from all the other success stories that house building of a traditional earth style would be possible in the near future. In perhaps 50 years there would be sufficient tree life to provide lumber. Martian sand could be fused into glass, and it appeared to me that whatever successes found elsewhere in the solar system, only Mars would be able to support life in the true sense of the word.

What did I say about madmen? Grandad tried taking his helmet off, but he soon put it back on! However perhaps he wasn't entirely as mad as those others who regularly did this, after all it was his 100th birthday.

Mars had put in a request for a nuclear station and earth had agreed in principle. A design based on the Titan and Europa ones was under consideration. Mars had confirmed large deposits of copper noticeable by blue green streaks in some of the hills following rainstorms, and needed power to reclaim it. In the final analysis, earth's designers selected a site as remote from the known useful areas on mars as possible. The whole nuclear plant with its cooling water would be in one of the great Martian lakes that was filling a large crater. This water was isolated from other lakes and streams and so could not easily spread contamination. The control room would be the other side of the crater walls to offer some protection against radiation in the event of such a problem. The five legs would be long enough to rest on the crater floor and the central anti flooding tube would be sunk into and fixed to the crater floor before being pumped dry.

In this instance there would also be a flood door so that the reactor room could be flooded in a real panic emergency. This does not exist yet, but the design seems sound to a woman such as myself, and I will admit to an unreasoned fear of nuclear radiation.

Since the innermost planets of the solar system appear to have a common ancestor, it would be reasonable to expect that most things found on earth would eventually be found on mars.

Sonny is still shining brilliantly and this reaction is the subject of furious study. As yet the best brains on earth have still not come up with a suitable theory to explain its operation. One idea being pursued is that there is an amount of iron involved. At the very high temperatures the iron becomes a gas, and this gas is somehow helping sustain the reaction.

I tried Martian steak while we were there, and unlike Grandad, I really like it. It is very tender and has a delicate flavour.

Corn was one of the GM modified crops grown on mars. It makes lovely bread! I would still be worried about eating this long term, but the taste is so good, I am sure others will not worry. I trust my worries prove to be unfounded.

CHAPTER 37

BACK ON EARTH

GRANDAD MAKES IT OK

The visit to mars had given Grandad's muscles time to rebuild and yet he still found his own weight on earth almost impossible to support. It took him three weeks to reacclimatize, and then just on shear will power he heaved himself out of his chair when Eric and I went to pay him a visit. He said, he thought he had needed about two more days in the giddy room with that room running at top speed, but he hadn't done that and found earth very tiring.

He admitted to me that he had feared for my life when I had europan flu, but swore that the wine we had given him simply banished the virus from his system while he slept. He is still struggling on but I suppose I have to expect bad news in the near future.

An unexpected result has come from Titan. Samples of hydrocarbons found on Titan had been taken, and it was found when these were dissolved in petrol, the calorific value of the fuel was increased by 30%. This would mean that earth's oil supplies could be eked out for many years yet. This set the scene for more visits to Titan, and provides a good basis for raising the money, and research avenues regarding fuel additives are already being pursued.

From my perspective it appeared that Titan having produced its own basic life-forms was a safer place to be than Europa, which seemed to be in a virulent beginning of such things. None of any of the gas giant's moons could ever be colonized in the same way as Mars, but Titan seems to me to be second only to Mars. I expect that Titan may yet have a penal colony as an alternative to prison on earth. Carefully chosen inmates could open it up much as the chain gangs in America made many of the large highways there. There would of course be no need for chains.

I don't think that Eric is set to retire from captaining the Solar Orbiter for many years yet, but I will not be able to accompany him for some time yet as our family is due for an increase shortly, and I hope Grandad will still be here at that time.

The lust to explore the solar system has been partly assuaged, and the whole scale of things will be greatly reduced in the near future. I hope that such reports as there are can be handled on a part time basis, because I am going to be busy!

The Martian elixir is now being sold world wide, although some supermarkets are struggling to obtain sufficient supplies as its popularity grows. Time for a bit more investment!

I'm off to see Jane Johnson, and talk mom talk. Whenever anything else of interest crops up in the reports, I will write further addenda. *Bye for now, Catherine Whistler.*

CHAPTER 38

DOES THIS EXPLAIN SONNY?

An idea being bandied around earth just at the moment seems to go like this. An atomic bomb is an uncontrolled nuclear fission reaction. An atomic power station uses the same principle but controls the ferocity of the reaction with carbon rods. The sun and other stars have a fusion reaction when atoms of hydrogen get squeezed into atoms of helium due to the pressure caused by enormous gravitational pulls, and the temperatures caused as the gas is compressed. Now sonny, on its own is no where near large enough to cause a fusion reaction. The latest explanation says that the original bang out in space was a simple nuclear fission reaction. However there was probably enough uranium to make 500 atomic bombs, but the original bang threw all of the remaining constituent parts outward, thus reducing the proximity of the individual masses of unused uranium. The gravitational pull internal to this new moon however was just enough to keep the uranium within its sphere of influence. When the uranium began to fall, there was sufficient to sustain the basic fission reaction, this being a gentler thing as the material is supplied rather slowly and on a continuous basis. This in turn acts just like an early hydrogen bomb and drags some hydrogen into the atomic maelstrom at the core of the moon. This hydrogen gets converted to helium, as the gases are trapped by incoming uranium. The combined effects raise the core temperature of sonny so high that some of the uranium is simply split into other elements such as iron, and this in turn suffers further massive temperature rise, so much so that it first evaporates then splits again into lighter elements. The combined effect of the relatively small gravitational pull and the core temperature causes many atomic elements to form and many of them to shortly be destroyed by the actions within this moon. Some reactions consume energy but some give energy out. The net effect is that a reaction is sustained and the life expectancy is 25000 years. I know that this is a poor description but the issue is so technical that it's the best I can do. Remember the issue has baffled far greater brains than mine.

Eric and I are now the proud parents of a small son. Grandad enjoyed the baby for a few weeks but then one day simply didn't awaken. I am missing him terribly.

Bye for now. Catherine Whistler.

CHAPTER 39

THERE IS SOMETHING SERIOUS GOING ON OUT THERE.

Hello this is Catherine Whistler again. It has been some time since I added to Grandad's journal, but some of the reports coming in lately have given me a certain unease. As you may recall the colonization of mars has been going on at a slowly increasing rate, but suddenly the number of applicants has quadrupled. This coupled with the content of certain rumours has simply given rise to worrying disquiet in my conscience. Earth now has a small fleet of space vessels. The Freeloader is still going about her rounds; the Solar Orbiter has been on several missions captained either by Captain Johnson or my husband Eric Whistler. Other senior men have captained the other ships of the fleet.

The Whistler, my grandfather-in-law, had achieved stunning success with galactically engineering asteroid movements that have been instrumental in reviving mars, and reading between the lines it appears that others have tried even more ambitious plans but without real success.

Unfortunately their failures appear to about to unravel, and many of earth's politicians are still spouting twaddle and they imagine that the populace is blithely unaware that there are dangers to be faced. The dangers facing earth's people are not defined, yet are rumoured to be immense, hence the sudden popularity of life on mars. There is a rumour that we have a ship lost in space, though no reports coming to me for archiving have confirmed this as yet.

The irresponsible attitudes of certain factions within the space community are breathtaking and seriously life threatening. So far I have not been able to divine the whole truth from the filed reports, but suddenly financing has been found for a twin mission, involving both Captains Johnson and Whistler, and before I could speak to Eric about it, they were both under strict orders of silence. Their mission starts tomorrow, and I will be following reports avidly.

Amazingly it has come to my ears that both the Prof, who was fully retired and the Whistler as top scientific officer, have been requested to accompany the missions, the Prof with Captain Johnson and the Whistler with my husband.

CHAPTER 40

ABOARD THE SOLAR ORBITER

Captain Johnson called an open meeting on the bridge of all the senior men under his command.

"Good afternoon ladies and gentlemen. As you know we are on an emergency mission, and this calls for emergency measures. The Prof, here used to be my second in command and on this mission even though he is technically retired, you will still accord to him all of the respect for that position. Is that clear? No? Well should anyone not accord him the respect I demand, that person will spend the entire mission in solitary." He waited for the surprised murmuring to die down.

"Many of you will have voyaged under other captains and may find my disciplinarianistic style of control difficult to swallow. You will swallow it. Is that understood?

I am approachable however, but I will have no truck with bullshit. I am appalled at how the standards of discipline in the space service have been allowed to decline in the last couple of years. Our mission may involve the utmost danger. The only way that we can proceed is to be fully professional and earn the mutual trust of our colleagues. Earth is relying on us to complete this mission safely. Now your loyalty is to me and the command of this ship. Other past loyalties must be forgotten and will not be tolerated if they impinge in any way on the ability of this ship to achieve its mission aims. Is that absolutely clear?"

There was a deathly silence.

"Perhaps the Prof here would like to add a few words!" added the captain.

The prof stepped forwards his hair previously an iron grey was now flowing white.

He began "as you can imagine, dragging an old fart like me from pruning my roses means that something is afoot. As yet the whole truth has not been revealed. We have sealed orders, not to be opened until after we receive our slingshot from the sun.

As you know, I have only had three days to re-familiarise myself with the ship's log, but I must say that the record of discipline across all functions leaves a lot to be desired. Now that we have a commander whose record is second to none, you can rest assured that this ship will be run hard but fair. If anyone has anything to say now is the time to say it!"

There was a mumbled comment from the floor.

"What was that?" snapped the captain.

One of the older men squared his shoulders and said simply "thank god for that!"

The Prof asked the man to remain behind after dismissal.

This crewmember was an ordinary able spaceman. He had no hidden agenda to think about, and did not have the verbal skills to describe what exactly had been upsetting him in the recent past. The Prof questioned him quite carefully but could find nothing amiss, and yet the Prof knew that there was some element at work which had undermined this man's faith in the space administration.

CHAPTER 41

ABOARD THE SPACE ADVENTURER

At about the same time Eric Whistler called an open meeting aboard the bridge.

He addressed the senior men.

"When this mission was mooted back on earth a decision had to be made as to who was to captain each vessel. Now when you here stories over the jungle telegraph you may feel thankful to be aboard this ship. Captain Johnson is an iron disciplinarian, but I learnt all that I know of space vessel operation from him, including how to maintain discipline, and do that I will! I am approachable, but I will take no evasiveness or bullshit! The success of our mission may yet depend on mutual respect for your professional colleagues. Back stabbing will not be tolerated. You will at all times conduct yourselves in a professional manner to the sublimation of your own personal feelings. Should any man have comments, on any issue at all he will be free to speak to me after dismissal.

Just for the record, this vessel has a number of guests on board, and amongst these is the man universally known by his nickname. He is the Whistler. He is also my grandfather. He carries no operational rank in the space service but, he is the head of space administration. You will accord him the respect that would be required if he were my second in command. We have sealed orders that I will be permitted to open once we receive the slingshot effect from the sun. I trust that you will convey what I have said to your men, any procedural breaches will be punished with the harshest penalties. I as captain am the law aboard the ship and I will change the rules if I find it necessary. DISMISS!"

One man remained where he was shuffling uncomfortably.

"Name?" barked the captain.

"I am Jim Roberts!"

"Well?"

"As you can see sir, I am in the second half of my career, and I welcome the return to discipline. I feel that I may have information regarding the safety of Earth.

"The safety of *Earth*?"

"I fear so sir"

"Well you will come to my quarters now and explain!" the captain then barked a request into the ships communications "James Whistler to the captain's quarters immediately please."

The information revealed was so surprising that Eric used the secure transmission to let the Solar Orbiter know at once.

Captain Johnson gave the information to the Prof and asked what he thought of it.

The Prof was quiet for a minute and then spoke.

"Either this man is a plant with an ulterior motive or he has been released from some overburdening fear and has allowed his conscience to speak." For the moment the Prof considered further.

"This information is known to the two captains, me, the Whistler and Jim Roberts only. Should anyone else get to hear about it, it means Jim Roberts is spreading it about and therefore cannot be trusted."

This valued opinion was sent back to Eric Whistler. A decision was made to keep eyes and ears open, but for the moment to keep the information close. Jim Roberts was allowed a loose tether.

The orders when opened were rather vague, and mentioned pandemics and avoiding contamination. The two captains discussed their orders, and were frankly puzzled. At about this time however there came an urgent communication from earth and this was sent via the secure system to both bridges simultaneously. "Use headphones, and for captains ears only," came the curt request, "use coded headphones, the information will be scrambled". Both captains obeyed, selected the days coding and listened intently.

"Earth has received a demand from somewhere out in space that it cannot meet. The demand is to cease all space travel and to prepare to meet its doom. The essence of the messages is that earth will be showered with new life forms that will be guaranteed to eliminate all existing life forms. We imagine that the madmen behind all this do have some means to do what they threaten and even if we were to comply, we believe that they would take over mars, to ensure their own survival and throw Earth to the wolves. We are missing one spaceship that we thought had been lost in space but now we think it is the home of these renegade nutters. We suggest that a severe question and answer routine be set up on both ships to try and glean anything that you can, in the way of information. You have the best brains already with you, so please track down and destroy the source of our worries. Earth out."

Eric Whistler sucked his teeth, opened the secure transmission channel to his sister ship then said "I want to tell the Whistler and the Prof, and I think we should hold a head to head at the earliest opportunity."

"Agreed, Johnson out."

CHAPTER 42

JIM ROBERTS

As the Prof had suggested, a quiet eye was kept on this individual, but after a few days there was absolutely nothing to report. Checking through his service record revealed an honest stolid intelligent man. There were no black marks against him at all. Even Eric Whistler had got a couple of black marks for his moon bicycle incident, but Jim Roberts, absolutely nothing. This in itself was not reassuring.

His record showed his field of expertise as psychology, and he had been proficient rather then brilliant. He had served on the Freeloader, the Solar Orbiter and one other ship named as the Gravitas.

Eric Whistler made enquiries quietly through normal channels, as to just what the specification and present mission of the Gravitas was. The answer gave no comfort. The Gravitas was similar in specification to the Space Adventurer and the Solar Orbiter, but had failed to return from its last mission.

Eric gave the bridge over to his second in command, a rather intellectual chap known as Doctor Barry.

"Ok doc, you have the bridge, I am going to check on the emergency evacuation procedures!"

Quietly collecting the Whistler on his way he launched one of the landing craft and skipped the few miles of space across to the Solar Orbiter then hailed Captain Johnson without fully identifying himself.

"Permission to dock?"

Within moments the top four men were ensconced in the captain's private quarters.

Eric Whistler and his grandfather the real Whistler fished out some small battery powered pens, and skimmed round Captain Johnson's abode.

"Seems to be clean" murmured Eric.

They discussed all of the implications of the information so far gleaned. Their suspicion that the renegades, if there really were any, were in the Gravitas.

"Well what about this man Roberts?" questioned Captain Johnson.

"He is simply too clean" said Eric Whistler, "and he served on the Gravitas."

The Prof then interjected "I have given the matter some thought and it seems to me that somehow or other space has been invaded by politics. Whatever this organization is, it seems to have bizarre aims and must be headed by a madman. The snag with a madman is that he always knows it and will be strikingly clever at hiding it. I think the Gravitas is lurking somewhere near Europa, and that the crew are harnessing the virus producing capacity of the damn place, and have found some means to deliver this to earth.

The chief is a megalomaniac who wants to control the world, and he is willing to destroy Earth leaving his target as Mars. At the last count Mars has now got a thriving population of about 2 million, so it would feed his ego enormously if he thought he could control it, and of course if he had already destroyed the entire population of earth, he would have Mars in the palm of his hand.

The Gravitas has a laser weapon system similar to ours, so I suggest we get the best brains to develop some protection against it. Once this is done I further suggest that we split the mission into two. For sake of argument, the Space Adventurer could visit mars with a view to weeding out possible sympathizers and the Solar Orbiter could try and locate the Gravitas with a view to disabling it!"

The Whistler added, "Meanwhile we should spend a few weeks researching space administration records and trace the whereabouts of every member of the crew of the Gravitas who are not still aboard it.

Captain Johnson, if you have known suspects aboard the Solar Orbiter, send them across to the Space Adventurer in a shuttle, under the guise of an evacuation procedure check, and we will observe behaviour."

This was soon done and the Whistler boys noticed that Jim Roberts was seen briefly in the docking area, this underlined that there was every likelihood that both ships in effect had spies on board. The shuttle from the Solar Orbiter was sent straight back before there was any chance of any chatter between the crews.

The Whistler demanded that all communication transmitters in the shuttles be given an actuating code to be revealed only to the assigned captains at the time of launch, and that this would be changed on a daily basis. This piece of advice was followed on both ships.

The communications officers were instructed to monitor all forms of transmission, and the auto transmissions back to earth were stopped. When earth demanded to know why this was done it was told that one James Whistler would reveal all at some future date, and earth then responded with a deafening silence.

The spies on board realised that a net was tightening and went to ground, the research into their activities however continued.

Here, best use was made of the Prof's history. He had been at the epicenter of so many disagreements that he was the ideal man to approach for help.

CHAPTER 43

ABOARD THE SOLAR ORBITER

An awkward question

Captain Johnson asked the Prof to see him in his quarters, and the Prof went along curious to know what was afoot.

Captain Johnson then gave the Prof the following deduced details.

"Prof we want to look into the service record of any man or woman that has had some sort of disaffection with the authorities. Now as with any scientific investigation, it must begin on a firm basis so the captain began "Prof, the man we are so eagerly looking for, it isn't you is it?" and with that awkward question he stared straight into the Prof's eyes.

The Prof was startled for a second and openly returned his stare but then chuckled "well I can just imagine me at home tending my runner beans and pruning my roses, and running a vicious space empire in my spare time! Just for the record I am not the man you seek!"

Captain Johnson nodded grimly. "Also just for the record, my time and energies have always brought ample reward and I am content with a captaincy, I have no desire to be a dictator! These questions and responses are now part of the record of this investigation."

This time the Prof's eyebrows raised as he realised that the captain really was going about things in his characteristic way, but even more thoroughly if that were possible.

"Well on quick reflection, I see that no one is above suspicion! And I think that is good."

"Ok old friend, I had to ask did I not? I have also cleared the two Whistlers, in much the same way! Now though this is a two ship mission I am the most senior commander, and thus the heaviest responsibility falls onto me. I can only have one source of files of suspects and this will be kept as a disc which I will keep on my person at all times. A copy of the record will be kept on the Space Adventurer but coded and compressed transmissions will be used at some time during the day to eliminate as far as is possible, the chance of anyone else listening in, to update the copy record.

I want you to use your personal laptop to aid your investigations, but at any time even if you only suspect that your security has been compromised you must inform me."

The Prof then mused "do you think that we have been living in a fool's paradise when for the last twenty five years or so we have fully occupied ourselves with scientific and engineering issues generally for the good of mankind, with no political considerations even on the fringes of the picture?"

"Both the captains eyebrows raised as he considered this. "Prof you are usually correct about such things, and I suppose anyone with a political agenda has had total freedom to recruit others to his cause. I do think however that as this has only just come to light that the mastermind behind it all has moved cautiously at all times until now, and therefore our investigation should start as far back as possible."

The Prof's face took on a curious expression as he said "I am damn sure you're right about that. Now perhaps there is more life left to me than just tending runner beans. I will have some information for you at the end of the day. I suggest that we do not meet in your quarters but in the canteen during main meal times where it will be busy and noisy!"

The captain nodded assent and nodded assent again as the prof stood to leave the bridge.

The bridge had an enclosure, away from the ship's section commanders, where they had been sitting. The captain decided to have this bridge quiet room swept for bugs every day as a matter of course. He further decided that he would use his hand held bug detector before and after any further meetings held there. In his mind he gave thanks to Eric Whistler who had swept the captains quarters at the brief head to head meeting for the idea.

CHAPTER 44

MEANWHILE ON THE SPACE ADVENTURER

The Whistler read the latest information from the senior ship. "You know we must find some way of giving the Prof a real professorship. Although I can probe thought channels regarding technical fact to a considerable depth, he seems to be able to do the same with human frailties, and that is a fantastic ability!"

The Whistler then said, "Ok Eric we must start at the beginning, and commence with the oldest wallahs that we know. I think that there are many issues for us to fret about and I will name these as follows. Firstly the Prof is right, there has been a political vacuum out in space, and this has now been claimed by a very devious man. Secondly no one man can do whatever he wants to do on his own. Therefore he has allies, and I think his allied partners are all over earth and mars as well as the space ships. Thirdly, he now knows that we are looking for him and so will be doubly difficult to flush out. Fourthly, In common with other dictators he is without conscience and thus utterly ruthless. Fifthly he has some means to carry out the threat he has made against earth. I think that he has found a way in which to control europan viruses and has found a means to deliver these in great quantities to earth. Sixthly I think that I myself may have been instrumental in providing him with the means of delivery of the viruses to earth!"

"Keep talking!"

"Asteroid displacement is the means of delivery. And I think that this conscience free rat does not mean to deliver a known virus to earth, all that he has to do, is to place a number of frozen amino acid chains harvested from Europa and plant these on a small asteroid, then send the asteroid on a collision course with earth. Many of these viruses would die as they burn up in earth's atmosphere, but some will be bound to get through. The viruses, legion in number would then develop inexorably with no means of knowing the overall effect."

"My wife experienced the first effect of that but you felt the effect of a mutation and that nearly saw you off!" said the Captain with a malicious glint in his eye. "I know I must remain professional but things now have a personal edge."

Casting his mind back the Captain suddenly flinched. "Christ!" he exploded "I remember just one man who was not pleased when we ejected all of the virus cultures into space! Now what was his name???? Bradbury, er no, just a minute, Cadbury er no, *ADBURY*, yes that was him, Jack Adbury."

The Whistler was already scanning the manifest of the Gravitas. "Eric, that may be an inspired bit of deductive work; he is listed as a crew member of the Gravitas." Seconds later Captain Johnson and the Prof were mulling this new shaft of light over.

But there was another revelation about to break.

Eric Whistler suddenly remembered that as his Grandfather had been fighting for his life it was Jack Adbury who had come up with the idea of the microwave heater and refrigerator to treat the Whistler's blood. So James Whistler owed his life to a man now thought to be on the brink of destroying life on earth.

CHAPTER 45

BACK ON THE SOLAR ORBITER

The Prof found that he was enjoying himself. All his life he had had this ability to defuse disputes, but now he faced a gigantic challenge. During the noisy lunch break he sat as usual with Captain Johnson.

"The tadpole now has a tail and it is growing," chortled the Prof. The captain raised his enquiring eyebrow. "We can be fairly sure that this guy Adbury is at the heart of things. He may not be the leader but people who are known to have associated with him and with Jim Roberts are now fixed on our viewing crosswires! The leader is going to be a man of some intelligence to command the respect of men such as these two. You know I used to read science fiction stories by the bucket load when I was a young man, and I remember one story where there was this guy referred to as "the mule" and he was so different that he almost caused a breakdown in the history of the universe. Can I suggest that we borrow the name and use it in all references from now on?"

"Agreed. I never met this man Adbury, but I have met Jim Roberts, and I must say that he doesn't seem to have enough mental fire to fulfill the role of first space emperor."

"If I remember rightly, neither did the mule in the book! But thinking of this guy in the book, he had the ability to get people to perform above themselves, and because of this he had dominion where no normal man could get; and that was inside the minds of others.

"Well", said the captain, I trust that we are dealing with an ordinary nutter if there is such a thing!" however a cold shiver ran down his back. "Now has anybody shown any practical skill for protecting this ship against an incoming laser beam?

The Prof suddenly said "not that I have heard, but how about signal dispersal. We need a host of crystalline mirrors to deflect a beam at all different angles and thus weaken it, don't we?"

"Once again Prof, you have come up with a possibility that is better than some of the drivel I've been presented with so far!"

Back on the bridge the Captain barked out his orders and a number of technicians came rushing in. The Captain outlined the idea, and of the twenty or so men one stood deep in thought and did not here the dismiss command. The captain bellowed the command a second time, but the technician stood stock still and imperiously waved the command away. The Captain presented his face within six inches of the technician's own and quietly repeated his order. The technician awoke as if from a trance. As his cognizance returned, he said "Captain I think I've got it!"

"Ah" said the Captain "then speak up!" The Prof meanwhile had returned to the bridge, smirking as he came, and had seen the exchange.

The technician, whose name was Antonio Anthony, would you believe, then began to speak.

"It is my considered opinion that the notion of a mirror is sound. Further to that however, rather than disperse the signal it occurs to me that it would be justice if we could send it or at least some of it back to its source, and blast the bugger from the skies!"

Even the captain permitted himself a small smile at this outburst.

The Prof then joined the conversation.

"Just what means would you use to do this?"

Antonio warmed to his theory. "I would use liquid crystals sir! You know the sort of thing used in early calculators. It should be possible to control the crystals to either deflect the beam at one angle or to control the deflection to another angle and hence destroy the source."

"Costs and time?" grunted the captain.

"The idea is fresh in my mind so with regard to either I can only give a guess. The materials can be found from aboard the ship and we are already being paid, so costs would probably be acceptable and we may be able to try a test run if we can find a suitable laser signal in a bout 7 days time depending on how many men are assigned to the team!"

"You are in charge of this project from this moment on. You may take as many men as you wish, and I will give this top priority!" DISMISS. He heard this time.

Speaking to the Prof a little later the Captain said "You know I learnt an invaluable lesson on a sales course that I attended whilst I was a young man. The course was run by an Irishman who really knew how to get the best out of people, and he told me that if you ever wanted a hero, then ask for one and one will step forward! Antonio is our current hero".

Over the next few days the men on the project produced a parabolic disc lined with highly polished cubes of stainless steel all designed to reflect any incoming beam back from whence it came. At the centre was a liquid crystal control and this was wired up to a laptop computer. The captain ordered that the system be set to deflect mode, and then ordered the Space Adventurer to fire a low intensity laser beam at the target dish. The target dish glowed briefly as it performed it's function-successfully! The captain then asked for reflect mode, and watched as again the beam was dealt with and was duly reflected back from whence it came.

The captain was satisfied that the bones of a system were in place and gave orders for the work to continue. He also invited Antonio to his quarters to discuss any foreseeable problems. Antonio was a little uncomfortable to be in such hallowed quarters, but the Prof put him at his ease.

"Look lad, in the short time taken that was a very gratifying demonstration. Now at the top of the command structure in any enterprise, the gaffer can not proceed on the basis of bullshit, so we always go for straight fact. Have you got any issues that give rise to any feeling of discomfiture? Just remember you are not in competition with your peers you are here on your own!"

"The test was only carried out at low power sir, and there was a large rise in temperature on the reflectors even so. According to my calculations it would take a full power blast of 38 seconds before the reflector begins to melt, after that it would be down and the control system would have ceased functioning after only 14 seconds. I have a viable idea to improve the 14 seconds up to 47 seconds, but the melting issue may be a stumbling block."

"Alright, I will get the metallurgists to look for the highest melting point alloy available, if that is any help" said the captain.

"That would likely be some alloy of tungsten, Captain" replied Antonio.

"What about pre-cooling?" said the Prof.

"I have considered that, and it would be possible to make an improvement of the melting time, but the liquid crystals are already struggling to cope with the low starting temperatures at the moment"

"Where are you domiciled at the moment?" enquired the prof.

"Lab j14- x22" was the reply. "Ok" said the Prof "if I have any ideas about it perhaps you would do me the honour of not laughing in my face if I mention them to you."

"Laugh *at* the Prof", I don't think so, sir" said Antonio.

"Nothing else yet then—no, ok dismiss" said the captain.

CHAPTER 46

MORE THOUGHTS ON THE LASER PROTECTION SYSTEM

The Prof thought quite deeply about the issue of protection against lasers and muttered "we must make the dish large enough to cover the frontal area of the ship. Although we would still be vulnerable from a broadside attack, from a distance all we would have to do is to point the ship at the enemy and we would have a realistic chance of survival."

The captain murmured then that all things being equal "if an incoming blast reached the ship, it wouldn't remain on exactly the same spot on the reflector for the entire length of the blast, and therefore the melting issue wouldn't quite be as severe as had been shown during their tests. If luck was with them, the reflected beam though not as concentrated as the incoming beam would be powerful enough to do severe damage and in the final analysis could result in the enemy shooting themselves down!"

"There's a nice thought, but somehow life doesn't usually turn out to be quite that neat!" grinned the Prof. "and by the way, here's the disc of the personnel I think might be worthy of investigation. I have wiped all traces of downloads away from my laptop so that is the only copy."

After a few more days the design of the full frontal shield protector was given to the engineers from both ships but only after every man went through a stiff vetting procedure. Antonio solved the melting problem quite simply. He had heard the captain's comment that the incoming beam would not be concentrated on the same spot and extrapolated the thought by introducing an oscillation to the reflector.

The Prof voiced the opinion that the renegades would still have got wind of what was going on. Whilst the Solar Orbiter remained within the asteroid belt, and effectively got close enough to an asteroid to use it as camouflage, the Space Adventurer went into geostationary orbit above mars. Now James and Eric Whistler went down to Mars unaccompanied by other crew members, and stayed a few days in Medusa city as the largest settlement had become known. The city has spread like a multi headed snake and now rivaled many of earth's great metropolitan districts.

They were met by the lord mayor of the city who quipped that Mars was now under martial law! It had adopted the laws from earth and simplified them to suit its own needs. His name was Ken Lee. He knew nothing of the latest mission from earth and was alarmed at the fact that virtually anyone with a small army could take over on mars because the planet was undefended.

Eric Whistler said as he understood the threat facing earth, mars was safe for the moment as the miscreants planned to use Mars as a haven. Ken Lee did not like the sound of what he was hearing at all. Those on mars were by the fact of being there very resourceful, and Ken Lee hatched out a plan to flush out any sympathizers.

Unlike those in charge on earth who had a fear of public panic Ken decided to broadcast the plain bald truth to those on his home planet, and that night he broadcast to every nook and cranny on the planet what he thought may be going on, and demanded that any known weirdos with aggressive oddball views be rounded up and brought to the detention facility in Medusa.

Only the following morning there were 23 rather miserable men and women all complaining vociferously of their innocence, ready to be interviewed. Five of these had in the recent past been members of the crew of the Gravitas. These five were moved to the second stage interviews and they all found themselves sitting before a trio of judges two of whom were the Whistlers.

One of the others apprehended seemed to have a quiet control and was a very dignified person. She was taken aboard the Space Adventurer for further questioning. The others were held until the next visit of the Freeloader and were shipped back to earth in irons. Two of these had a terrified air about them. Possibly, because they thought they knew what fate awaited earth.

Back aboard the Space Adventurer, the lady prisoner was placed in the brig. She demanded to see Captain Johnson. She was told that he was elsewhere in space, but she then clammed up and would speak to no-one else.

The results of the Martian exercise were relayed over the secure transmission system to captain Johnson and he handed control over to the Prof before using a shuttle to get over to the Space Adventurer.

He observed this female prisoner and felt that he knew her from somewhere. He racked his brains and finding no solution went down to the brig.

She looked up at him and said "you are older than I remember!" he could still not bring to mind where he had seen her.

She said "you surely remember Helena?"

"I do, but she died in childbirth, then you must be her daughter" he murmured, realizing why she seemed so familiar.

"That I am but more to the point I believe I am also yours!"

The captain then said in a kindly tone, "well if you are we will soon prove it, we will use DNA."

The results were back within the hour. "It seems that I am not in fact your father!" he informed her and gave her the results to read for herself. She openly wept. "I have been living a lie all this time and, well, I just don't know what to say!"

"As a matter of fact I think that most men would be proud to call someone like you his daughter, I most certainly would have been."

"My grandmother told me that you were my father" she sobbed.

"Old Cressida?" he said, and she nodded.

"That is strange because your mother was my first real girlfriend, after we had a humdinger of a row, and I stalked off a full 15 months before you were born. I must say I did feel terrible when I heard that Helena had died in childbirth, but I just assumed that her new man would not like it if I turned up at the funeral. Look, I think you have had enough shocks for one day, stay where you are get some sleep and I will be back to talk to you as time permits me. By the way what is your name?" "Helen Johnson," came the reply.

10 minutes later he was talking over this revelation with Eric and James Whistler.

"Opinions, gentlemen, if you please, I know you were watching via the observation cameras."

As one voice they replied "She is a plant!"

"Ok so what do we do with her?"

Eric Whistler considered then spoke "if she is a plant, we must keep her away from our senior mission commander, so she stays in our brig, though perhaps you could send the Prof across to see if he can wheedle anything out of her!"

The Whistler then commented that perhaps a few doors should be left open to see if Jim Roberts was interested in her, and to monitor things very closely but discreetly.

Captain Johnson's departing remarks were "what a delicious idea, just has the Prof's subtlety about it, James you are learning!" with that he returned to his shuttle and returned to the Solar Orbiter. The last thing that he did was to sweep the shuttle for bugs. He got a positive result. His technicians soon found the device, shorted its battery out then placed it back where they found it.

The captain headed for the bridge. "Ok Prof I am back, anything to report?"

"Not a thing!"

Well listen to this then. The captain brought the Prof up to date including the discovery of the bug device. "Tomorrow I want you to go over to the Space Adventurer to see what you can wheedle out of our lady prisoner, and tell Eric to keep a discreet watch on the bug device because someone is bound to replace the battery, and we all need to know who does it."

"Well that should find me something to keep me out of mischief for tomorrow. With your permission Captain I plan to turn in, I am fair shattered!"

The Prof didn't get much sleep that night. He mulled over Jim Roberts, Jack Adbury, Helen Johnson, bug planting, the mule, and he knew he was in the middle of a thriller but this was no book it was real with dire consequences unless they could close the net on the would be perpetrators.

I am inserting a note here, relating to transmissions from this mission as there have been none at all. There are other transmissions from other ships, but nothing from the twin mission. I am hoping this is just for security reasons, but I have spoken to Jane Johnson and she has heard nothing either. This is a worrying time for us back on earth.

Catherine Whistler.

A junior operative was seen to replace the battery in the bugging device and a close watch was kept of his movements over a few days. It was obvious that he had merely been carrying out orders, but a few discreet questions revealed that Jim Roberts had been involved.

CHAPTER 47

HELEN JOHNSON

Using the shuttle the Prof went straight to the Space Adventurer as soon as he had breakfasted. He had with him a transmission detector and as soon as his shuttle was on its way the bug started transmitting. With a shock, the prof realised that it was not a sound bugging device but was a tracking device. He kept silent about this notion.

He arrived at the brig and introduced himself to Helen Johnson. He apologised for the absence of Captain Johnson but offered inescapable duties as the reason.

"Helen as you are aware we are trying to remove a threat to our home planet, and we trust that we can rely on you for some information to help us," he began.

"We already know that you have expressed views that may be interpreted as dangerous but we hope that you will be better understood after I have talked to you."

Her expression was one of puzzlement, but she said "well what would you like to know?"

"Have you ever come across anybody on this ship that you already know?"

Well there is Captain Johnson of course and in spite of the DNA results I still think I look like him and then there is a doctor, er no, a psychologist that I met down on mars. I saw him briefly yesterday, not to speak to, but he was in that doorway over there." She pointed.

"Where is the Gravitas?"

"What is the Gravitas?"

"Do you know any crew member of the Gravitas?"

"Oh, it is a space ship then?"

"Do you have a qualification in any related space venture skills?"

"I am a decent mathematician" she answered, "and as a matter of fact I am also hungry, what do I have to do to get fed?"

The Prof nodded to an orderly who brought in a breakfast menu. The Prof's wrist bleeper went off and he excused himself and wished Helen bon appetite.

The Prof took his leave of Helen Johnson and went to the bridge. Eric Whistler and to the Prof's surprise, Captain Johnson were both there eager to know what the Prof had learnt. The Prof chided them both "I barely had time to ask her any questions!" he moaned.

Captain Johnson fidgeted slightly and agreed that they had terminated the interview so that the Prof would not be unduly swayed by her charm.

"My honest opinion is I just don't know. She fended my questions so easily that she is either the most adept manipulator, or is as straight as they come. I do hope it is the latter. She hasn't entirely accepted the DNA results you know and still thinks that she looks a little like you!" he said glancing at Captain Johnson, "and I am struck by the fact that she does indeed resemble you."

"Are we the subject of a massive effort to dupe us here?" chipped in Eric Whistler, "I think we should redo the DNA tests but independently, with the labs on both ships doing the work but not knowing of the other ship's involvement, and then there will either be no doubt as to the result or we will be able to root out another spy."

"I have just thought of a possible reason why a lab technician may have fiddled the results, and that is this. Suppose for a moment that Helen had been earmarked as a sympathizer. If she found she was related to me it would have probably changed her perceptions and her loyalty could have been split. Thus a move has been made to pre-empt that possibility."

The Prof gave a rueful smile and said "well I hope she is your daughter, because whatever the case she is a lady of quality. Remember with DNA and cloning experiments there are more ways to produce offspring than there used to be!"

Captain Johnson and the Prof returned to their shuttle and set about returning to the Solar Orbiter. The Prof's bug detector started beeping, and irritated he fished it out from its hiding place and removed its battery. "Make a 180 degree turn and head away from our ship, he directed. Captain Johnson obeyed with a wicked grin on his face as they headed in the opposite direction. He then made another right angle turn and asked the prof to place the battery back in for a few seconds and then remove it again. He kept to the new course for about half an hour and used the gravity motor to impart a fair speed to the shuttle. The Prof then gave the battery another few seconds back in its place, but this time left the battery in and discharged the bug via the rubbish chute. It went on its way transmitting merrily.

Captain Johnson resumed heading for the Solar Orbiter, but decided that he would dock surreptitiously. The two men hoped that they would have thrown a spanner into the works of the spies, who would now be tracking in the wrong direction, and hopefully making wrong deductions.

CHAPTER 48

SOME MORE DNA RESULTS

Once back on board the mission command ship, the captain summoned his lab technicians and demanded a rapid DNA test be carried out on the two samples, with a view to proving parenthood. Then they put their heads together.

The captain spoke first. "You know I had quite a nasty wrist injury when I was going out with Helena, and she took me to a hospital and using stem cells they managed to regenerate the bit of flesh and bone that I was missing. I suppose they could have stored that data and generated more stem cells," and his voice tailed off as a truly horrible notion swam through his mind.

"Christ I wonder if that was why Helena died in childbirth, due to some unforeseen complication?"

Within the hour the DNA came back with a positive result. Shortly afterwards the Space Adventurer confirmed the original result. Eric Whistler had two men in solitary confinement within 10 minutes of the discrepancy being known.

The Prof said "Captain, I know the lab uses an automated process for the checking and I further know one of the junior technicians, who has not been involved so far. This is of paramount importance for both of you testees as well as the mission. With your permission, I will proceed for further confirmation!" the Prof left without waiting for the captain to confirm permission.

Captains Johnson's mouth opened with a reprimand but no sound came out. He was very nervous when the prof returned 50 minutes later.

"She is your daughter" smiled the prof, "shall I go over there and tell her or bring her back or what?" he asked.

"Bring her back with all possible speed" said Captain Johnson. I will clear it with our sister ship, and give Eric the all clear for serious questioning of his two suspects. Eric Whistler transmitted an affirmative reply and told how he had threatened to put a shuttle on full auto pilot to return to earth with the two miscreants chained up inside it. He then knew by the terrified reaction of the two men that they were as guilty as sin and decided to use truth drugs on them. He reasoned that normal decency and crew member's rights had to be suspended due to the horrifying prospects awaiting all those on planet earth.

The men were forthcoming with some very interesting information.

Within two hours the Prof was back and he had Helen with a solid bar wrist restrainer across her two wrists. Captain Johnson was enraged, but his rage melted when she slipped out of them easily and he realised that his daughter had had the presence of mind to play a prank on him, she smiled artfully.

"Helen, I don't know what my wife and children will make of you, but I hope to welcome you into my family. We are on a most horrifying mission and I am going to take a frightening gamble. Prof I want you to bear witness to this. Helen do you know that there has been a threat to wipe out earth?"

She blinked and blanched. "But surely no-one can wipe out a whole planet?"

"What did you do on Mars that got you arrested?"

Suddenly she looked rather tired, "I thought that the famous or as I used to think of you, the infamous Captain Johnson denied me and had let my mother die. I blamed you for that, and as a result I was against the space authorities, so I had been invited to attend a meeting. I never got to it because I was arrested before it happened. I honestly thought that I was going to be swept under the carpet and I admit I was very bitter about that."

"We refer to the renegade leader as "the mule" began captain Johnson but he stopped when he saw a slight smile creep onto her face, "Oh I read some of the Asimov stories, they were simply brilliant!"

"Unfortunately this character that we are dealing with has had years of quiet endeavour and has established a wide network of sympathizers. He is a very able man and so far we do not know who he is. We have lost a ship in space and think that the renegades have it but we don't know where it is. When I took on this mission I was horrified at the degradation of discipline, and I thought it was due to weak captaincy. I now think that the captains have in fact been strong and have had to work against a current of malcontentedness spread by this dreadful organization, culminating with the seizure of the Gravitas."

"Oh dear, oh dear, oh dear," said Helen. "It will be obvious to everyone within a few hours that my loyalty is to my dad, and my mathematical mind tells me I will be a target. They don't know what I know, which I might add is probably pitifully little, but they won't be able to take the risk!"

The Prof and the Captain looked at each other and realised that she was right.

The captain then looked at Helen directly and with his gimlet eyes boring into hers demanded to know if she was a member of the mule's organization.

She physically started at the ferocity of his gaze, and reluctantly tried to hold it.

"I am glad I'm not against you dad, and no, I am not a member but if I look back and read the signs now, I think they were going to groom me!"

"Ok, the future of Mars, Earth and all other solar system human activity rests on what I am about to tell you. I trust you, come here!" he opened his arms.

She rushed into his arms and smothered him with kisses which left him pink with embarrassment. "Plant Prof? he said.

"For what it is worth, I have changed my mind; I was wrong and am pleased to find out that I was wrong!"

"Helen, you have just witnessed a cataclysmic moment. The Prof was wrong. He has been right so many times when others were all wrong I had thought of him as infallible."

"Well I was close" grinned a delighted prof. "body armour for you young lady. The latest stuff is quite light weight and no one will ever see you without it and so they will not notice that slight additional bulkiness, I suggest that you hide until I have a suitable costume made up.

The captain then strode out of his inner sanctum onto the bridge proper, and demanded that 25 woman aged in their mid twenties should volunteer for special duties, reporting to the bridge immediately, he also mentioned double pay!

Over the next quarter of an hour a number of grinning ladies of all shapes and sizes reported for the special duty. The captain chose 19 of them. He told them that purely as a precaution they would wear body armour. They all trooped off to get kitted out. When they returned he lined them up into two rows, and 20 young women were given a dining room rota, and then they were all dismissed talking about what was going on, but only one of them knew. They all returned to their duties and Helen had been found some secretarial work to do. Yes even spaceships have girls who are better typists than the men.

The Prof nodded at the captain. Beautifully done, the way everyone mixed in no-one noticed the extra girl, so Helen had got anonymity.

"Prof, the chances of a spy being amongst that lot is very low, but we must keep an eye on them all to see who they associate with etc". Now the Prof fully appreciated the subtlety of the captain's move. He knew that the spies would probably know that Helen was on board, and they would find out that she was his daughter, but he had made it vastly more difficult for them to know which of the women she was, and they would have to take more risks to try to find her. The women he had chosen though varying in height and hair colour had a similar slim build. Fortunately the crew of the ship was so numerous that the chosen women only knew each other as slight acquaintances, and this helped Helen to hide. In a rota they would each sit with the Captain and the Prof at the dinner table. The captain had drawn the rota so that Helen was the seventh woman to get her place at the table. Helen had of course been given a new identity, the Prof had been looking through personnel records when he had come across one woman who had been taken ill just before the ship had set off and had had to remain on earth. A little bit of skill and he had transferred her name to Helen's cabin, the name of this unknown party was Miriam Johnson. Retaining the surname made it less likely that Helen would make a revealing mistake.

CHAPTER 49

STEPPING BACK IN TIME A FEW HOURS

On board the Space Adventurer Eric Whistler had been enraged when he had received the false DNA report for a second time. He had summoned an armed guard and proceeded at the double down to the laboratory. As his group walked in two lab technicians looked at each other and were promptly arrested.

"You have one chance now to tell me the whole truth," he spoke through gritted teeth" or be assured the whole lot of you will placed in the brig and will face a full court spatial as soon as I deem it necessary."

He stood and glowered round the lab, and was just about to issue orders for the arrest of all personnel in there when a young man stepped forward and admitted that he had delivered the envelope with the results in it.

"Who gave you the envelope barked the captain!"

"Senior technician Jones!" said the lad pointing at one of those arrested.

"Anyone else have anything to say"!

Two men stepped forward. "We have plenty to say but we need protection" they spoke almost in chorus.

Eric Whistler was nothing if not decisive. "Right, you lad, will be grilled in my quarters, go and wait outside the lab door, and let no-one in, not even Captain Johnson if he should appear!"

"You two guilty men, will be pumped full of truth drug and you will spill the beans. SILENCE!" He roared as one technician began to speak. "You will be given a chance to speak first without the drugs and the words spoken will be noted and compared to the drug induced words. The rest of you will remain under house arrest. The doors to your cabins will be electronically locked, and you will remain there at my pleasure.

Just at that moment another technician bolted for the door, but he was shot before he even got there.

Eric Whistler strode over and pulled the dart from the man's back. And he spun round with savage speed.

"If you think this is just a game, think again. It may take every ounce of courage that you have to speak out, but speak out you will. I will find out what hold these bastards have over you and it will be broken!"

"Escorts, take each man to his quarters, one at a time." Eric Whistler demanded to know the cabin location reference for each man, checked it out against the ship's manifest, and when satisfied that this was true dispatched each man to house arrest.

Eric Whistler was left with the two technicians who had stepped forward.

"Just what hold has the mule got over you?"

The first to speak said "it's my wife sir, they have got to her and should a regular call from this ship not be received, they will execute her."

"It's my daughter and my son sir they are at university and face the same threat." said the second man.

"They are using insurance men to make the threats sir" said the first man.

"They are using the mentor connection to threaten my children, sir", sighed the second man. "The mentor has a loose sort of roving role, so he can appear anywhere at any time without raising questions."

"Do either of you know whether the messenger boy outside is involved in any of this?" both men shook their heads in the negative. "We will continue this conversation in my quarters."

Once outside he glowered at the trembling messenger boy. "Who tried to get in while you were on guard?"

"No-one sir, but a technician walked right up and seemed to change his mind at the last second! I think his personnel number was XJ29."

"Never give me reason to doubt your loyalty, DISMISS!" the lad visibly relaxed and turned to go back into the lab. The captain however instructed him to join the number 2 lab, and to spread the word about what had happened.

At this juncture the situation on both ships needed an urgent discussion. The Prof and Captain Johnson were due to arrive within the next half an hour. Eric Whistler told the two technicians that he could not guarantee the lives of their loved ones but would make every effort to increase their security. "You must realise that the survival of planet earth has to be top of my list, but I give you my personal guarantee that every possible protection would be applied to the situations of those under threat. DISMISS, rejoin the lab team and go about your duties in the number 2 lab."

Eric pressed the broadcast button, "James Whistler to the captain's quarters immediately please!" Seconds later the door opened and in walked the Whistler, the Prof and Captain Johnson.

Eric said "Welcome. I have news and some conjecture for consideration. The issues that we face are still unresolved. However in view of what I have just learned I have reviewed my opinions." He related the events just so recently finished and followed this up by adding "Captain Johnson has the highest reputation amongst earth fleet captains. He is known to be hard and fair but is also known to be a savage disciplinarian, with a terrier like disposition for following things through and it is accepted that his thoroughness is second to none!"

Captain Johnson dipped his head in acknowledgment as Eric whistler continued "in my view, because of this, I believe that my ship has the greater preponderance of disloyal crewmembers on it. In my opinion the mule's team has made a serious error of judgment in discounting my own terrier qualities. Being younger than captain Johnson, I admit that I am hotter headed, and I have learnt what I have learnt today because of it. We have two technicians who are undergoing drug therapy as we speak, and I will give those men no sleep at all until I have squeezed every last drop of information from them.

It is my belief that the Gravitas is the ship that has fallen under the mule's malign control and we have to figure out who he is and where the ship can be, before this meeting is over. I believe that the mule was ranked as either a captain, a vice captain or a ship's doctor on the Gravitas because only personnel of that rank could wrest control from the official captain without causing scuttlebutt which would have come to our ears."

The Prof then mused "we had already thought that the Gravitas was not lost because the mule would not have means to deliver his knockout blow to earth without a big ship. I must say that I think you are right in your assumption as to who has control of the Gravitas, and if you would do me the honour of waiting just one second, ah, (waiting for his laptop) yes here he is, one Albert Trueblood. He is the ship's surgeon on the Gravitas and on the occasions that I have met him, I could not get on with him. He was full of unnecessary politics, and was very opinionated on virtually any subject!"

"He sounds like an ideal disciple to me." growled Captain Johnson.

The prof suddenly sucked breath over his teeth "my god, while I was chatting to Grandad during the europan flue outbreak, he told me of this doctor Trueblood and said how he found him almost impossible to converse with, because he was so self centered and self opinionated, but he also told me how some other guy had got his measure because he could shut Trueblood up in mid sentence! Now who the hell was he? YEEEESSSS! I remember he was a mathematician, Professor Jackson. Captain Johnson cut in "this meeting is closed and will reconvene aboard the Solar Orbiter just as soon as we can get across there!"

CHAPTER 50

BACK ON SOLAR ORBITER

Miriam Johnson was enjoying a cup of coffee along with two other girls in the canteen when the captain's voice was plainly heard requesting sandwiches for five in his quarters. The catering staff was at full stretch just at that moment, and none of the other girls with Miriam noticed what she had noticed; the double click from the microphone, at the end of the captain's request.

"Well I am off duty now so I'll take them to the old fart" she irreverently joked.

The canteen manager asked what sandwiches the captain would like.

"How the hell should I know?" responded Miriam, "I'm doing you a favour just make him something up!"

The request was fulfilled and Miriam wheeled the hostess trolley to the captain's quarters, but left it outside and carried the plates in manually. The captain spent a few moments checking the trolley for bugs and then went back in to his quarters just as the Prof was finishing scanning.

"Hello miss err???" enquired the captain

"My name is Miriam captain, as you can see by my badge!"

"Now Miriam, we would like you to cast your mind back and tell us if you have ever met a doctor or professor Trueblood."

"A more self opinionated prig would be hard to find, and I must say I was tempted to be rude to him on more than one occasion. The only man I ever saw shut him up was Professor Nick Jackson. One word from him and Trueblood clammed up!"

"Who was Professor Jackson?" asked the Whistler.

She froze in her tracks. "He was the one that originally invited me to that meeting I never got to on Mars, he was a professor of mathematics, but he made his mark as the chief scientific officer on board some big spaceship or so I believe!"

Everyone waited with bated breath as the prof skimmed over the keys of his laptop. "It was the Gravitas and he was on board when she went missing!" he nodded.

Captain Johnson rejoined the conversation "Miriam, do you recall saying that you knew precious little of the mule's organization. I think that has turned out to be true but what little you did know was precious!"

"Oh dad!" she whispered.

James Whistler then made the running. "I think that the Gravitas has made landfall on Ceres and is hiding there. I think it may have a polluted asteroid in tow ready to release on a collision course with earth, when the time is ripe." James Whistler was frantically tapping numbers into his laptop and Miriam was stood behind him and suddenly whispered quite audibly "clever boy!"

Without pausing in his task the Whistler said, "you can come and work for me any time you like," then glancing round gave her the benefit of that rarest of his facial expressions, he smiled. The smile lit up his face and Captain Johnson realised with the delight only a parent has, that his daughter had made a big impression on James Whistler.

Three voices chimed in union "its time to go public!" captain Johnson with both eyebrows raised asked if anyone wanted a vote.

"Unanimous!" said James Whistler.

"My reason for saying that is that according to my calculations we have about four days to find and disable the Gravitas, after that galactic conditions will be perfect for the mule!"

A hastily composed message was compiled and sent to earth requesting instant response. A few seconds later the secure audio link was running. Within a few minutes Captain Johnson had brought earth fully up to date and told earth that he was about to go public on both ships. Earth agreed and set the security forces in motion with a view to protecting as many of the space crew relatives as possible.

"NOW HERE THIS, NOW HERE THIS" went the loudspeakers on both ships blaring out in full American naval style. "This is Captain Johnson speaking on behalf of this mission and the earth's authorities; we have identified the mule and his closest henchmen. We now know of the number and names of those spying for the mule aboard both ships on this mission. (This bit was a bluff) We also know that some of you are under duress because of threats made to your wives and children. Earth is on red alert and has mobilized its security forces so that wherever possible armed guards will be deployed in your homes. Every member of the operational crew on board this and the sister ship will have armed guards sitting down to tea this evening in your homes. This is the moment of truth. Should any man be found to be guilty of aiding and abetting the mule without owning up to it he will be placed in the ejection chute and will be blown into space. We have no time for courts spatial. All guilty men report to the brig immediately. All personnel doing so will get a fair trial after this mission is over. At my discretion I may offer full pardons before that.

We have less than four days to disable the mule's spaceship, which is the Gravitas. That's right the Gravitas. Those of you with friends aboard her may take some comfort in that. We will not reveal the destination of our mission as that would only confirm to the mule that we really do know where he is lurking. We want to put the fear of god into every man on the Gravitas, and every man on this and our sister ship. Bridge out."

Within minutes the threat was working, there was a steady queue filing down to the brig; some faces looked very worried others looked relieved.

CHAPTER 51

THE SPACE ADVENTURER IS CLEANED UP

James and Eric Whistler shuttled back to the Space Adventurer and found that their brig had almost twice as many men as the Solar Orbiter's. Eric had been correct in his belief about where the spies would be ensconced.

Eric sought out some of the men from the guilty laboratory personnel.

In particular he wanted to talk to the runner.

"Name?" he barked.

"Peter Ford" came the sullen reply.

"PETER FORD *SIR*," he was reminded.

The man stiffened, "Peter Ford sir," he intoned.

"We have already deduced much of the mule's methods from other prisoners, and the vast majority of them were under severe personal distress. However we do not think that the mule could have only used the stick, he must have offered the carrot as well. Just what form did the carrot take?"

There was no reply.

"Guards, prepare this man for ejection, full space suit but no helmet! Now Ford, understand this. We now know that the mule has an organization consisting of over 100,000 people, so the only carrot we can see is that he has offered you some elevated position in his new order. He is a rank liar. There will be no elevation, he plans to execute all except his closest allies. I have to put the fear of god into the crew of this ship and I am going to film your ejection!"

"You can't do that, it's against spatial law!"

"Ah, suddenly you want our spatial law to protect you and yet you wish to tear down everything that we have built in that respect. You are a disgrace to humanity."

"Guards continue with your instructions, and bring the suited prisoner to the canteen!"

Taking up his captain's microphone, he spoke to the ship's crew.

"This is the captain of the Space Adventurer, all operational crew assemble in the canteen forthwith."

The canteen had an ejection chute large enough to take a human body and everyone knew that.

"Bring forward the prisoner!" the guards frog marched the space suited Peter Ford across to where the captain stood.

"Now then Ford, what have you to say for yourself?"

Peter Ford spat on the floor and with malevolent defiance, said "I will be the third in command of the new order!"

Eric Whistler laughed outright. "You are the ninth prisoner to tell me that! Is there any other fool here that has swallowed that guff?" he demanded.

There was a sudden movement from those assembled in the canteen as about 85 percent all moved to one side leaving others wondering what as going on.

One man stepped forward "sir, with respect we are all clean, those men are not!"

"Guards, shoot any man from the smaller group that moves."

Peter Ford capitulated. "I will tell you what you want to know, but only if you don't eject me!"

"Take him to the ejection chute", said the captain, "prepare for ejection."

The inner door was opened and the sweat stood out on the forehead of Peter Ford. "Ok, ok I will tell you" he squeaked.

"Temporary stay of execution! Right Ford, *Mr. third in command.* You will give chapter and verse of your knowledge. Fetch this man a laptop."

Eric Whistler looked round the assemblage and went straight to a sweating man stood in the clean group. "I notice you are sweating. Are you in the correct group?" his eyes bored into the man's.

"I am sir, but just for a moment I thought of myself in Ford's shoes and it made my blood run cold. I wasn't aware of the sweating until you spoke."

"All you men in the traitors group sit down where you are use your personal notepads to provide all information at your disposal, including details of any carrots offered by the mule.

Surprisingly quite a number had been offered positions high in the new order, ranging from third down to eleventh.

Eric whistler counted eight men who all believed that they would be third in command. His bluff had scored a direct bull's-eye hit. He placed these under a scanner and displayed them on the screen for all to see. A murmur went round the room as every man there now believed that their captain did indeed already know details of the new order. Those providing details relaxed and decided to give everything. After all he already knew so what was the point of hiding anything, particularly as space ejection was not a pleasant way to die.

"As each of you finishes your signed account, you will place your pads on the canteen table here. Guards will then escort you to the brig. "Guards" he addressed them all "do not leave with a prisoner until the previous guards have returned and confirmed that they carried out their task correctly".

"You" he barked at the man who had organized the division of personnel. "Come here. You will be in charge of this clean up operation from this point onwards, erm Mr. Mills" said the captain, reading the man's name tag. "You know what to do with anybody who is rebellious" he said glancing across at the still open chute door. "After this duty you must come to my quarters and give me full disclosure of how you achieved that division, this mission owes you a debt!"

Eric Whistler returned to his quarters and swept them for bugs. Finding none he brought his senior captain up to date. Captain Johnson mulled over this astounding result and said he would get the Prof to apply himself to the same task aboard the Solar Orbiter, but in fact he did it himself.

CHAPTER 52

THE NEW BROOM SWEEPS THROUGH THE SOLAR ORBITER.

The Prof thought Eric Whistler had acted on impulse but was driven by shear genius. He was already mentally giving Captain Johnson credit for cleaning his own ship and he set about plotting himself into the mule's mind set.

He set himself apart and went into the ship's library.

Captain Johnson meanwhile had assembled the operational crew in the ship's canteen.

He made full disclosure of the events aboard the Space Adventurer, and looked round the room.

"Eric Whistler has just shown why he was placed in charge of our sister ship, and if you think his actions were a little harsh, well as the saying goes, You aint seen nothin' yet". He glowered around the assemblage.

He pointed at three men. "Guards, suit these three up immediately and open the ejection chute!"

All three men looked ashen.

The captain continued "we rightly considered that due to past disciplinary records the mule installed more spies on our sister ship than on this one. We also consider that the spies on board this ship are more senior than those on the Space Adventurer. We really have no time to lose here and I intend to weed out the guilty just based on suspicion. I apologise to any innocent man, but your life will not have been sacrificed in vain. This ship will be clean within the hour. After that each man in the brig will be individually monitored. Should any semblance of data transmission be detected, that man will be ejected into space. All crew's right are suspended until I say otherwise".

A voice then sneered "it will not be like that in the new order!" the man was suited and ejected, within a few seconds of making that statement. The chute door closed on the cursing man, who promised death and destruction to all his erstwhile colleagues. There was the characteristic hiss then silence. A pregnant fear driven silence lasting for several seconds ensued, then a furious fight started between two men. They were separated by the guards.

The smaller of the two combatants snarled "come on you other bastards, show your true colours. You all know who is tainted and who isn't. All those for the old ways stand by me; you know your families are protected now!"

Only nineteen men were left stood apart from the others, after the division. The captain cajoled them. "Sit where you are and write me a love letter, and you can tell me just how brilliant the new order is and what rank you think you will hold in it, and you never know you may persuade me of the advantages of your argument." Captain Johnson smiled, that is to say his mouth smiled but his eyes were hard as diamonds.

After half an hour the guards collected the scribblings. The captain read them all carefully. Again, five thought that they would have a rank equal to third in command others were lower except one man who did not claim an offered rank. He was number xf213 a Mr. Allison.

"Do not eject xf213, Mr. Allison. He is the mules second in command. Each of you other men will now describe to me who by and how the offer of senior rank was put to you." Most men named Mr. Allison. The offers put to each man were skillfully worded. The offer of elevation to the mentioned rank was contingent upon carrying out their duties faultlessly, and there was the thinly veiled threat against the man's family.

Those of a stronger character had not accepted the offer but were living in mortal fear for their loved ones, whereas those of lesser inner strength had succumbed and accepted the mule's dominance.

Captain Johnson realised that virtually every member of the crew below the upper ranks had been approached, and the scale and shear effrontery of the mule's operation shook him.

"Fetch the ships doctor to the canteen at once, and tell him that he must bring a large amount of truth serum with him, as we have the mules second in command!"

He arrived and the captain instructed him to fill a hypodermic with as much truth serum as a man could stand. He watched the doctor then calmly took the syringe from the doctor and pressed it hard into the doctor's arm, and waited with his thumb poised over the plunger.

The doctor flinched, went white and stood silently as the cold sweat gradually formed on his forehead.

Before the doctor could speak, the Captain quelled the words in his throat.

"You will note Mr. Allison that the doctor here looks worried. That is because he has put enough truth serum in this syringe to kill at least two men. He was trying to shut you up!"

"You stinking bastard!" spat Allison.

"He has conned you, you fool" moaned the doctor.

"I am afraid it was you that I conned" said the captain, "most men named Allison as their recruiter, but three named you. You should have left such things to other ranks. Now if Mr. Allison really is the second in command then where does that put you, it would put you as the mule himself." He paused and watched as the ghost of a smirk came to the doctor's face. The captain continued "No I think that you are the second in command and that Mr. Allison is in the same boat as all of those recruited from the crew of this ship—a fool who has believed a completely empty promise!"

The ships doctor stopped smirking as the captain pressed the plunger about one third of its travel and then called a secretary in who could still do shorthand, and told her to write everything down no matter how bizarre that the doctor may say. He also called in Miriam Johnson and asked her to look at the doctor. She just said "well it is him, the prig professor, you know, Trueblood!"

The captain withdrew the syringe from the doctor's arm and asked for a medic to step forward. "The medic took one look at the syringe and said "captain it is possible that you have given surgeon Veritsang enough to kill him even though you have only used about 30 percent!"

The captain grunted and shrugged this off.

The drugs were working.

The captain said "well now surgeon Veritsang, I suppose you thought we would never decode your half French caricature of your real name!"

"Well it lasted ok till today" bragged Trueblood.

"Yes" murmured the captain encouragingly, we will give you that. We have deduced where the mule is and who he is but we don't have time to act to defend ourselves, so you can tell us all about it. You have Nick Jackson's full permission. Oh and by the way I was converted weeks ago but I need details from you so I can play my full role."

Trueblood flinched at the mention of Nick Jackson but as the drug took hold, he relaxed and prattled on and on and every so often he divulged something not previously known. After about one hour the drugs were wearing off and Trueblood was exhausted.

The secretary said "Captain I have about an hours typing here. I hope I can read my own shorthand, I don't get to practice it much these days!" the Captain nodded his assent and the secretary zoomed off to complete her work.

"Remove all of Trueblood's clothing and put him in the brig. Give him a blanket for his embarrassment but only after a full invasive body search," the Captain instructed the guards.

"I am now returning to my quarters, and if any member has suspicions or information, I still want to hear it!"

Within the hour he had the neatly printed report from his shorthand secretary, and then there was a knock on the door.

"Come in" he bellowed.

Miriam entered almost dragging a reluctant crewmember with her. She made to leave but the captain asked her to take notes.

"Ah, I wondered if you would show up" he said addressing the fighting crewman.

I see that you are able crewman Clarke "he said,

"That I am, captain but I must tell you that I don't think all traitors have been weeded out yet."

"How many more are there then?"

"I only have one suspect myself but he is a radio communications officer, and he had the presence of mind to attach himself to our group during my little fracas."

"Yes, your little fracas. Normally fighting brings a month in the brig, but in your case it could mean two months." He smiled at the shear dismay on able spaceman Clarke's face. "It is much more likely though that you will receive the highest commendation!"

The captain knew that in the bar that night there would be stories abounding regarding these few remarks. "You may tell your entire loyal group, and that includes your suspect, that the beer ration tonight will be three pints. Frankly I am going to leave the traitor in circulation. After all it is him that we rely on to keep the mule up to date with the shenanigans aboard this vessel! Keep a watch on this guy discreetly from a distance; we want him to think he has avoided detection, he obviously hopes that no-one suspects him. Leave me his name—here write it on this pad. Yes, ah, thank you.

I think this mission owes you a debt so DISMISS and enjoy your extra pint.

Helen aka Miriam, commented that she had watched with horror as the hardline crewman had simply been sent to his death.

"The captain sighed." I had no choice; that man could have caused us time and trouble and we simply don't have the time. I also think that he had enough fire in him to be a rallying focus for some of the other members. I needed the crewmen and women to be more afraid of me than of the mule, and I think it has worked. I am not fool enough to think that we have cleaned the ship completely, but a good deal of the simmering discontent amongst the lower ranks has now gone, and the mule's ability to garner information from us has been dealt a severe blow. This gives us an important edge. I have the Prof working on the mule's psychology, and he and I along with the Whistlers, will have to work out a battle strategy. None of us are of military background, so an awful lot rests on us getting in the first significant blow. There is going to be a fight, a big fight, and the first galactic battle. I want you to play a part in this too."

"She looked slightly alarmed and said "What part?"

"I want you to issue space suits to all crew members, of a non operational nature, you know, the shopkeepers and so on. I will give you full authority to disclose whatever of this operation is deemed necessary. There could of course be another swathe of new order sympathizers amongst them, so arm your self, and defend yourself vigorously, if you have to. Should you shoot anyone it will be deemed self defense. I suggest that you leave here immediately and make a start. You may show a video of the happenings in the canteen, and I trust that that will be enough to stop sympathizers dead in their tracks.

Here is your letter of authority, together with a disc of today's proceedings.

Please be careful" he smiled while saying "DISMISS!"

Using the secure link to the Space Adventurer, he advised the Whistlers of the recent proceedings, and he asked for a full face to face meeting, and suggested it be held on the Solar Orbiter.

CHAPTER 53

Helen gets started

Helen had scarcely ventured away from the operational side of the ship, and she was truly daunted by the size of the innards of the ship. The shopping mall had a great hall and she proposed to call a meeting of as many of the undercrew as she could muster. Although there was no gravity, so there was no up or down, the mall was designed with a top and a bottom but everyone relied on space boots to keep them standing upright.

Similar to the operational crew the undercrew had a quartermaster and he had a lady assistant. Helen presented the quartermaster with her letter of authority and demanded to see a copy of the ships manifest, and a duty roster. The quartermaster blinked in surprise and asked his assistant to bring the latest duty roster while he found the latest copy of the ship's manifest.

"Thank you for your cooperation" Helen began. "I must call a general assembly and the only place large enough to hold it will be the great hall" she continued. "Now I have a video showing what all the fuss is about, and I wish to show it on the big screen there!"

Within minutes there were undercrew members scurrying around, and Helen realised that to run an enterprise on the scale that big in a spaceship, required just as much discipline and organization as the operational side.

Two hours later, there was a gathering of a great proportion of the undercrew.

Helen hooked her laptop into, the TV screen system and took the microphone offered her.

"Today" she began; "I am going to inform you all as to the purpose of this mission. Normally the undercrew only gets to hear scuttlebutt. Here is the unvarnished truth." Helen outlined the purpose of the mission, the threat posed to earth, and the threats posed to personnel who had been recruited to the mule's cause.

"We were all brought up as children on Star Trek and Doctor Who, but this threat is real. It doesn't go away when you switch the telly off."

She paused and glanced round the room. "Should any person have fallen under the malign influence of the mule's organization, he will be given one and only one chance to recant, watch this video carefully because what you see has pretty well been done on the Space Adventurer as well, so things are twice as bad as they look. With that she hit the run command and the video began.

There were incredulous gasps from the floor as the full extent of the mules new order was revealed.

There was a stunned silence as the undercrew watched when the discharge chute was seen to operate.

When the video was over, Helen asked for reactions from the floor. One woman said "I wondered where the hell he had got to!"

"Are you his wife?" asked Helen, "and do you share his views?"

The woman nodded and said "I most certainly do not. He was an angry man. He was angry at just about everything including me, so I may weep a few emotional tears but I am not sorry to see the back of him!"

"Helen realizing she had uncovered another link demanded, "all undercrew members who have a spouse in the operational crew, stand over to the right please!"

"All others stand over to the left except anyone wishing to declare a support for the new order stand in the centre."

At first there was no-one in the centre but a few minor squabbles broke out and finally reluctantly those backing the wrong horse were lined up.

"Quartermaster, please issue those on the left and those on the right with space suits"

"I fear ma'am that we will run short" said the quartermaster.

"I expected as much, so you will set up a space suit production line forthwith, you only have 48 hours to complete your task. Those with sympathies with the mule will work as slave labour on your line. They will be permitted meal breaks but no sleep until the job is done. Should there be a shortfall in the number of space suits, those in the centre rank will not be issued with one. You will all need a space suit as a life support system in case the mule manages to disable or depressurise this ship!"

Just as she said this a man stepped forward from the ranks of those recruited to the new order. "I remember you" he snarled "you were going to be recruited at the next meeting!", and with that he rushed towards the dais that Helen stood on. Helen recognized him and ordered that he be detained. No- one moved so she took out the firearm calmly removed the safety catch and shot him in the leg.

"You cow!" he howled. Helen stood her ground; put the firearm back in its holster behind her back, and said "yes, but for a happy change in my circumstance I could well have been recruited. It did not, however, NOT happen. I was bitter because I had been brought up to think that my father denied me, but when I met him I found out that he did not know of my existence, yet within hours of meeting me had shown me a love and respect that was hitherto missing. My bitterness simply disappeared and hence I find myself here entrusted with this very difficult job. Take this man to the brig and find out what he knows!"

One woman from, shall we say the loyal group said, "Well are you all blind or what? It is obvious to me that she has Captain Johnson's blood running in her veins!"

Many of the undercrew had never seen Captain Johnson in the flesh, but they all knew precisely what he looked like, and a murmur of recognition rippled through them all. The whole attitude of the undercrew underwent a subtle change, shown with acceptance on their faces.

Helen then asked them to return to their quarters but to sign out on their way, except for the disloyal members who were asked to stay behind.

There was a little nudging and pushing, and suddenly one of the disloyal number was propelled forward.

"Yes?" enquired Helen.

"Please ma'am, we know we have been weak, but the mule has people all over earth who were going to murder, no assassinate our loved ones. We have been working under duress!"

"The last I heard, earth's security forces who I admit had given first priority to protection of the operations crew, had traced just over 16,000 of your relatives and each one should have an armed security companion as we speak. Should there be difficulty in finding some folk then we are hoping that the mule's men are also finding it difficult. Surely now you realise from the video that not only were your loved ones under threat, the whole of the animal world is at the same risk. The Captain has promised anyone that recants, a fair trial, and he may even give free pardons at his discretion. Please Mr. Quartermaster, give out pens and notepaper to all those left here. Write an account of who recruited you and when, and disclose to me anyone else who has been coerced or otherwise into the new order organization."

Helen did the same again around two hours later when the rest of the undercrew was examined.

The spouse link was investigated fully on both ships and the responsibility for the action coherence was assumed by Helen. Captain Johnson watched via video link and felt a delighted pride in the way she had comported herself particularly when faced with a personal attack that did of course have some basis of truth. He suddenly realised when he had found out about her being Helena's daughter that it wasn't her likeness to Helena that had puzzled him it was her likeness to himself. Amazing how he had not spotted it and yet a crew member found it so obvious. He suddenly felt quite stupid and yet more confident that Jane would like her, and he so wanted that to be the case.

CHAPTER 54

WHAT THE PROF THOUGHT

The Prof had been considering the situation as more and more information came to light. He knew he was working against the clock, and he also knew that age was finally catching up with him. He was tired.

Just before the four way head to head was organized however he had managed to snatch nearly 6 hours sleep. The Prof spoke first;

"Perhaps captain I should tell you what I think and then you can tear into my notion and bend it all as you wish!" he said in a rather despairing voice.

The captain however asked the meeting permission to bring Helen in as she had the final picture regarding the on board situation.

Whilst they awaited Helen's arrival Eric Whistler commented that the Prof looked tired.

"Yes I dare say it is a bit obvious that I am," declared the Prof, and then continued as Helen arrived, "I have considered all that we know of the mule, this Nick Jackson. He is a very clever man, so I think we must try to be at least as clever. This will not be easy. I suggest that we preprogram a shuttle and send our recent surgeon Mr. Trueblood on an automatic trip back to earth, somewhere remote like the Sahara desert. At the moment I think that the mule's ship is hidden from us and we in our turn are hidden from him. I think we should start a rumour that Trueblood has escaped! By the time the shuttle is on the blind side of the sun, we should have engaged the mule in combat.

Now bear in mind that he has tentacles reaching even into the undercrew on our vessels, I think it is likely that he has taken the vast majority of the undercrew of the Gravitas and with false promises of high rank in the new order has trained many thousands of willing soldiers. He has had several years to do this, we have only a few hours but we must do something or else we will simply be overrun.

We have two ships and he has only one. We think we have developed a reflective protection against laser beams but without doubt he has men of ability who could have developed his weaponry further. None of our captives have mentioned this but it is inconceivable that he would try to take over the solar system without having some advantage up his sleeve. He could for example have developed a lower power laser and equipped each of his shuttles with them thus in effect giving him several fighters capable of operating not only over a very long flight range, but at close quarters in the field.

I think we must attack him from opposite directions or at least very diverse directions and this would split his fighting forces. I further think that our attack would have to be synchronised. During WW2 a Japanese aircraft carrier was destroyed because it couldn't repel sea and air attacks at the same time. We must adopt this policy right from the outset. I think that we just have enough time to fly outside the asteroid belt and going at carefully calculated speeds we must arrive at Ceres at the same time.

Now with regard to where he is lurking, I have considered various options. Ceres is the favourite because it is a dwarf planet. Once landed on it the Gravitas would have no problem getting back off it as its gravity is only a fraction of that of earth's moon.

I think that the major difficulty faced by the Gravitas is that though it can get off easily enough it is in a remote part of space and will not be able to find a gravitational source large enough to accelerate quickly. If I were him I would use two or perhaps three of the shuttles and help the Gravitas back into orbit using the two way effect of the shuttles smaller gravity motors to achieve this. I also think that he will probably have posted a couple of shuttles out in the main asteroid belt, and will use their on board radar as early warning of our arrival."

The prof stopped to draw breath.

No one spoke so the Prof continued "I think that we should approach from opposite directions as I said before but initially we should use our asteroid capturing skills to send at least two asteroids to collide with Ceres. With luck that would avoid a direct battle and it may completely destroy the Gravitas. Once we engage the Gravitas in a fight it will be down to you two captains to cohere and simply shoot the bugger out of space! We have conjectured that the Gravitas has a virus laden asteroid in tow. I think this is most likely, they may even have several, and our asteroid strike could just upset their apple cart somewhat. Now if the mule successfully manages to launch an asteroid at earth then we will have to use our gravity motors to divert it to say a collision course with Venus where the asteroid's viruses would simply be burnt up. If one of us remains engaged in combat with the Gravitas then, with any luck the Freeloader could be seconded as a second source of gravity motor power. I hear that she has undergone a refit and now has the latest gravity motor giving her about half as much power as our ships.

Having got it off his chest so to speak the prof looked relieved and nowhere near so tired.

James Whistler spoke." Firstly I think I will need Helen to do what I propose because there is an awful lot of maths involved and I know she has the abilities in that regard. Again the Prof has shown a grasp of the situation and we all trust that the mule will behave as we expect him to. I have been checking our records of known asteroids, and I think that the asteroid belt is missing one or two. This means that the mule has them stashed away somewhere. I think he will have put them into a wide orbit round Ceres. We must ask earth if Ceres has developed a wobble at all, because if it has then that is certainly what he has done. With regard to using asteroid capture I think we will have to try to capture two and aim them at the disease carrying asteroid of the mules in order to speed them up and send them in an orbit towards Jupiter, not Venus. Other than that I think the Prof is to be congratulated. His expose is food for thought.

The Captain interjected, "Helen how is the space suit situation coming along?"

"I have the traitors working non stop on that problem. They are working hard because failure to meet the target means that they are the first in line not to have a suit!"

The Prof smiled "I'm glad that the mule never managed to get his hands on you young lady!"

She smiled slightly, mentioned that other volunteers were also working hard but dipped her head in acknowledgment of the compliment.

They sent an urgent communiqué back to earth asking for the latest observation of Ceres.

There was no wobble, but earth could detect three moons going round it.

The prof smiled thinly "so the bugger *is* on there but he has three possible disease asteroids. At best we can only knock out two, so a battle is inevitable. Eric Whistler then said thoughtfully "not necessarily. I can man a mission in one or perhaps two of our shuttles, and we could pull one of the asteroids away so it would fly off towards Jupiter. We would need to carry whatever armour that we could because we may have to fight off the Gravitas' own shuttles!"

"Ok" said Captain Johnson, coming to an immediate decision. Helen you are with James on the maths. Eric you will mount a three prong attack via shuttles, we will loan you one of our shuttles so as to more equally deplete both of our ships. Our other one will carry Trueblood back to earth. You however Eric, are forbidden to take part yourself; select the three most able pilots, take your pick from either or both ships. I insist that you look after the Space Adventurer!"

"How did I know you were going to say that," grinned Eric resignedly.

"Prof, get some sleep you have earned it."

"Action stations everybody!" were the captain's last words at the meeting.

CHAPTER 55

ERIC GOES THE LONG WAY ROUND

The Space Adventurer was destined to take the long way round to get to Ceres.

Eric Whistler set course for the sun, intending to use the long pull and sling shot effect to give him maximum speed.

On the journey he allowed his technicians to spacewalk and to unfurl an enormous coil of aluminium foil, and this was trailed some half mile behind the space adventurer. When asked what it was for he declined to comment except to say that "Walls have ears!"

He demanded that the technicians come up with a miniature version of the laser gun and fit it to the three shuttles at his disposal. This was a tall order but the technicians had some success but were unable to get the focus correct. There was only one point where the rays were dense enough to do any damage and that was about 3 miles from the laser emitter, after that the rays diverged and were effectively harmless.

Eric decided he would call the attack shuttles attackers 1, 2 and 3. Original, perhaps not, but straightforward yes. He outlined his plans to the pilots, and stressed the importance of radio silence. He and the pilots knew that their radar signature would be very low, thus making them hard to find, but radio transmissions were a different kettle of fish. Each pilot was given some target practice and found that these weapons though not brilliant were far from useless.

The shuttles were victualled for a week's mission, and all three shot off on different courses.

The Space Adventurer attained warp factor 0.9 on the way to the sun and maintained this thereafter.

Earth was tracking both ships and used a hastily arranged code to transmit the positions from each to the other. Captain Johnson used his on board computor to calculate Eric's estimated arrival time and adjusted his speed to match the arrival time. The Solar Orbiter would be on a narrower orbit than the Space Adventurer, and would most likely be detected on the mule's radar first.

Eric broke radio silence to transmit over the secure link "have been joined by the Freeloader. She is hot on my tail and will not be detectable as a separate ship on the mule's radar."

Captain Johnson had had to guess what Eric Whistler was playing at but acknowledged the signal quickly.

Eric hoped that the senior captain would guess that this was an attempt at giving the mule some disinformation.

Within a few hours Ceres was on the radar and Eric's attack ships combined to pull one asteroid out of its orbit round Ceres and accelerate it thus diverting it to head towards the Jovian group. There was no response from Ceres. They attacked and diverted both other asteroids with the same success, still no response from Ceres.

The leader of the attack shuttles sent a compressed coded message back to the Space Adventurer, and their message was sent to the Solar Orbiter.

The Prof observed that it looked as if the mule had outwitted them because it did not appear that he was on Ceres after all. He commented "the mule appears to be a master of obfuscation!"

Back on the Space Adventurer, Helen was staring at the information presented on her screen. The Whistler had asked her to investigate as many asteroid courses as possible and calculate any courses that looked like they were unusual. This was a quantum leap from anything that she had hitherto attempted. But she had constructed a program and this had shown fifteen asteroids travelling seriously slower than the others and she knew that they could not sustain their positions in the asteroid belt.

"James, would you look at this please?"

James Whistler carried on for a moment then broke off what he was doing and came over.

She put her prediction maths program into action and showed a screen full of millions of asteroids. Visible because she had set up a lingering trace amongst these there were traces of course changes on these fifteen satellites. He stared for a moment, asked a few pertinent questions, checked on their own position in the cosmos, and turned the ship's radar to look at the largest group of these. There unmistakably was the outline of a non asteroidal shape.

"Helen, you are clever and lucky all rolled into one. You have located the Gravitas!"

Within minutes a secure link signal was sent out with certain codes in it. The attack shuttle pilots returned to the Space Adventurer. Captain Johnson was astounded to realise that they were at the opposite side of the asteroid belt to the Gravitas.

"See what I mean about obfuscation?" commented the prof Eric Whistler had already focused his gravity motor onto Jupiter to get another sling shot and this would take him into the region of the Gravitas within the next day.

He ordered that any more known suspects within the crew be suited and ejected and prayed that this information would not get to the mule. He further realised that Captain Johnson would be some hours behind him and that he might have to attack on his own.

CHAPTER 56

BACK ON BOARD THE SOLAR ORBITER

Captain Johnson knew instantly that Eric Whistler would get to the Gravitas some hours before the Solar Orbiter. He knew from the character of the man that he would attack the Gravitas.

He requested the Prof's presence on the bridge and brought him fully up to date with the situation.

The Prof was struck by the mule's clever strategy. The mule had known of the skills aboard earth's mission ships, and had relied on it to drag the mission to a far flung place to give him more time for his new order to propel disease at earth.

Captain Johnson had found out that there was still one new order adherent in the under crew who was actively sending intelligence to the mule.

The time was ripe and the protesting man was suited and ejected. Captain Johnson hoped that Eric Whistler had taken a similar action. He decided to send two more shuttles ahead with a view to providing some support for the Space Adventurer at the earliest time. The shuttles being lighter described orbits that were a little straighter than that of the main ship, and hence could get to a destination a few hours more quickly.

The coding for the secure signals was changed every two hours with Captain Johnson himself selecting the new code. The Space Adventurer had an automatic decoder on board and so would always be able to interpret any signals. In so far as anyone knew, the Gravitas did not have this facility.

The Prof meanwhile, was musing at the courses of the satellites and realised that only one of them needed to carry the viruses. Thinking of the mule's action so far he also thought that the mule would have the virus on at least three of them. Other asteroids would simply cause massive damage to earth and the resulting damage to the ecosystem alone would wipe out most of life. The prof also thought of the longer term implications of all this. Assuming earth was wiped out; the mule would have no problem in subjugating Mars. He could establish a reign of terror, and in a hundred years when earth had settled down again his descendents could recolonise it. He really was trying to establish a regime that the Prof thought of as the Fourth Reich. In fact the more he thought of it, the less use he could see for a pandemic set of viruses. The only reason that anyone was thinking of pandemics on earth was due to the original communiqué from earth. It seemed to him that the mule's plan was typically devious, and that the mule only used that threat to frighten earth into looking for the source of the threat. Imagining that life somehow survived the impacts of the asteroids, civilization would regress so much so that a handful of technically competent soldiers could overrun the entire set up. All this made sense to the Prof.

"Captain Johnson I have new intelligence for your urgent consideration!" the Prof murmured.

The very way in which the Prof delivered this message caused the Captain to suddenly sit bolt upright. "Go ahead Prof, you have my undivided attention!"

The Prof related his latest thoughts and as he expounded his views, Captain Johnson became more and more convinced that the Prof was on the right track.

He ordered the rest of his shuttles to a state of readiness, and sent an urgent communiqué back to earth demanding the use of the Freeloader, but with only an operational crew on board. Earth immediately complied and sent orders for the undercrew to take an extended break on mars. Fortunately the Freeloader was already in geostationary orbit above mars.

The captain then sent an urgent secure message to the Space Adventurer.

The essence of the message was to leave the Gravitas unattacked, and to concentrate on diverting the asteroids, this being a priority order.

Captain Johnson then sent another message which outlined the Prof's reasoning, and advised that the Freeloader would be joining the Space Adventurer some hours before the Solar Orbiter could get there. He advised that all armed shuttles be used as attack or diversion vessels, but only to try to down the Gravitas if it showed any aggression. Other shuttles were to join in the asteroid control. All shuttles from all three ships were to be employed, this being some 52 vessels in all. Captain Johnson scrambled all his remaining shuttles, ceding command of these to Eric Whistler.

CHAPTER 57

THE APPROACH TO THE BATTLE ZONE

As the Space Adventurer closed in on the Gravitas, Eric Whistler was heartened to find the number of shuttles at his disposal increasing. He knew there would be a fleet of 52 vessels plus his ship and the Freeloader which was hurtling through space to his assistance.

He had control, now it was only required that he formed some sort of plan.

He barked "James Whistler and Helen Johnson to the bridge immediately!"

Both parties shot into the command section of the bridge on their wheeled magnetic boots. They were both travelling so fast as to find it difficult to stop.

"Yes very efficient!" he chuckled "I want you to listen to this, put these headphones on please!"

The recently received orders and messages were duly played, and considered.

James Whistler spoke, "it looks as if the Prof has cracked it. Everything he has reasoned seems very likely to me. The Prof has easily the most accomplished mind with regard to unraveling the complex situations, and again based on very little intelligence he has come up trumps. I would say commit 80 percent of your reserves based on the prof's reasoning, and leave 20 percent for contingencies, what do you think Helen?"

"I have no experience of life yet so I am not competent to judge, but I can appreciate your line of thought. Since we are dealing with a very clever individual I think that your reserves ought to be split into three groups, in order to give you some elbow room. Just in case!"

Eric Whistler growled "I have taken a gamble and slowed our approach down. This should give a better chance for the Freeloader to arrive. In fact the Freeloader will arrive in time, and as she is travelling the fastest, I have ordered her to make a pass in front of the Gravitas. The Gravitas radar may not be sharp enough to tell the difference between her radar echo and ours, in spite of the size difference. Just at that time our shuttle fleet will be up to full strength. I will split the shuttle fleet into the attack section, and the diversion section. The attackers will comprise 38 vessels in three wings, two of 12 vessels and one of 14 vessels. The other fifteen vessels carry no weaponry and will assist in diverting the asteroids. If we can slow these down we can perhaps get them to miss Earth and hit Venus.

James perhaps you could set up your programs and using fifteen computors we can track each one separately, and work out what to do to achieve our ends."

James Whistler's face took on the glacial calm expression typical of him when he was deep in thought, "we will only have the tiniest margin for error. Each asteroid will have to be carefully controlled. The mule has chosen well. He knows that we could deflect an asteroid, and he also knows that the most likely collisions are with earth or the sun. He knows we cannot risk hitting the sun as it could cause untold reactions with no certainty of outcome, but there is a window whence the asteroid will just miss earth and will hurtle inwards, with the most likely target being Venus. Now Venus has no moons so it is possible that it may capture some asteroids as moons, others would crash into its surface. Not much is known about Venus itself, but we have to assume that there will be no dangerous galactic outcome from our actions.

Should any asteroid miss both Earth and Venus then we will have to calculate its orbit and see if it a dangerous one and if it is, then chase it and drag its orbit away from the inner solar system and try to put it somewhere else, otherwise it may get us on a subsequent orbit.

"If we engage shuttles from the Gravitas how will we tell them from our own shuttles, and what is to prevent the Gravitas' shuttles mounting a daring raid with us as the target?" enquired Helen.

"Our shuttles are instructed not to engage with any shuttle painted yellow, because it will be one of ours. I just hope that the Gravitas hasn't used the same colour as us, because that would make things difficult!" chimed in the Whistler, "sometimes the simple ideas are best."

Eric Whistler held up the conversation with a wave of his hand. "We are so close to the expected engagement zone, that I am about to break radio silence. All shuttle commanders report to the Space Adventurer. In alpha numeric order please, and report on the colour of your ship!"

All except one reported that they sported a bright yellow finish.

"Give your reason for remaining unpainted!" barked the captain.

"There was no paint left sir," came the reply.

"Dock immediately with the Space Adventurer! Laser gunner, train your weapon on the incoming shuttle."

"ARMED GUARDS! Go to docking bay 9 and escort the entire crew of the arriving shuttle to the bridge, and leave three fully armed men to guard the shuttle. Let no one, not even me past. *Is that understood?*"

Eric Whistler knew that all shuttles had been painted with the possible exception of those arriving from the Freeloader.

Nine rather harassed looking men were shepherded to the bridge. Every other person on the bridge was armed and stood with weapons at the ready.

"Account for the colour of your shuttle, forthwith," Growled Eric Whistler. "If by any chance you are on a mission from the Gravitas, your existence is hanging by a thread. If you admit complicity in this, you will be placed in the brig and will receive a fair trial.

If I suspect that you are from the Gravitas and admit nothing you will be ejected into space fully suited but with no helmet, is that understood?"

All nine men stood ashen faced, but one man stood forward and admitted his guilt.

"You stinking traitor," howled two of those remaining standing. The others looked glum. "10 seconds" barked Eric.

All of them admitted their guilt.

"Right then, what have you done with the shuttle that you tried to replace?"

"She has been disabled, and left drifting, she has no electrical supply."

"SIR," glowered Eric Whistler. "If there is one word of a lie, in anything you tell me you will go through our ejection system as I described earlier. I might tell you that earth's security system has been on red alert for the last few days and every person in space who has loved ones back on earth, no matter what ship they are on has armed guards providing family protection, if that is of any interest to you" Eric noted that four men's shoulders slumped as he said these words.

"We are frankly amazed that so many people recruited to his cause have been offered a high rank in the new order, and by high, I mean in the top 10. We have already elicited that 27 people thought they were going to be third in command and a further 52 men thought they would be no lower than tenth."

Eric Whistler wished that Captain Johnson had been there to watch the reaction of these latest captives. Eric continued, "You do know that he is targeting earth with his towed asteroids and plans to wipe life from earth completely, then go and establish his new order on Mars?"

One crewman gnashed his teeth and spat out the following "he swore us to silence with regard to the rank to avoid petty jealousies he said, and he told us that mars was the target, and when he had wiped that out he was going to return to earth triumphantly, whereupon all threats to our wives and families would cease."

James Whistler then commented "I am the Whistler; I dare say you may have heard of me. The mule as we call him is a very skilled, cunning and convincing liar, but a liar none the less. We have already sent one professor Trueblood back to earth to face trial, so what do you make of that?"

"You've captured his number two, yes we heard about that but we were told that he had escaped!"

"That I am afraid was a rumour started by us to give the mule something to chew on!" interjected Helen.

There was some murmuring amongst these men, then one man, the man who had first admitted guilt, stepped forward and asked to be reinstated as loyal to earth.

Eric Whistler could not offer them a pardon, only captain Johnson had that authority, but he told them that, then invited the men to fill him in with details. "Fresh clothes" he ordered, and in the meantime you will strip naked and undergo a full invasive body search. Other functionaries on the bridge were asked to form a tight circle around the men. Helen politely declined this instruction. No hidden weapons radios bugs or any other devices were found.

"Right we will now interview you singly. This interview will be conducted under armed guard. The guards will not touch you so long as you remain passive. Any show of anger or aggression and you will be ejected into space. This is a no brainer; does anyone not understand their predicament?"

The captain was rewarded with total silence. "You remain here, he said selecting the man who wished to realign his loyalties, you others will be escorted to the brig. Whilst there you will write me a dissertation on precisely how you were recruited and what has happened to you since. You will also detail your shuttle mission. DISMISS!"

Eric Whistler knew that time was running out and had taken a gamble that the man's desire to realign his loyalty was genuine.

"What was the purpose of your mission?" he growled.

"Sir, we expected perhaps 6 shuttles and our purpose was to disable them.

We would close in, converse with the pilots over the short range radio and tell them that we had some protection to install. As the shuttles are not armed we expected to be welcomed. Once we were aboard then we would reverse the connections on the stand by battery and tell the pilot to revert to standby power for a moment. The reverse polarity would effectively ruin all on board computers and auxiliary systems, including life support. On the shuttle that we got on to the pilot ordered his crew to don full space suit and helmets as a precaution"

"We just said sorry and that we had made a mistake and would fetch a few new parts across and then we made our exit. Shortly after that you asked this strange question about the colour of the ship and then ordered us to dock with you. We knew the game was up but we hoped to bluff things out."

Just at that moment Helen Johnson gave her captain a piece of paper but said nothing.

Eric Whistler read the contents and smirked. "Colour check all shuttles again please Helen!

We have just received intelligence that all our shuttles have now reported in, and so you have done us a favour by disabling one of your own!"

"Perhaps I should have smelt a rat, sir, when it was so easy to board her! As you know captain, we didn't give up our allegiance to earth easily. Nick Jackson told us that the way earth was going it would soon be uninhabitable and it needed someone with far seeing vision to restore it. He mentioned the banking scandal of the early 21st century, the political dogma being followed relentlessly by traitorous politicians who thoughtlessly force people of widely differing beliefs to live cheek by jowl, and the gradual disenfranchising of the man in the street, the ivory tower mentality of political adherents, the emergence of aimless terrorist organizations, the slide backwards into lawlessness, and how he couldn't imagine any right thinking man wanting this for his children. All of these things when totaled up painted a pretty grim picture. He offered me, because of my grasp of such things the rank of ninth in command when the new order was running, and swore me to silence lest it caused petty jealousy amongst other recruits. My initial gut reaction was to disbelieve what he said, but I kept this almost to myself. Slowly however the duties he asked me to perform began to offend my sense of fair play and I realised that I had been sucked into a maelstrom of political intrigue. At about this time I was told that should my actions compromise new order security in any way, not only would I be executed but my family on earth would also be assassinated. I think he still has a core of fanatically loyal disciples but most men were like me, coerced with promises of milk and honey, until they were in too deep to back out. I used to sneer when I read in the history books of men claiming that they were only following orders, and I was horrified when I found out that I was doing exactly that.

He and his senior aides told us that the present command structure in the ship left much to be desired and that there was a golden opportunity to begin the rightful fightback. He had of course recruited most of the security forces on the Gravitas and as ship's scientific officer he carried considerable authority. He waited until the captain and his number two were almost alone on the bridge and simply had them thrown into the brig, where they still are. This act occurred whilst I was asleep, and the new order was in command when I reported for duty that morning. He still has the full undercrew on board and he thinks that this fact alone will prevent you from mounting an armed attack!"

"He is wrong there, it gives me a moral dilemma but I cannot weigh the lives of the crew and the lives on a whole planet up, without regretfully concluding that there may be those who will be sacrificed. I would however resign my commission as soon as I got back to earth if this should prove the case.

If you wish to earn a full pardon there is one means by which it could be done. You could lead a raid onto the Gravitas. If you could broadcast over the internal communications the situation with regard to armed guards providing protection for loved ones then you may be able to provoke a mutiny or at least cause enough dissent to render her less efficient!"

"Captain, my name is Henrik Svensson, and I do not wish to go down in history with a reputation as a Quisling. I will consider your request as an order. Of my crew there are only two that I can trust to back me up, but perhaps you could make the complement up to 9 men. I cannot believe though that your men would submit to taking part in a mission led by me. The risks would be enormous; the mule as you call him is always surrounded by a ruthless armed guard. I could get the message across because I know where to tap into the video system. I could leave it playing and perhaps we could get back off and wait to see what happens. I do not think that a team of nine men no matter how well prepared could simply put the mule out of his stride. Of the operational crew perhaps a quarter would remain loyal to the mule no matter what circumstances prevail; of the others no-one would have access to any arms. We could carry some arms on board but the security system would detect them and in effect all we would be doing would be to give them additional weapons."

"Nevertheless, it may be the only option giving a chance for the undercrew to survive. Do you think you could dock safely?"

"Yes captain, this shuttle has had malfunctions on its gravity motor, and this is well known, I think if I request to dock with a requirement for a new static field generator for the motor it would not raise any suspicions."

"Do you know if the mule has set up any auto self destruct functions for the ship?"

"I am not aware of anything like that but the mule is a clever man, and he may have done that."

"Do you know if there is a spare shuttle still on board the Gravitas?"

"All shuttles are deployed except the one designated for emergency lifeboat duty!"

"Ah, that will be the mule's escape pod of course!"

"Ah well sir, it is stocked with food and medicines, in case wee need to evacuate anybody!"

"And just how many will the arc take, do you think?!"

"What fools we've been. We swallowed what he told us, he gave us assurances that every person on board would be treated equally and there would be no elitism at all!" Henrik Svensson's mouth set in a determined line. "In so far as I dare say, I volunteer for this mission, SIR!" he snapped to attention. "As an aside sir I only got into the mules setup by default. I never attended the induction class that every one else did, but until today I was trapped!"

Eric Whistler made a decision. "Very well Svensson I am going to trust you. If I put a double crew on board your shuttle, can they disperse amongst the under crew, without being detected?!"

"That I don't know, sir. Thinking about things though, it is possible that the usual guards may have been assigned other duties for the forthcoming battle, so the docking ports may be empty; but that is pure conjecture!"

Svensson then gave the captain the names of his two associates who he hoped would switch allegiance back to earth.

Eric Whistler put each man through a question and answers routine, and generally liked what he saw. He ordered fifteen of his most trusted men to join him on the bridge.

Introductions were made and two of his own men refused point blank to go on the mission with traitors. "Convince them otherwise Mr. Svensson!" he ordered.

Svensson stood still for several seconds and said finally. "No one here regrets his own actions more than I do. Let me tell you how I was inveigled into the mules command structure." With that he regaled the men with what he had told the captain, not word for word, but in every sense of the words that he had told the captain from start to finish.

"Ok so I am weak, I am gullible, and I am greedy, and I wanted to survive, aren't we all like that? The mule relies on it!

All this I acknowledge, but I, no we three, are not Quislings. We are grateful for a chance to atone for our misdeeds, but the Captain has already said that regardless of the outcome of this part of the mission we are all to stand trial on earth. Though it is no defence, all I can tell you is that Nick Jackson, the mule, is so damned convincing when you are in his presence."

The doubters were convinced, though they still threatened to watch his every move.

Henrik Svensson actually smiled and said it would make a change to have his back covered by someone that he could trust.

The team spent the next hour on the logistics of the mission, and spent five minutes finding out what a Quisling was and why those of Nordic descent abhorred the idea of being one.

Eric Whistler received a secure message that Captain Johnson would be with him in about one hour.

Eric Whistler puzzled over this; he knew that Captain Johnson could not have made the journey in so short a time unless he had exceeded the speed of light for some of the distance involved. "It looks like the Prof has made another discovery!" he smiled, and ordered the Freeloader to forego her planned flypast and to take up station with the Space Adventurer as soon as she could.

CHAPTER 58

GOING BACK A FEW HOURS ON THE SOLAR ORBITER

Captain Johnson was worried for the success of his mission. He knew Eric Whistler was not as rash as he once had been, but he also knew the man's nature. He confided to the Prof that there was an even chance that he would make a rash or headstrong move. He knew that in a very short space of time that the Space Adventurer may engage the Gravitas. He knew that the shuttles would arrive half a day before he could arrive himself, and that basically the mission was robbed of its supreme commander, right at the crux.

"Hey Prof, got any ideas for exceeding the speed of light?" he asked.

The Prof said "well remembering old Scottie of Star trek, I cannae rewrite the laws of physics for you!" the Prof chuckled, "mind you I have often wondered, when we are at warp factor 0.99, which is just about our top speed, what would happen if you shut the gravity motor down and give a good blast on the rocket motors! You know down in Europe using the Large Hadron Collider they discovered some sub atomic particles that could be made to go faster than light so perhaps it isn't only a dream"

"Captain Johnson's mind raced. "You know we normally don't exceed about warp factor 0.85 or 0.9 but right now we are flat out at 0.95, and still creeping upwards.

He gave the orders to close the gravity motor down and give a blast at 100 % thrust on the rocket motors. The ship shuddered alarmingly but then was smooth.

"There you are you've done it!" chuckled the Prof. However when he looked on the large screen the video was completely blank there were no stars visible at all. The Prof went to a viewing window and again saw nothing but blue velvet, but with faint red spots on it. "Christ I think you may have found a hole and we've gone through it, so how do we get back!" he spluttered.

Captain Johnson used his pilot rockets to turn the ship through 180 degrees and then gave another full power blast on the rocket motors. For several seconds the ship moved with its usual smoothness but then there was a violent shaking followed by a return to smooth travel and all stars resumed their normal appearance.

A check on the ships instruments showed the warp factor digital indicators on 0.999, they wouldn't read any higher. Bearings were taken and the ships position was checked. Now the estimated time of arrival at their destination was only just over one hour away.

The two men looked at each other and knew they had done it. Captain Johnson sent the secure message that we know the Space Adventurer had received.

The secure message screen beeped and Captain Johnson looked at it. It was from James Whistler. "Congratulations on being the first ship to break the light barrier. You are welcome here right now. We have an undercover mission to board the Gravitas and this was started 14 minutes ago. Eric Whistler is NOT leading the mission. Suggest top level powwow, as soon as you arrive, regards, The Whistler."

The Solar Orbiter had started its deceleration some minutes before and then at last on the screen the captain saw the first shuttle, recognizable by its bright yellow livery.

Only minutes later the Space Adventurer came into view with her long aluminium foil tail. Captain Johnson in essence hid the Solar Orbiter behind the long tail, boarded his shuttle along with the Prof, and handed the bridge over to his second in command. Just a few minutes later he demanded to be brought up to date. Eric Whistler told him the absolute facts so that within minutes Captain Johnson gave his opinion.

"Eric that is a bold move, it will either succeed or fail but if it succeeds we will have the Gravitas back under our control with minimum loss of life. How confident are you with regard to the revised loyalty of Svensson?"

"I suspect captain that it parallels your own dilemma with regard to Helen. You were right about her so I hope I am right about him!"

Both decisions were an act of faith, so it was really simply a matter of judgment.

Within the hour the shuttle was requesting permission to dock again. "Henrik Svensson was accompanied by one crewmember from the Space adventurer.

"REPORT" barked Eric.

Crewman Jones stood forward, and spoke. "We had no difficulty in entering the ship so far as we know we were undetected. Our crew members accessed the undercrew quarters, and have hidden amongst the masses. Henrik Svensson here linked that digital disc player into the ships communications cable and as we left, the entire ship reverberated to the sounds of your voice, sir, giving details of earth's security operation and demanding the crew to recant and realign their loyalties. We scarpered sir as soon as we could because there will be a root and branch search of the ship. The small transmitter you gave us with additional crewmembers data was activated. We don't know if the ship's manifest has successfully been changed. Our spies are relying on it as proof of crew membership but neither of us have the technical skills to understand how to check for success."

"Ok Jones, I think you left the ship at the right time. *Very well done.*

Now Svensson, this is Captain Johnson, the only man who can give you a pardon".

Henrik Svensson blushed to the roots of his hair, but snapped to attention.

Captain Johnson murmured "a commendation may be possible but you will still have to face trial on earth."

"Thank you sir, I hope my trial will at least in part exonerate me but I can go to my maker when the time comes, with a great stain almost wiped out, even if I have to go to gaol."

"If this mission is successful, I will testify on your behalf," Eric Whistler assured him.

"Right ho Mr. Svensson. If you can get back on board the Gravitas, you could be useful to our spies on there," said Captain Johnson. "I realise of course that if you decide to throw your lot in with the mule again, our men could be doomed, and so you can see by this that I trust you implicitly. I would never knowingly take such a risk with my men's lives."

"I will not let you down sir!" said Svensson and with that he returned to his shuttle. Half an hour later his shuttle docked without detection on the Gravitas.

Captains Johnson and Whistler decided to give the mule a show of strength. Eric Whistler hailed the Gravitas and demanded to speak to Nick Jackson. The Gravitas responded immediately, and Nick Jackson alias the mule, appeared on the screen. "Well we meet at last Captain Whistler" he said jovially.

Eric Whistler immediately enquired as the health of Captain Cortez, the official captain of the Gravitas.

"Ah yes" said the mule smoothly, "he was not quite up to requirements and is detained in our brig, under sedation!"

Just at that moment Eric Whistler did a double take. There standing directly behind the mule was non other than the Prof. Eric Whistler contained his surprise and anger, and informed the Gravitas that a defence against the standard laser gun had been developed, and that if the mule would care to look out of the viewing window he would see that the Space Adventurer was pointing directly at him and in effect was hiding behind its newly developed protection, and furthermore had the bridge area directly in line with his own laser. "Our protection is such that should you aim a laser blast at us, it will be directly reflected and you will blast yourselves out of space!" Eric Whistler spoke calmly.

The mule was unfazed. He said "Captain Whistler, I know that you, by reputation and your record on humanitarian issues will not attack the Gravitas due to the severe risk to the ship's undercrew."

"You are wrong on that score I assure you, but perhaps if Captain Johnson were here you would react differently!"

"Possibly, but Captain Johnson would have had to have travelled faster than the speed of light to get here at this juncture!"

"Correct!" interjected the Prof.

The mule spun round, and was visibly shaken by the unexplained appearance of the Prof.

"Now then Prof" he began fighting for time to sustain himself in these unforeseen circumstances, suppose you explain your presence here!"

"Perhaps you had better explain the presence of the Solar Orbiter out there!" said the Prof indicating the viewing window.

The mule spun round again and was as they say gob smacked. As the space Adventurer had turned 90 degrees its long aluminium tail had suffered a gentle whiplash effect, and was no longer hiding the Solar Orbiter. Captain Johnson had got his second in command to bring the Solar Orbiter into full view, and just to compound the surprise it was plainly obvious that a third ship was there bearing the name Freeloader.

"We have made a breakthrough" smiled the Prof, and as a side effect we have also discovered Teleporting. Now you know how Captain Johnson got here so quickly and how I got aboard so easily. To be truthful we had never tried it over a distance greater than about fifty feet before today, but the Whistler was positive it would work so here I am." This was of course a 100 percent bluff. The mule however displayed a slight loss in his composure.

The Prof said "if you check down in your brig you will find Captain Cortez is not there! We teleported him back across to the Solar Orbiter."

He let this sink in then informed the mule that this was the fourth teleport operation, the first two being to install the message of mutiny to his crew some little while before.

The mule began to sweat, but the Prof continued. We have over fifty shuttles out there some of which have a crude but effective laser gun on board, (again an exaggeration) and all of ours have a bright yellow livery, so your observers can see them. I might tell you that your efforts to disable our shuttles started brilliantly well except that the only one that you disabled was one of your own, which is now drifting slowly in space. We captured the crew of your attacker and one of those men, a certain Henrik Svensson has been most cooperative!"

"I always suspected he was not fully convinced of our cause, the stinking RAT!" yelled the mule.

The Prof continued calmly "I have come over here to point out to you that as of this moment your threat against earth is just that, merely a threat. You have committed no major death sentence crimes, as yet and so I ask you to formally hand over command of this ship to me!"

"Check in the brig" yelled the mule. Some moments later he was told it was empty.

He slumped into a chair. "I admit to being outmaneouvered and so I will hand over the command of the ship but first I will put a bullet between you eyes" he snarled snatching at his side arm. The gun was only partly drawn when there was a report from across the bridge as Henrik Svensson took his revenge, the mule dropped dead on the spot. The Prof looking around seized the initiative.

"I have command of the Gravitas, Mr. Svensson you will assume the rank of second in command. Please inform the earth mission of the situation on board this ship.

Two of the mule's henchmen had already drawn weapons but a loud rapping on the wall as the earth spies together with a few crewmen, about thirty men in all, also armed, suddenly appeared.

The Prof continued as if this were an every day occurrence "Mule's men. Lay down your weapons no harm will come to you. One man made as if to fire but was cut down in a hail of bullets. "Last chance, LAY DOWN YOUR ARMS" roared Svensson. First one then another slowly the renegades began to lay down their weapons.

The Prof grabbed the ships intercom, and enthusiastically said. "To all crew members, hear this. The Gravitas is now once again under the control of earth and a return to full normality is immediate!"

"Release Captain Cortez" ordered the Prof. The Captain was brought to the bridge, but was still in a state of muzziness partly from drugs administered by the mule's men, and partly caused by the speed of events. The ships communications screen flashed up a part anxious part angry Captain Johnson.

"What the hell is going on over there?" he thundered. The Prof appeared on the screen at his end while saying "take this lot to the brig" then turning said "Captain Johnson, I am happy to report that the Gravitas is under my control!"

The Captain frowned, then smiled and said, "Find someone to leave in control and get over to the Space Adventurer pronto. I will meet you there!"

"Mr. Svensson, you have the bridge that is if you can hold such a position. Questions?"

"When the Prof gives me that sort of order, I would never refuse. I can handle it *sir*!"

"Mr. Svensson. I am sure you can, and thank you for your timely intervention back there, I thought I had overplayed my hand" said the Prof who had just then begun to shake.

Henrik Svensson looked at the Prof who was still shaking and said "Well you are human after all; I trust you will have recovered by the time you get to the Space Adventurer."

As the Prof was leaving the bridge he heard Svensson demanding that Captain Cortez be his second in command until the positions of everyone could be finalised. He didn't here the outcome of this but instinctively he knew Svensson would be up to the mark.

CHAPTER 59

THE PROF EXPLAINS HIMSELF

Captain Johnson gave the Prof a good measure of single malt from Eric Whistlers reserve.

"Here we were trying our damndest to sort out a strategy for dealing with this menace, and you, only a guest on this mission sneak in and steal our thunder!!!" complained Eric Whistler "I am supposed to be the hothead round here!"

"If you have it on tape I would be glad to see it," said the Prof.

"Tapes went out 150 years ago but we have burnt it onto a flash memory" said Captain Johnson.

After a few minutes the Prof said, "I cannot believe how calm I looked, because inside I was furiously trying to decide what to say next, and I was scared stiff!"

"You will always be my hero" said Helen Johnson and she planted a big affectionate kiss on the Prof's surprised face.

"I took the opportunity to beg a lift off Svensson, and made some suggestions to him. Luckily he followed my suggestions to the letter and got all of them done. He released Captain Cortez from the brig. By a stroke of good fortune the brig guard was just going off duty and he accepted Svensson as the next man on the watch. The new man was a couple of minutes late so the outgoing guard didn't even see him. Svensson told the new guard that he had been relieved due to other military requirements, and told the guy to wait in his quarters for orders. He went without even a question. Svensson had given Captain Cortez a message for our other guys, and as he escorted him to the undercrew, about thirty men were activated as an armed attack party. The mules escape pod was disabled, and Svensson is the expert on that, and after that fortunately he made his way to the command area on the bridge. The mule was going to shoot me you know!"

"Really?" said Captain Johnson drily.

"Well you saw how the conversation went, and when you got the Solar Orbiter in the viewing window, it shook him and I knew he was open to suggestions, so I invented teleporting. He already knew you had to have flown faster than the speed of light and I ad-libbed the idea of teleporting, and he believed it! I was truly hoping for surrender from him and so I was unprepared for his murderous response. Fortunately Svensson was there!"

Eric Whistler commented, "We were fortunate in the extreme to have achieved so much with so little blood shed, the scene panned out like a play. But the all important element in this play was timing, and the whole thing in that particular regard was a complete fluke!"

"Agreed, said Captain Johnson, but I give you the man of the moment!" all present raised glasses and sank a good mouthful of Eric's whisky, whilst acknowledging the Prof.

"It's a good job we are all friends, or you could have put our noses well out of joint, after all you're not even attached to the space service!" chimed in James Whistler.

He continued "I have been going over the data from your time warp jump, and yes, you really did it. I would advise against a repeat attempt because I do not understand how you did it!"

"It was the Prof's idea" smiled Captain Johnson.

"Not him again" laughed the Whistler, I think we shall have to confer a professorship on him at the earliest opportunity, as it is the only thing that will keep him tending his beloved runner beans!"

"They should be ready for picking when I get back," chuckled the Prof, I suppose it would be quite good to be a professor of runner beans!"

Note from Catherine Whistler: it was about this time that the news blackout was lifted, and a vast amount of information suddenly winged its way across the ether and landed on my desk for archiving. Some of the information was astounding to say the least, and as it is part of the story here, so I have included a chapter about it.

There were many loose ends to tie up before this matter could be confined to the history books, but on earth, it was now possible to relax. I haven't bothered with the details of how the asteroids were dealt with, but the Freeloader made her contribution in this regard and no asteroids hit earth though there were some spectacular flypasts.

CHAPTER 60

BACK ON EARTH

Hello again! This is Catherine Whistler. Down on earth we worried incessantly about what was going on. Jane Johnson and I who both had a husband away on duty had perhaps more reason than most to worry. As it turned out due to the unbelievable skills and shear daring of the Prof, neither of them had to face the expected dangers. Then I read about the breaking of the light barrier, well truly I don't believe that yet, but as I caught up on the archiving I phoned Jane up and invited her over for a barbecue. When she came the weather was appalling and the rain pounded so hard that I extended my invitation to a stopover. I was going to do that anyway because we live hundreds of miles apart, but now I had good reason. My one and her three all beamed when I said this, so after we had finally got them all tucked up and in bed I told Jane that I had something to show her.

I admitted to her that I was a little apprehensive because the knowledge I was about to give her could be life changing. Being privy to this information and keeping it to myself was a none starter. She was and is my best friend.

I showed her a personnel file photograph of Helen Johnson then waited for her response.

She looked at the photo, mentally drank in the detail and said "she is the spitting image of her father, and he will have some explaining to do keeping her a secret all these years!"

I then let her read the pertinent parts of the archives and she gasped as she realised that Helen Johnson had appeared out of the blue so to speak, and that Captain Johnson had been unaware of her existence.

Her grandmother, referred to only as Cressida, had somehow inveigled her mother Helena to allow herself to be impregnated with genetically engineered seed generated from samples taken when Captain Johnson had been in hospital for reparative surgery.

Jane suddenly smiled, only a small smile but still a smile. She turned and thanked me and was aware of just how much I had had to screw my courage up even to broach the subject.

Fast forward now three weeks, we were expecting our Captains, the Prof and the Whistler, at a private welcome home party, over at Jane's. Captain Johnson was first in, and he strode across the room to embrace Jane, and said "I have a big surprise for you!"

Jane spoke quite loudly "well bring her in then!"

Both his eyebrows shot up, but it was Jane who said "come on in Helen Johnson!"

Helen came in rather diffidently and then walked into Jane's outstretched arms. Both women burst into tears.

Captain Johnson looked round the room and his eyes fastened onto me "Ah" he said as full understanding hit him. "Catherine, I think I owe you massive thanks. Logic told me that these two" he thumbed behind him at the chattering pair of women, "would get along just fine, but when it came to it I was in a quandary, I don't mind admitting."

The relief on the man was palpable.

Helen was just regaling the room with how clever James Whistler was, when he said "yes, I know I'm a clever boy, but I have here a letter for you from my department offering you the post of my assistant. Now this is a research post not a P.A. post, I already have a P.A.!"

Helen sat down, read the letter twice and dissolved temporarily into tears again. "My dad already knows that I was almost conscripted into the mule's new order, because I was brought up to believe he was my dad but had denied me. I was bitter. When I met him for the first time he had DNA tests done and these revealed that he was not my dad. He was very kind if a little abrupt in the way he broke the news to me and when I told the Prof that I didn't believe the DNA tests because I think I look like my dad, he got them done again. Suddenly dad opened his arms and all my bitterness melted away completely. I realised right there and then that no matter what I would never go against my dad, and that

I had had a really lucky escape. One man who didn't have a lucky escape was Henrik Svensson, and I think the earth owes him a debt, which no doubt it will pay by putting him on trial!"

Jane Johnson quietly intervened, "you are your father's daughter, there is no doubt of that, not only do you look like him, you think like him. Even in an emotional cauldron as we have here today, your thoughts turn to someone else's predicament. It's time I introduced you to your half brothers and sisters, or step family or whatever they are" she said chuckling.

"I think I would like to be their big sister" said Helen smiling. Introductions were made and any shyness felt initially was gone in seconds as the smaller children competed for Helen's attention.

The Prof suddenly spoke up "I have taken another liberty ladies and gentlemen" he said scanning the room, "possibly how you receive another guest will determine how the world sees him!" he dialed a number on his mobile. Seconds later a knock on the front door, and the Prof said "Helen, I think you should answer that."

"Me?" she queried looking rather puzzled, but she got up and answered the door, and came in only seconds later holding the arm of Henrik Svensson.

"Svensson, you do have the habit of turning up just at the crucial time!" smiled Eric Whistler.

Helen looked round the room and locked eyes with the Prof. "how on earth did you know. I never said anything, not even to dad or to Henrik!"

The Prof smiled serenely. "There won't even be a clue in the archives, is that right Catherine?"

It was right; there was nothing in the archives. I knew the Prof however and readily acknowledged that he even outdid my Grandad for drawing conclusions based on evidence not apparent to anyone else.

"While you are here Henrik," interrupted Captain Johnson, perhaps you would like to read this. Henrik Svensson read the pardon and citation that was before him, and said, "Captain have you not overstepped your authority?"

"There will be those who deem that I have, but I have scrutinised my mission command documents carefully, and believe I am within my remit. Even the mule doubted your allegiance to him, and so taking all in all, particularly as my daughter almost fell into the same trap I think that far from being a Quisling as you said, you will be a hero, and I truly believe that you are man enough for my new found daughter." Helen blushed with absolute pleasure.

"What a swell party this is" she grinned, and turning to Jane and me she asked "is it always like this?"

"Usually a bit quieter!" we replied in unison, and then Jane said "you like music then?"

"This is the highest society party that I will ever be at so it just seemed an appropriate phrase!"

After that the party devolved into small talk and chit chat but it was still probably the best party that I ever went to.

Towards the end of the evening, I got Jane on her own, and then asked her a question that had been bubbling away inside me and wanting to surface for some time.

"Jane what is your husband's first name!"

She went all deliciously conspiratorial, "well you know the books and that old TV serial, Inspector Morse?"

"His name isn't Endeavour?" is it I asked.

"No it isn't, his father though was an engineer and his hero was Isambard Kingdom Brunel."

I waited with baited breath.

"I am afraid it is Kingdom!"

"Well what do you call him?"

"Cap, what else!"

CHAPTER 61

AND FINALLY

As anyone who reads this will have deduced the space crews were made of a wide range of nationalities. The Prof though was an Englishman. King Charles sent a personal letter to the Prof inviting him to Buckingham palace. The British were no longer world leaders, but still could out pomp and out ceremony most other nations.

In the letter, King Charles asked if the Prof would be good enough to bring the entire senior team with wives and girlfriends and children, somehow WAGS doesn't seem to fit, to the palace so that a grateful nation could show its pleasure and respect.

It took a while before other inescapable commitments permitted, but finally the day arrived and the entire team was at the palace.

The Prof was accorded the duty of introductions, right the way from Captain and Jane Johnson, down through each family finally reaching Henrik Svensson and Helen Johnson. The children were uncharacteristically quiet.

The King was curious. "Henrik how was the mule able to persuade so many people to his cause?" he asked.

"Well your majesty" began Henrik, but the King cut him short.

"Henrik, protocol has its place but just for today, inside these private rooms, please for God's sake, call me Charles!"

"Well erm Charles, the mule was somehow unbelievably persuasive, I found myself within an environment where I was with his disciples, and I felt I had to go along with it, even though I couldn't espouse many of his views. Several times when I wished to discuss a point, he always seemed to second guess what I was going to say and even before I had said it he gave me his reply. I never could find a way to stand up against him even though in my heart I knew what he was doing was wrong. Then I made a mistake and got myself captured by Mr. Whistler and his crew. That mistake gave me a lifeline and when the opportunity arrived I shot him. Had I not shot him I think none of us would have been here today!"

"Well I certainly wouldn't have" said the Prof, "the mule was intent on putting a bullet between my eyes, and I am too old to move quickly enough to avoid the forthcoming shot. Henrik though was quicker to the draw and thanks be given, dead accurate."

The King nodded as he took all this in, and turning to Captain Johnson, said "how did you manage to break the light barrier?"

Captain Johnson warmed to the situation. "Charles, it was once again the Prof's idea. We knew we could approach the speed of light that is warp factor 1.0, but for general conservatism we did not normally run above about 0.9 during our travels. The situation required us to support Eric Whistler here, so we were running at as high a speed as we could attain. The Prof said, he had often wondered what would happen if we were at warp 0.99, switched the gravity motors off and gave a good blast on the rocket motors. I can't remember now exactly how fast we were registering, but it was over 0.95 when we tried it. The star view from our flight deck suddenly changed to one of complete blue-black with red dots, and the Prof joked that we had done it. In fact we had done it, and then the Prof wondered how we were going to get back to normal times. I was in a sweat about that, I don't mind admitting. But I did the only thing possible; I turned the ship through a 180 degree orientation and gave another long blast of the rocket motors. Fortunately it worked!"

James Whistler then cut in, "we in the scientific community do not know why it worked. We are struggling to find any suggestion as to why it worked. It appears that Einstein's laws of physics have been bent or broken. Great efforts will be made to get to the bottom of this of course!"

Charles then added "it is so refreshing to get information straight from the horse's mouth so to speak. The well meaning wallahs round here dilute most of what I read for fear of offending my sensitive ears. They forget that not only am I King, I am also a man.

However in the case of this situation I sent a royal security box to bring me unexpurgated facts. I must say Catherine that you and your Grandfather before you have done a magnificent job, filtering the story from all of the interminable reports!"

"Oh sire, he would have been so proud to have been here!"

"Charles" he reminded her.

"I also listen to the odd bit of gossip now and then, I think Catherine that you used that delicious American word scuttlebutt for this, and I believe that romance is in the air!"

"Possibly Charles, but if we can come to that later, there is something that you can do to help us all you know!" she was not going to let this opportunity slip. "My Grandad was intending to publish this story but he died before he achieved that aim, is there any chance that you could endorse the story?"

King Charles started at the directness of this approach. He grinned, and his grin widened into a broad smile, then into a good hearty chuckle of genuine pleasure and said "well I suppose in some small way it would make me part of the story. It would be the least I could do, but before that I have another rather pleasant duty to perform. Usually this particular duty is performed at the behest of recommending politicians, but in this case I am taking the initiative myself."

"Kneel, Prof" he commanded. The Prof knew instantly what was about to unfold but was unprepared. Nevertheless he managed to get down and the King tapped him lightly on each shoulder with the ceremonial sword that he seemed to have produced out of thin air.

"Arise Sir Prof now knight of this realm."

The Prof needed assistance to get back up and then while he was slightly flushed from the effort, the King handed him a scroll. "Within that scroll is a brand new title. You are Professor Emeritus of Professors. This title is recognized by every university in the land, and I suspect it may be some time before that honour is awarded again. If you were a military man I would have awarded you the Victoria Cross but as you know the George Cross is the equivalent for valour not involving enemy troops. On reflection even that didn't seem appropriate to cover your deeds, and so it is with great pleasure that I confer upon you the Great Charles Spatial Cross. You are the first recipient of this award!"

The Prof for once was left speechless, but his ears did not miss the spontaneous applause from the gathering.

The King continued, "What on earth made you go into the lions den like that, Sir Prof?"

"Charles, my real name is Bill Wild. I suffered all the slings and arrows that a name like that brings to a lad, but when I did something a little out of the ordinary, with a good idea, suddenly I acquired the nickname of "the Prof", it has done me well for nigh on 70 years so I will stick with it under most circumstances. None of my colleagues knew my actual name, not until now!"

The King looked round and saw that every one was nodding, though Captain Johnson was noticeably quiet.

Catherine though could not suppress her innate sense of humour and wanted to play a small joke. "A spaceship, a spaceship, my *kingdom* for a space ship," she misquoted. Captain Johnson flashed her a quick glance and he knew the game was up. "Ok, ok" he admitted defeat, "that is my unused first name!"

Charles though was quite impressed. "Kingdom Johnson!" he said. "You know that has quite a ring to it, I wouldn't mind having that name myself!" he thought for a moment and said "Brunel?"

Captain Johnson nodded in assent, then looked round and gazed at his grinning wife. "I recognize your hand in all this!" he smiled.

Charles then said "come on Prof, why did you do it?"

The Prof sighed and exhaled slowly. "Sometimes I wonder that myself, but the dynamics of the situation were that Henrik Svensson had just agreed to go back on board the Gravitas, an act of extreme courage I may add.

I, only being an advisor was not subject to the military style discipline and I begged a lift from Henrik, telling him that I need to speak to Captain Cortez.

I am sure that Henrik didn't believe me but he knew I was acting on my own initiative, so he agreed.

The mule had dispersed the guards from the docking area to other duties, so we got on board without mishap. Now the Gravitas is a sister ship to our two ships and the layout is of course identical. As I made my way to the bridge, one or two people probably recognized me and gave me some funny suspicious looks but I got there in the nick of time. I watched unobserved for a few minutes and then when our mission told the mule that Captain Johnson was expected any moment, the mule knew he would have had to have gone faster than the speed of light to achieve this and said so. This was my cue, I said *correct,* and my appearance shook the mule. While he was trying to gather his wits about him he asked me to explain my appearance. Just at that moment the Solar Orbiter came into full view and I retorted that he had better try to explain the appearance of our second ship. This shook him even more, particularly as he could also see the Freeloader. I bragged that we had made a breakthrough, and further added that as a consequence of our breakthrough we had discovered teleporting. I used this to explain how we had infiltrated his ships public address system, and that we had teleported captain Cortez back to our ship. Actually Captain Cortez had been rescued by Henrik Svensson, and he had only just hidden him when the mule's men came looking for him. The timing of events would have done a west end comedy proud, but in fact were fortuitous as will be revealed by the forthcoming enquiry. The mule was going to shoot me but Henrik drew quicker and shot him instead. I went where angels fear to tread, I am a danger to the space service and I will not be making any further contributions!"

The King muttered "fortune really does favour the bold! But what about the virus issue"

"I was pondering that at some length, added the prof, "and suddenly I struck a line of reasoning that made me realise that the mule was trying to establish a fourth Reich, or similar. A poisoned planet was of no value to him. At that point it seemed obvious that his threat, which could have been real, was in fact a blind and a very clever one at that. While we were chasing those moonbeams he was on the opposite side of the solar system continuing unmolested.

"Well we were cleverer than him, but it took our combined brains to defeat him. It is truly a pity that a man of such ability was not able to keep within accepted guidelines. I suspect that had he been brought to trial it would have taken a very gifted brief to nail him, but it won't happen now!"

The King looked around his guests and said, "I pride myself as being able to recognize all of the different accents in English but I am at a loss with some of yours. For example Catherine where exactly do you call home?"

Catherine smiled and said," Grandad was Canadian but I was conceived and born on the Falkland Islands, but I have settled in England in Shropshire!"

"Ah! And you Eric?"

"Well, I am half Canadian and half American, but I was brought up in South Africa! Though Shropshire is home for the foreseeable future"

The king's eyes rested momentarily on Kingdom Johnson, and he raised enquiring eyebrows.

"My grandfather was an immigrant to the USA, so I hail from Boston, and Jane here is a native of Melbourne in good old Oz."

James Whistler was next. He thought for a moment, paused a moment more, and said "my family are all so called intellectuals, except Eric," he grinned, "grandfather was English, mother and father were both American but I was born in France. My upbringing was partly in France partly in South America, and then in any university that would accept me. Home at the moment is in Switzerland."

"And you Henrik?"

"Now, my family has roots in Denmark, Sweden and Norway; but for some time most of us have lived in the United Kingdom, which is why I don't have a Nordic accent! My grandfather was a world champion speedway rider!"

"I know all about you Prof, but that still leaves Helen. Come on Helen give!"

Helen smiled, and admitted that up till recently her home had been in California, but she was not sure what to say just now "So where do I live Henrik?" she purred.

Henrik grinned delightedly. The King smiled as he watched this romantic moment.

The King also noticed that each of the Prof's friends seemed to have connections with only one grandfather, which was of course impossible, but he was steeped in the traditions of protocol and politeness and swallowed his curiosity as to why this was so, simply accepting the situation as fact, which was precisely true. He realised that being part of the space exploration set up, each and every present member lead a truly international life. The King quietly envied them their freedoms.

The day was drawing to a close. The King shook everyone by the hand as he said goodbye, and spent a moment or two longer with Henrik Svensson than anyone else. Each person was given a small medallion that the King had commissioned to be made to mark what he called a truly exceptional occasion. They were all ushered out in a fashion that only exists in Great Britain.

Note from Catherine Whistler: at this point I thought the story had run its course but this turned out not to be the case.

CHAPTER 62

THE ENSUING COURT OF ENQUIRY

It took some time to organize the trials of those who had irrevocably thrown there lot in with the mule. It was decided that the court would hear the whole story and then each man would be tried for his part in it. It was a big story and took some time to tell. The court would here everything under English law as this underpinned many of the legal systems throughout the civilized world, and perhaps had better standing than any other system. A single judge would preside, but he would be backed by a quintet of judges who would argue points of law. The court was fundamentally a court of enquiry but it was charged with finding the traitors and committing them to be tried in another court of law.

The first major shock came when Kingdom Johnson was called as a witness. To say that the presiding judge was hostile would have been a massive understatement.

Everything went along in the usual fashion, Captain Johnson swearing the oath of truth. Captain Johnson was asked to account for his actions with regard to Henrik Svensson.

When he agreed that he had given the man a pardon, the judge, to use modern parlance, went ballistic.

"You have exceeded your authority and this man Svensson will accordingly be accused of complicity in this affair and could face the death penalty!" he roared.

Kingdom Johnson stood his ground stoically and said. "This planet and everyone on it including your lordship would now be dead if it were not for the actions of Henrik Svensson. If your lordship would care to peruse the articles and terms of my mission command you would see that I was well within my terms, and frankly it is only because of people such as yourself that the mule had any chance of success."

"You will be held in contempt of court!" roared the judge.

"No, sir you will be held in contempt of this court as you have not declared a material interest, in these proceedings!" replied Captain Johnson, with glacial calm.

The judge sat open mouthed.

"I took it upon myself to carry out certain investigative procedures before coming before this court, on the advice of a man universally known as the Prof. I offer this information to the court as material evidence of the accusation I am now about to make."

"Inadmissible" spluttered the judge.

Captain Johnson continued. Here are DNA profiles of yourself, our presiding judge and of the mule, One Nick Jackson. I have had these analysed and the result is that you are the mule's elder brother!"

The senior judge of the quintet stood and calmly beckoned the court bailiff. "Take his lordship down to the cells whilst we formalize these irregular proceedings. I will step up to the duty of trial judge and we will now adopt one of our reserves into the quintet."

The bailiff took an ashen faced judge down to the cells. The new presiding judge immediately called for a 24 hour recession, then signaled Captain Johnson over to the bench.

"Captain Johnson, the court owes you a debt of gratitude. We on the quintet knew there was something wrong but we couldn't pinpoint it! When the court resumes, it will not tolerate outbursts such as we have seen today.

"I trust it will not. But I must say that I had never in the entire history of my command been so angry, as when a man not even in court is threatened with the death penalty. I wondered how the mule had managed to infiltrate so far into earth's society, well we have just seen the link. I believe that he hasn't got any more brothers or sisters. Remember I sent men to their deaths without trial during this mission, but I had no other option when you consider the gravity of earth's perceived peril! But his lordship wants to condemn a man who is not only truly innocent, but was instrumental in saving earth."

"All that can now come out during these trials, and I assure you the trials will be unemotive and scrupulously fair."

"I now have no doubt that this will be the case, but perhaps I may make a suggestion, after all the whole of earth, mars and other outposts will be watching. Before the court is declared to be in session, each judge could volunteer to take an oath that he has absolutely no connection, or sympathy with the mule and his views, on pain of death.

"Yes the eyes of the worlds will indeed be on us; I accept your suggestion and will take the necessary steps to make this oath legally binding, and then we will see what effect this will have."

Even Kingdom Johnson was surprised that when the court reconvened, there was not one but four new faces on the quintet. So the influence of the mule was even more all pervading than hitherto assumed.

Each judge including the presiding judge swore in open court that he knew of no impediment that would prevent him sitting in judgment, and that he had no connection familial, commercial or any other with members of the so called new order, on pain of death. In effect, volunteering for the death penalty if such a link be proven.

Captain Johnson glanced across at the presiding judge and caught his eye. The Captain's eyebrows rose, but there was no reaction from the judge at all. Captain Johnson felt reassured by this.

The new judge settled the court down and spoke openly of a scandalous slur that had been made in court yesterday concerning one Henrik Svensson. Is Mr. Svensson available to the court?"

The usual echoing sound "Calling Mr. Henrik Svensson" rang out and a few moments later he entered the court.

The presiding judge spoke, "Yesterday Mr. Svensson an appalling attack on your character was made, by an officer of this court. Should you wish to sue for compensation then you will be at liberty so to do! However, before you do anything you must be sworn in."

After taking the oath of truth, Svensson spoke "I need to cleanse my name your honour, I have no interest in financial compensation!"

"Please tell the court in your own words the circumstances of your induction into the new order, and perhaps you could shed some light as to why the leader was known as the mule!"

"May it please the court; I was never actually inducted in. Some of my colleagues were though. There had been a few days when there was a palpable undercurrent of discontent on the Gravitas, nothing that I could put my finger on, but one morning when I reported for duty, the captain was in the brig and everybody was talking about the new order with some enthusiasm. I was not happy about it but I went along with things as there was an element that would have murdered me if I had not. I performed my duties as best as I could, and when I had the chance to ask a question of the mule, he always seemed to second guess what I was about to say and gave me plausible answers before I had asked the question. This was very disconcerting as all around me there were those who revered him. Some months went by and I spoke carefully to a number of my crewmates and there were quite a number who felt as I did, but quite a number who were wholeheartedly for the new order. I could see no way out.

When it looked as if a space battle was about to unfold I was given command of a shuttle ship. The plan was for me to mingle with the approaching fleet of shuttles and gain entry with a view to disabling them. At that time I did not know that all of the shuttles under the command of Captains Whistler and Johnson had been painted bright yellow. The first shuttle that I approached unbeknown to me was actually one of the mule's, and I successfully disabled her. I have heard that the men have since been rescued. At about this time Captain Whistler I think it was, demanded that all shuttles radio in to confirm their colour. I took this to mean their allegiance. By an absolute fluke one of the yellow shuttles was out of radio contact, but I assumed it was the one I had disabled. I radioed in, and was commanded to dock on the Space Adventurer immediately. I decided to bluff it out and complied. I had no chance, and realised that an opportunity to put right the wrongs aboard the Gravitas had fallen into my lap. I openly requested the opportunity to swear allegiance to earth saying that I did not want to be a Quisling, and some of my crewmates called me a stinking traitor. In my view they were the stinking traitors.

Captain Whistler had to make a snap judgment as to whether or not I could be trusted and he decided that I could. Looking back now, I can see what a difficult decision that must have been.

The main architect in my view, behind the demise of the mule was the Prof, who I am proud to call a friend and has just been knighted by the King of England! He was only on the mission as an advisor, but he begged me to give him a lift over to the Gravitas on my shuttle. Well I was going anyway under orders so decided to take him knowing our lives could well be forfeit if things went wrong. The Prof gave me a few tasks to do which included getting the release of Captain Cortez of the Gravitas, and I succeeded in these.

Having done my errands so to speak I decided I would go to the bridge and entered the command area just as the Prof made his presence felt. I saw a battle of wits between two masters, one of them a liar and the other not afraid of exaggeration or small porkies as we say."

"Small porkies?" enquired the judge.

"Cockney rhyming slang your honour, pork pies equals lies" said one of the bailiffs.

As the judge showed a ghost of a smile Henrik Svensson continued "the mule had not known of the last two or three dockings that we had done, and so the appearance of the Prof shook him particularly badly, as the Prof used the situation to confirm the thought train in the mule's mind about going faster than the speed of light. He mentioned me during the discourse and the mule said "I never trusted that man" or words to that effect. The Prof took the chance to plant fear in the mule's mind, he mentioned about a side issue discovery from going faster than the speed of light and that was teleporting. A science fiction means of transporting people about. The mule believed this crafty little fib, as the Prof used it to explain his presence on the bridge. The Prof asked him in the most gentlemanly fashion to cede command of the Gravitas.

The mule believed that he had been outmaneouvered and said that he would cede control of the Gravitas, but I knew by his tone of voice that he was going to do something drastic. Suddenly he threatened to put a bullet between the prof's eyes he was drawing his sidearm. I had about a half second advantage and had already drawn mine, I shot the mule in the chest and he died on the spot. Immediately the Prof seized the opportunity to assume control of the Gravitas, and told the mule's men to lay down there arms. The hard core of those close to the mule would not do that. Fortunately we had smuggled a few men aboard the Gravitas earlier on and I had given them the names of a few crewmembers that I could trust and the whole group arrived on the bridge just at that moment. One man was again going to shoot the Prof and my men opened fire and he died in a hail of bullets. I by then was bitterly angry and I shouted loudly at the remaining men to lay down their arms, they were completely surrounded and first one, then another complied and within a few seconds the mutiny was over.

"Mr. Svensson" said the presiding judge, "Quisling, never, you sir are a true hero, do you by any chance have the pardon given you by Captain Johnson?"

"I do your honour."

"Bailiff if you would be so good as to bring the document to the bench, gentlemen, the court seal please."

The judge stamped the document and he and his quintet all signed as "approved."

"Mr. Svensson, you leave this court not only without a stain on your character but as a shining example to us all. You found yourself, entrapped in a most invidious situation but you kept your head and waited for an opportunity to extricate yourself and you did that with some skill and determination. You are free to go, though you didn't explain where the name, *the mule* came from!"

"I am sorry sir I simply don't know."

Henrik Svensson walked through the main courtroom doors smiling, but even that did not hide the tear that threatened to fall from his left eye.

He reappeared moments later in the public gallery with Helen Johnson proudly clinging to his arm.

Captain Johnson was recalled to the dock.

CHAPTER 63

THE COURT HEARS MORE EVIDENCE

"Captain Johnson, the court reminds you that you are still under oath and is curious as to how Professor Nick Jackson acquired the name *the mule*." asked the presiding judge.

"If I remember correctly it was the Prof who first coined the name based upon a space science fiction novel by Mr. Isaac Asimov. There was a character in this book that caused mayhem and we simply adopted it." Three of the quintet were smiling, presumably Asimov readers.

"Perhaps you could account for sending men to their deaths, a most serious issue?"

Captain Johnson drew a long breath. "I ask the court to understand the following. The authorities on earth had received a threat from a space ship previously considered lost. The threat was that earth should cease all space exploration forthwith; otherwise, asteroids carrying viruses would be diverted so that their orbits would cause them to crash into earth, and wipe out life. From my own direct experience I knew that this was possible, and I knew that the viruses would certainly wipe out any life left after earth suffered a massive asteroid impact. What I did not know was the extent of the mule's organization. I was shocked to find that we had many adherents on both the Solar Orbiter and the Space Adventurer in both the operational and undercrews.

Almost right from the outset I was horrified to find that since my last mission the standards of discipline had been allowed to crumble. Later on I realised that this was due to the mule's malign influence. A certain crew member named Jim Roberts let me know that there were problems on board and that they affected earth's security. I left the man on a loose tether and observed, and it soon became apparent that we had a major security infiltration problem. This was far worse than earth was aware. Our next stage in the discovery of what was going on was when we found that a number of so called new order adherents were in fact working under duress and had genuine fears for the safety of their loved ones. I realised that I needed the crew to be more frightened of me than of the mule. I started a program to check on the cleanliness of every man on the mission including both myself and the Prof, James and Eric whistler. Our responses to the questions I put are now a matter of record on the ship's log.

I discovered that I had a daughter during the course of this mission and it was only by a stroke of good fortune that the mule did not get his claws into her. As it finally turned out she played an important role in the location of the mule. I found her amongst a group of dissidents on mars. Ken Lee there broadcast the full known threat and demanded that anyone with funny antiestablishment views be rounded up. My daughter was amongst those, but I can swear on oath before this court that she was as innocent as the driven snow. At about this time Eric Whistler had two crew members who said they would spill the beans but needed protection. As a result of this earth was informed and sent armed guards to every mission crewmembers houses. That move allowed me to remove the fear element and get some results. However, amongst the mules adherents there were some very determined characters involved and the more senior they were the tougher they were.

Captain Whistler was the first to threaten a crewmember with ejection and he promised to film the event so that others could see exactly what fate awaited them. The demeanour of the men who were exposed was twofold. Some looked relieved others looked worried. In my view the worried ones feared for their fate on earth because they knew of the impending doom facing the planet.

One individual did not like the prospect of facing life under Johnson Law, and sneered that it wouldn't be like that under the new order. I had him suited and ejected within a few seconds. He was cursing and yelled of the fate that awaited all the fools on earth as he was ejected. This started a furious fight and the man who started the fight was loyal to earth, he demanded and got the loyal members to group themselves with him. This man at a stroke weeded out the traitors from the true men and the mission owes him a debt. He was able crewman Clark. Able crewman Mills had meanwhile done the same thing on the Space Adventurer. The ships' logs show who was ejected, and when. Just at this juncture we uncovered the true identity of our surgeon who was on board as surgeon Veritsang. His real name is Professor Trueblood and he was dispatched back to earth. He was the mule's second in command. Thus we had been proceeding on a mission when the second in command of our arch enemy was operating as a ships surgeon, a position that gave him free run of the entire mission. An unbelievable coup, for the mule.

Initially the mule fooled us into thinking that he had made landfall on the dwarf planet/asteroid Ceres. While in fact he was at the opposite side of the asteroid belt planning his strategy. Whilst I can give you a reasonable account of what happened next, really the court should in my view hear from the Prof."

The judges conferred for a moment and finally the presiding one agreed.

"Thank you Captain Johnson we may call on you again if the court deems it necessary.

The court has noted that the Prof as he is referred to seems to be a major player in this saga. You may step down." The court didn't as it turned out deem a recall necessary.

The Prof was called to the dock, and sworn in. The presiding judge welcomed the Prof and for good measure told him the point at which captain Johnson had deemed him the better raconteur.

Before the Prof gave evidence the court thanked him for the debt it owed him.

"I believe the damning evidence against several trial judges was obtained on your suggestion. How did you know about the original presiding trial judge?"

"This is a prime example of my particular talent," said the Prof, "I looked him up on the internet and looked at his career. There was of course very little to go on as not much is in the public domain in such matters. But there were a few videos. I was struck by the man's general demeanour, and though he didn't look like the mule, having seen both men either in the flesh or on video I had overwhelming suspicions. I mentioned to Captain Johnson that it would do no harm if he commissioned a DNA check. All peoples DNA is now on an international database. Captain Johnson got the results and blanked the names out then had them analysed, by experts. Well DNA testing is now an advanced science and they were able to confirm the connection between the two samples as being fraternal. There was no proof that the judge was involved with the mule, but I reasoned that he should have declared his position, and when he did not, both myself and Captain Johnson knew that our mission still had someway to run."

"The court is indebted to you; please now proceed with your evidence"

The Prof began "I suppose the point at which I should take up the tale is when I suddenly realised that the mule had duped us good and proper. He was cunning, and deep thinking. He knew we would be looking for him and he knew that we had deduced that he had the Gravitas under his control. He couched his warning to earth in terms that we would recognize. He knew we would be looking for some sign of asteroid movement. We realised that if he had made landfall on Ceres, he would have an excellent base to start from and of course he would be hidden from earth's radar detectors. We asked earth to examine Ceres and earth reported that it had suddenly acquired three moons. We took this to mean that the moons were actually three virus carrying asteroids dragged there by the Gravitas under the command of the mule, and made plans accordingly. This really was a clever ploy by the mule, as he knew we would link the discovery of the three moons round Ceres to his presence there. When we discovered that we had been hoodwinked, we realised that we would have to conduct a full orbital analysis of any viewable asteroid. The task of examining the orbits of all viewable asteroids fell to James Whistler and Helen Johnson. Helen actually by a combination of intelligence and good fortune managed to finally find where the Gravitas hence the mule was. Captain Whistler was nearest and he sped off to engage the mule. We were expecting a full combat and made efforts to produce enough space suits to equip all of the operational and undercrew with space suits in case of sudden depressurization. Helen Johnson got a team of volunteers and pressed participants to set about producing enough space suits. These did not have a proper space helmet but were provided with a Perspex view window in the top of the suit which zipped up over the wearers head."

"What were pressed participants?" asked the judge.

"Ah, yes they were known dissidents, and they were told to work hard as they would be the last people in the queue to get a suit. Suffice it to say they succeeded. The Solar Orbiter was still some distance away from the combat zone, and we were going along just as fast as we could, when I mentioned to captain Johnson that I had often wondered what would happen if we switched the gravity motor off and gave a good blast on the rockets. Captain Johnson was already half way through doing this almost before I had finished thinking about it. The ship went through a period of shuddering and then settled down. I joked that we had done it, but when I looked outside through the viewing window everything was a silken blue-black. Minute red dots rather than stars were visible and we were travelling at a completely unknown speed. Captain Johnson's survival instinct kicked in, he reversed the ship and gave a good blast of reverse thrust. The ship again went through the shuddering, and then lo and behold all the stars reappeared, and by possibly some as yet undiscovered law of physics, we were still on our original course.

We checked our position and had gained a useful amount of time. All this time I was mulling over intelligence that had come our way, and I suddenly chanced upon a line of reasoning and realised that the mule was taking not only a short view but a long term one as well. I imagined that he was trying to establish an empire such as the fourth Reich, and like a bolt from the blue it suddenly dawned on me that a poisoned earth was no good to him. His descendants would have no use for a planet raddled with a million deadly viruses. That part of his threat was empty. No, the asteroids alone would do so much damage that should there be any survivors they would be forced back to the Stone Age. I imagined a technically advanced force from mars would then be able to enslave what was left of earth and rule both planets. I also considered that with human activity reduced to virtually zero, the earth would reforest itself and in effect be rejuvenated so in a hundred years time it would have returned almost to its virgin state. A marvelous asset for the New Order.

When we arrived behind the Space Adventurer, Captain Johnson hid behind the long aluminium streamer that Captain Whistler had used to confuse the mule's radar, with a view to coming into visual appearance at some advantageous moment.

I begged a lift across to the Gravitas, as I wasn't subject to the total discipline under which the mission was begun, and I asked Henrik Svensson to secure the release of Captain Cortez, take him down amongst the undercrew, and round up our advance party and some others still loyal to earth.

Then a real piece of good fortune fell into my lap. There was some discourse between the mule and Captain Whistler, involving the presence of Captain Johnson. The mule had just reasoned out that for Captain Johnson to be at this point in space he would have had to have travelled faster than light. At that moment I only had one word to say and that was *correct*. The mule was startled by my presence and he tried desperately to gather his wits and demanded that I explain my presence. On the hoof I just said that he had better explain the presence of the Solar Orbiter that had just appeared from hiding and was plainly visible to the naked eye, and although of less significance the Freeloader was in plain view as well.

This shook the mule further and I then claimed that as a by product of going faster than light, we had invented teleporting and that was offered as an explanation for my presence. Some hours before Henrik Svensson had connected a disc player into the ship's public video system and our message relaying earths security measures protecting all crew members loved ones on earth, had been broadcast for everyone to hear. I told the mule that teleporting me had been the fourth use of the teleport system, the first two being used to get a man on then off the Gravitas with regard to our message over the broadcast system.

I implied that the third use was to teleport Captain Cortez away.

The mule demanded that the brig be checked and fortunately Henrik Svensson had succeeded in his errand, the brig was empty and the mule accepted my bluff. The court has already heard how I would have been shot but for the intervention of the man I am pleased to call a friend, Henrik Svensson.

As you can see when the mission was put under weigh, earth had not had time for proper vetting. The result of which was that we had quite a preponderance of the mule's men in our crews. We were in an almost impossible position, finding ourselves charged with certain responsibilities and yet from the outset the mission was raddled with mule sympathizers, in all but the most senior levels. On both mission ships, there was a point of no return for the mule's men. Able spacemen Clark and Mills, each in a slightly different way managed to get the loyalists to declare themselves and simultaneously to isolate the new order sympathizers. We had to rely on scraps of evidence and deductive suspicion to weed the untrustworthy out. If we made mistakes then I wouldn't be surprised. In an enterprise like this the difference between success and failure is whether or not a seemingly small scrap of information is crucial or not. Luckily I have the sort of mind where I do seem to be able to sort the wheat from the chaff, but I am not perfect. When I first met Helen Johnson, my mind was already poisoned with the possibility that she could be a plant, and I thought she was. She very quickly changed my mind and I was delighted, when she turned out to be Captain Johnson's undiscovered daughter."

Someone in the gallery clapped loudly and as the Prof turned to see who it was the entire public gallery followed suit, and burst into applause.

The judge brought down his gavel and demanded silence, and the applause slowly ebbed away. The judge smiled but said, "any repeat of that and I will have the gallery cleared."

The court then took the Prof back through his discourse and bit by bit every significant point was examined in minute detail. From time to time even the Prof's legendary memory recall was stretched and he begged permission to refer to the ship's log. This was always granted. Finally the judges were all conversant with the mission and conceded that field commanders had to have limited legal rights to do whatever was deemed necessary without fear of falling foul of spatial law.

At one point the presiding judge called his quintet into a closed door session and upon return announced "this court, having examined the actions of the mission commanders in great detail, can find no fault with the mission commanders' conduct. All senior personnel are now free to leave. The court can foresee that several lower ranking players in this real drama could receive highest commendations and heartily endorses this prospect. This court will now proceed with the examination of the actions of all minor players in these events!"

The presiding judge and his quintet had now heard all of the significant evidence points, and so decided to split into 6 courts to speed events along.

Even so the trials of so many individuals seemed to drag slowly on and it took almost two years before every miscreant had been examined and been taken through the full judicial process. Of those found guilty, every one was shipped to the new gaol on Titan, where they would either get slowly more bitter or repent and make an effort while they were there. Well you can't win them all.

This is a final note from Catherine Whistler.

With the possible advent of space travel faster than light now dawning, the original space exploration tale is complete. I dare say as I get older there may be more stories to be told. I know I was brash in asking the King of England to endorse this tale. It worked though! Publishers have been falling over themselves for the rights to publish. All I have to do is to choose the most reputable one.

If you should buy a copy, I trust it will make interesting reading. By for now!

An original story, by DAVID DONALD KEIRLE August 2009. The author acknowledges that his ideas have been influenced by what he has read over the years and thanks all those who have gone before.